£1.00

Cut Short

Cut Short

Philip Keep

Published in 1992 by
The Self Publishing Association Ltd
Units 7/10, Hanley Workshops,
Hanley Road, Hanley Swan,
Worcs.

in conjunction with Philip Keep

British Library Cataloguing in Publication Data

A catalogue record for this book is available
from the British Library

ISBN 1 85421 204 4

Designed & Produced by Images Design & Print Ltd, Hanley Swan, Worcs.
Printed & Bound in Great Britain by Hartnolls, Bodmin, Cornwall.

For Madeleine

Chapter 1

"Do I have to follow suit now or what?" Avalon asked.

I assured her that she had to follow suit, rather than do the other thing, at the same time tipping my chair back to an angle at which I could see further up her skirt.

"Oh, Lord! I'll never get the hang of this stupid game," she said.

What I had taken to be a pair of gusseted and casehardened tights the colour of baby sick now appeared to terminate about halfway up those coltish thighs of hers. There was even the briefest glimpse of some crotch-concealing material of a similar colour. I looked at my watch. Quarter to midnight. Surely twenty-five - no, thirty-five minutes of this stuff counted as a decent and acceptable length of foreplay. Surely by now she must have got the message that what she had here was a serious and high-minded doctor and not just some filthy-minded slob whose only interest was in giving her a quick poke. Time to suggest that we might, well, as it were, just possibly, why don't we -

Before I could give voice to this sentiment, Avalon put her cards face upwards on the table and said "I'm bored with all this. Why don't we go up to your room for a nice cup of coffee?"

Controlling the quaver in my voice, I nodded. "Fine by me," I said. Avalon got to her feet, demonstrating - what was it now? - the whippet-like grace that had first attracted me to her. Perhaps that's not quite what it was. Avalon is a bit skinny - swimsuit-advert concave belly, pelvis like a saucer, and arms you can practically get your fingers round twice, but not stringy or bony in any way.

I picked up her handbag by its strap, and helped her put it on over her shoulder, deliberately avoiding any adolescent attempt at a grope. Plenty of time for all that later: this is a sophisticated stud-about-town your dealing with, sugar.

"After you," I said.

Avalon gave me a coy smile and blushed prettily. No matter how you set about it, this next bit tends to be embarassing. Somehow, you have to stage manage a smooth transition from standing up with your clothes on to laying down together with them off: from two virtual strangers talking about the weather to 'Oh, oh, baby you make me so wet.' Just to make it more difficult, the rules of the game state that neither of you has to appear to know what's coming - the blatantly obvious has to appear accidental and unforseen.

"Off we go then," Avalon said.

As we prepared to leave, I became aware of just what sort of impression the Mess Common Room must make on visitors such as her - greasy wallpaper, holed carpets, sagging and body-stained leatherette armchairs, and over everything an air of dismal resignation, of generations of junior doctors serving their time, crossing off the days like prisoners.

"Why does this place always smell of wet nappies?" Avalon asked.

What was it with this *always* stuff? This was - so far as I was aware - the first time Avalon had been invited into the Doctor's Mess of the Breckleigh Royal Infirmary (South Wessex Regional Health Authority [Non-Teaching]). The first time I'd invited her here, anyway. "Always?" I asked.

"What?"

"You said 'always'. Have you been here before?"

"Oh . . . no," Avalon said. "It's just a . . . just an expression, that's all."

I pulled on my white coat, and the bleep flew from its top pocket, struck the floor with a plastic crack and slid under the coffee table. "Ah, knickers" I observed, without putting much feeling into it.

"Have you broken it?"

"Let's hope so."

As I grovelled about on the floor for a missing bit of plastic, I could hear another bleep going off outside the door, and then the door opened and a tall white-coated figure strode into the room.

"Rossiter," a voice said. I looked up. The owner of this voice was standing within three feet of me, using the fingers of one hand to grasp a telephone, and those of the other hand to pick his nose with terrifying ferocity. "Yeah, alright, put her on," he said.

Duggie, or Dr Douglas William Rossiter, MB, BS (London), acknowledged my presence by grunting or possibly belching in my direction and then proceeded to look Avalon up and down, pulling out the bogeys the while. A female voice could be heard coming from the earpiece. It started off slowly and hesitantly, but gradually began to increase both in speed and in volume. Rossiter's breathing also deepened and quickened, until he was snorting through his nostrils and pulling faces at the dartboard on the wall next to him. "Oh, for crying out loud . . . " he kept saying. The voice would not let him interrupt, and his finger hovered for a few seconds over the telephone as if he were about to cut the voice off in mid-flow. Then it happened - the catch in the voice, the slight hesitation, and finally the sound of sobbing. "Please - please - I'm sorry," the voice seemed to say.

There was a silence, then Rossiter turned his back on us and, in a curiously formal voice, he said , "Look, we've been through all this. I don't really see any point in raking it all up again, do you?"

"Shall we go then?" Avalon asked. She was casting a series of uncertain glances in the direction of the man with the telephone who was now saying, "I thought I'd made it very plain... Well, don't start blubbering, for Christ's sake."

Duggie went on to say, "Yes, that suits me absolutely fine. Yes, let's just leave it at that, shall we?" Without waiting for a reply, he threw the receiver back onto its rest and started to scratch his genitals. A slight flutter of the eyelids indicated that he had already dismissed the telephone conversation from his mind and he was staring at Avalon again in a way which suggested that he would not in the least object if asked to share a bed with her. "Did Barrington manage to get hold of you?" he asked me without taking his eyes off her.

"Barrington?"

"Yeah, something about an old geezer with an acute abdomen or something."

"Where?"

"Don't ask me," Duggie said, and he threw himself onto the sofa. There was the unmistakable bass rumble of escaping gas.

"Sod everything," Duggie said.

"Who on earth was that extraordinary chap?" Avalon asked.

By this time, we had got through the shifty ritual of trying not to bump into each other/hoping not to be seen as we negotiated the squealing front-door of Bleak House, mounted the protesting staircase and finally made the short dash down the corridor to my room. Avalon had asked to be directed to, and had been shown what she tweely insisted on calling the smallest room, and I had taken advantage of her absence to have a crafty pee into the washbowl. (OK, so long as you aim at the plughole and keep both taps running.)

What passed for coffee had been drunk from two pixie beakers which I had invested in following an earlier fiasco with a physiotherapist called Jo or Joan or something. Duggie had assured me that this particular one didn't fuck, or at least that she wouldn't fuck him - no, wait, it couldn't have been that - had assured me that she was a lesbian, which was pretty much the same thing as far as Duggie was concerned, so imagine how I felt when - with no goading - this Jo character accepted a late evening invitation to come up to my room and *listen to a record of heart sounds.* Mind-boggling, I know, but there I suddenly found myself, looking down the barrel of a pair of 38D's, and counselling her in low and reassuringly doctorly terms about some shiftless turd called "Brian" who had been giving her a hard time.

There seemed to be no way in which this consultation could not end up with the patient in bed under the doctor, but I am not the sort of character who simply unzips his flies and shouts, "Help yourself, sweetie". A little finesse, if you please, a little decorum. At the very least, this lady warranted the Ceremony of the Instant Coffee. It was at this point I discovered that there were only two suitable drinking vessels to hand - a squashy red plastic job, which I could not - surely, a man of my social position - offer to a guest, and a pink china thing with a rose on it; a thing which had once held toothbrushes and toothpaste, but which had stood unused on top of the wardrobe ever since I had taken possession of the room.

So there we sit - picture us, if you will - a just-about- decent distance apart on the edge of the bed, steaming mugs in hand, and I have managed to get to page five or six of the seduction manual - the bit where I fix her with a half-serious look and say, "Has anyone ever told you that you have - No, honestly, you have got - Surely you must realise that you have - the most beautiful eyes/hands/shoulders I have ever seen?" No: not the other things. I speak as one with some experience in these matters. The lady colours slightly, looks coyly into her cup and takes a long draught. There is a sudden choking sound from deep down in her throat, but it is not emotion. No; it is not the poetry of my words that has moved her, but rather a gelatinous lump of inspissated goo - the congealed drainings of a thousand toothbrushes - which had hardened to form a false bottom to the china mug, and had now been dissolved by the heat of the coffee.

"Which chap?"

"That tall, awfully good-looking chap who answered the telephone."

"Who - Duggie? He's not good-looking, is he?"

"Don't you think he is?"

"Search me - I just can't tell with men." No bullshit, that, either. *Pretty* men - yes I've got no problem recognising pretty men, but Duggie is not one of those, and I've long since given up trying to work out what it is about, well, non-pretty men that women define as *good looking*. There have been these blokes that I have regarded as homely - ugly even - only to hear some group of women agree as to their bedworthyness. Why, there have even been cripples that have turned out to be some woman's idea of physical beauty.

"Well I think he's rather nice. Nice bum, too," Avalon giggled. "Who is he?"

Duggie and I go way back - no, further than that, even. Weren't we at one time incontinent toddlers together, in the sandpit at High Bank Infants?

"Where do I begin? Duggie and I go *way* back," I heard myself tell Avalon. "We went to school together. And medical school." And lots of other things as well, but surely you don't want me to give you a rundown of everything I've learned about him over the years? About his filthy personal habits, his phallic boasting, his tendency towards physical violence, his total inability to understand or care about other people's feelings? After all, we're not here to talk about him, sugar.

Apparently, that was precisely what Avalon did want, so I got through as brief a summary as possible of the way in which our lives had far too frequently been intertwined. Avalon rounded it all off by saying, "And you're still together now", and then, with a cheeky little dig in the ribs, she added, "like some old married couple or something."

"It just happened that way," I said. "Nothing deliberate." One thing I didn't tell her was that the reason we had ended up at the same Medical School was that, even in the second year sixth, Duggie hadn't got a clue what he wanted to do when he left school. Learning that I had got a place at The North London Medical Diploma Emporium, he had said that he "might as well" do medicine too, and had asked me what address you had to write to. So much for vocation.

"Is he mad or something?" Avalon asked. "I mean, the way he was going on at that poor nurse or whatever she was."

"He's usually like that," I told her. "In fact, he seemed rather calm and well-adjusted this evening - for him, I mean." Avalon giggled and drew up her legs. This was not good. Next thing, she would be asking me to bleep him and invite him round for coffee. How did we get sidetracked?

The conversation earlier on had been heading in the right direction. I had asked about, and been told at some length about, her family - elder daughter and second of four children of local vicar - and about that name of hers. Daddy had named his children, in descending order of size: Launcelot, Avalon, Guinevere, Merlin. I had listened with apparent attention to a wordy account of an entire family of weedy parasites. There was Big Brother Launcelot ("You ought to meet him - you'll like him - he's very *sensitive.*") who had at least shown the initiative to leave Breckleigh and move to London where he tried to justify his existence by sending unwanted advertising material through the post. Guinevere didn't seem to do anything very much, except lay around complaining of heavy periods, while Merlin - poor bastard - had added to the misfortune of his name by being interested in playing the accordion and getting himself a place at a local theological college.

And as for Avalon, now, how do you think she earns a crust? I've already told you what shape she was, now here's the rest of it: pale skin, large greeny-hazel eyes, very full, very red lips, jet black hair half way down her back and with a tendency to be all the way down her face, so that from time to time she scoops the stuff up with her wrist and throws it back over her shoulder. Uses expressions like, "Oh, yah," and "No, hunnestly," but not so persistently that you could classify her as some tight-bummed green-wellied County tart. Give in? Here it is, then: Avalon is the manageress of the Welbeck Gallery, which is another way of saying that she sits around all day talking to tight-bummed, green-wellied County tarts and tries to part them from their money.

The way I had come across her was this: Jimmie Materson, self-styled senior consultant surgeon, noticing that his houseman - that is to say me, Robert Fullen, MB, BF and general dogsbody - is scheduled to have his first half-day off in three weeks, hands him a brown paper parcel as he is leaving theatre and asks him if he will "pop in with it" to the Welbeck Gallery "when you're passing". This entails a detour of fifteen miles, and means that I have to find parking space in the hyper-trendy area down by the Barbican, dodging the tourist coaches, the great American matrons and the rat-faced Japs who are busy grinning into each other's camera lenses. The brown paper parcel turns out to contain a giant photograph of Jimmie himself, dressed up in a peaked hat and lots of gold braid, like some Swiss Admiral, which he wants them to frame. At first, Avalon had struck me as snobbish and condescending, but after a bit I quite got to like her, especially when - entirely unprompted by me - she opened the parcel and laughed out loud at its contents. Avalon had already cost me - there had been an expensive outing to a vegetarian restaurant - (yes, I'm afraid she's one of those)- and a Sunday afternoon trip to the zoo, which had given her ample opportunity to expand on the highly original proposition that it was *cruel to keep animals locked up in cages,* though this had not stopped her from taking the piss out of the baboons, nor making some unexpectedly salty remarks about the reproductive organ of the pygmy hippopotamus.

That's as near to sex as I got, though, and this evening was definitely her last chance. Still, if she did come up with the goods, this could really turn out to be a Night To Be Remembered, not just for anything I might do to Avalon - however enjoyable that might turn out to be - but because this would be the first time that Jimmie Materson had ever been instrumental in getting me a fuck and, even more significant, the first time I would ever have reason to feel even vaguely indebted to my consultant for anything.

"Anyway," I said, "we're not here to talk about him."

"Oh? And what are we here for?"

I give her the half-closed eyes look and move in for the kill. After all, she has walked in here on her own two feet and sat on my bed. We are consenting adults in private, if you don't mind: and so it's left arm round shoulder, exerting just the most delicate of pressure, drawing her towards me and into waiting trap of right arm. As I home in on those giant, almost rubbery, lips, right leg comes over to lend support as - oh, yes, I've done this before, all right. Avalon does not resist as I press her backwards with a slight twisting movement so as to bring her head into contact with the pillow. Two dull thumps as shoes are levered off by toes of opposing foot, and then the smooth body swing which brings me alongside and only a little bit on top of her. I open one eye briefly to check that all is well. Her eyes are shut and she is breathing deeply and evenly - relaxed and confident in the hands of the master. Right arm stretches out and turns off bedside light. The bed twangs reassuringly as it takes our combined weight and then - the telephone rings.

"God! Hang on a tick. Hello! Fullen. What - casualty? – Sorry about this," I said to Avalon.

"That's alright," Avalon said. "I'll get undressed if you want."

"Er – Ooh, yeah, great! Hello? . . . Dr Fullen: Surgical Take. You wanted me."

In the dark, Avalon climbed over me and walked to the far end of the room. There was just enough light coming through the curtains for me to be able to see her silhouette as she stepped out of her skirt and busied herself with the buttons on her blouse. From the receiver, I could hear the echoing clatter of Casualty and a drunken voice repeating, "I never arssed to come to bleeding hospital, did I? I never arrsed – it was him brought me."

The grating Adeladian tones of Max Waters became audible. "Look, mate, it's neither one way nor the other to me," he was saying. "You can bugger off home again as far as I'm concerned, but while you're in here, you keep your big fat gob shut, otherwise I'll shut it for you. Yeah. Hello?"

"Fullen."

"Rob? Gooday,mate.I've got something for you."

Avalon was now standing by the bed, wearing only the baby-sick stockings and matching accessories, and I could see that she had something for me, too. She knelt beside me and put her hand inside my shirt.

"You still there?"

"Yeah."

"It's a nice young gentleman by the name of Patrick Michael O'Malley."

"Don't tell me – a Pakistani."

"I don't wish to know that. Kindly leave the hospital." Waters cupped his hand over the receiver and muttered, "Tell him to go and see his own GP.Stupid bastard. Right, Bob, well this, er, O'Malley geezer. He's had pain in his left loin for about eight hours. He's a known case of nephrocalcinosis – "

"Renal colic?"

"Yeah . . . straight X-ray of his abdomen shows . . . "

"Renal colic is medical."

"Eh?"

"Renal colic is medical."

"Not in my book, mate."

"Well it is in mine - mate. Renal colic is medical."

"Not this one. You're having it."

"No way. Get the physicians."

"I already have. They said it was surgical."

"That pillock Pereira, was it? Tell him to get knotted. Renal colic is a medical emergency, and - "

"Look, matey, I've got other things to do. I'm sending him up to Ward Five."

"Like hell you are. Renal colic is medical. We all agreed that. Haematemesis is surgical and renal colic is - "

"Get stuffed." The phone went dead,which was probably just as well, since Avalon had started to make quite loud moaning noises - it only takes one hand to hold the phone,you see. She was only the vicar's daughter, I thought, but - by golly! If I didn't know better, I'd think that she was actually being turned on by the idea that people on the other end of the phone might be able to hear her.

"Look, I'm sorry, love," I said, "I'll have to ring him back."

I took my finger out of Avalon and put it in the telephone dial, using that digit to ring Casualty, in the dark, by sense of touch - just one of those little skills you pick up as you go along. As I saw it, there were two - no, three - ways of off-loading O'Malley and his known case of nephrocalcinosis:

1. Could plead illness. - "I'd love to see him, honestly, Max, but I've got this headache, I've been sick a couple of times, and . . . " - 2. Could ring Pereira - shifty brown sluggard of a medical houseman - and insist he gets up to see patient; 3. Could give in my notice, effective immediately.

"Hallo? Casualty."Indian sub-continent woman's voice.

"Can I speak to Dr Waters again, please?"

"He's busy at the moment. Can I take a message?"

"Yes, tell him it's Dr Fullen here. Say that I'm not going to admit that renal colic patient to Ward Five. Tell him that renal colic is a medical emergency, and he's got no right to - "

"Just a minute, please."

I found myself making moaning noises too, as Avalon took it on herself to demonstrate the physiological advantages of over-sized lips. "Jesus Christ," I breathed.

"Hello? Dr Fullen?"

"Ooh, God! That's wonderf – Ah! Er – yes ?"

"Dr Waters says 'Piss off'."

Chapter 2

In the Casualty Treatment Room, a Lancastrian night sister of great antiquity and appalling facial appearance was remonstrating with some foreigner, who might have been a seaman and might have been Spanish, but was probably neither.

"No. Wrong department, understand?" she was saying, "You want Special Clinic. Spe-shul Klee-nik - Clinica Especial. No look: this - this cazz-ew-al-ee-tee, see? Wrong place. Wrong department. Departmento incorrecto, savvy?"

She was brandishing a Red Cross language card of the type issued to all emergency departments. These rendered into foreign unlikely expressions such as "Does it hurt when you cough?" or "Please put out your tongue" - phrases which never cropped up in conversation with the sort of patients I came across. If it had been left to me, I'd have scrapped the lot and replaced them with a selection of really useful stuff like "Get back to your ship, you greasy Wop" or "Go home, Frog, you are stinking the place out with garlic", or, better still, I would have perforated them at one corner and hung them up in the nearest carsey.

Skirting the Treatment Room, I kept against the corridor wall so as to avoid any involvement with a boiler-suited yob who was expressing his dissatisfaction at the emergency dental service to the wanker of a desk porter, and headed for the fetid little Duty Room. There, between the unwashed coffee mugs and the half-eaten suppers, I came across a pile of Casualty Cards. The first lot had been written by whoever it was that had been on Day Duty, and I had no difficulty in recognising the Anglo-Indian scrawl of one character who had won my grudging admiration by repeatedly referring to the nursing staff as "White Trash". "Patient is complaining of flat feet, also losing his memory," the top card read. God help the bleeding National Health Service. O'Malley's card lay uppermost in the centre of the desk and, following the smell of festering liver, I traced its owner to the accident bay at the end of the corridor.

"Mr O'Malley?"

"You what?"

"Mr O'Malley - is that you?"

O'Malley actually took the trouble to look around him at this point, as if to check that there was no-one else of a similar name in the cubicle, and then he said, "Oh yes, that's me alright."He looked to good to be true, as though someone in the make-up department had been asked to make him look Irish and had overdone it. Eyebrows meet in the middle - check. Teeth like yellowing gravestones over grown with moss - check. Calloused bananas in place of fingers - check. Stained leather belt holding together over-large stained corduroy trousers - check.

"Have you still got this pain?" I asked robotically.

O'Malley grinned amiably. "What pain would that be, now?"

I seriously considered simply punching him in the mouth and leaving it at that. "Which pain d'you think I'm talking about?"

"Ah - you mean the kidney stones."

"Right. Have you still got the pain?"

"Well now," he said in a sing-song voice, "that sort of depends."

"No, it doesn't sort of depend. Either you've got the pain or you haven't."

"Well, I have and I haven't, if you follow my meaning."

"No, I do not follow your meaning. It's perfectly straightforward. Either you've got the pain or you haven't."

This argument seemed to break a lot of new ground as far as O'Malley was concerned. A new and fresh approach which shed a whole new light on the situation.

"Well, I've sort of had it on and off for a bit."

"On and off? How d'you mean - on and off?"

"Well, it comes and goes, like."

"For how long?"

"What d'you mean, for how long?"

Speaking very slowly and clearly, I said, "Look, Mr O'Malley, read my lips. How - long - have - you - had - the - pain?"

"Well, I've sort of had it on and off for a bit," O'Malley said blithely. Stunned temporarily by the cyclical motion of this last bit of dialogue, I looked again at the Casualty Card to see what Waters had been able to glean from the ramblings of this peasant. It said, "Known case of renal stones. Pain on and off for a bit. O/E: nothing definite. Looks a bit pissed to me. Admit to be on safe side. M.W."

Now the doctor-patient relationship is very special; it is a relationship and a trust normally as sacrosanct as that of the confessional. I am no different from several thousand other junior doctors making their way up the greasy pole of hospital life. I *can* care about my patients: their welfare can be important to me: I really can feel compassion, but this relationship is a two-way bargain.When you have had two hours sleep the night before and have been plucked from the nest in the small hours of the morning to see some geezer who has rolled up to hospital because he's got nothing better to do, you react in a very different way. I look at O'Malley again – the scrawny neck craning around in its grimy shirt collar, like some giant red-necked, boil-ridden tortoise; on his face an expression so artless, so lacking in guile, as to suggest a sheep chewing the cud.

I put my face very close to his. "Listen, Buggerlugs," I hiss with quite a lot of low menace, "I have had two hours sleep in the past two days. It is one o'clock in the morning, and they have got me out of bed because you've walked in here and told them you've got a pain. Now: I am going to give you one more chance. When I ask you if you've still got the pain, you will answer either yes or no – understand me?"

"Oh , yes," O'Malley said, as though nothing could be more reasonable.

"Right. Mr O'Malley, have you got the pain now?"

"Wheell, yes – I have had it for a bit."

"A 'bit' – how long's that? An hour, a day, a couple of years, since the end of the Second World War?"

"Well, a couple of days or so."

"A – couple – of – days?" I repeated angrily.

O'Malley nodded agreeably: "Sort of. On and off."

"A couple of days, eh? And what made you suddenly decide to walk in here with it in the middle of the night?"

A bewildered look came over O'Malleys face. "Well, the place is open, isn't it?" he genuinely wanted to know. "That's what the place is for."

Steady, now. I counted slowly from one to ten and then I asked, "And what makes you think that I want to get dragged out of bed in the middle of the night just to look at you, you silly bastard?"

"You're *doctors,* aren't you?" O'Malley said emphasizing the word doctors. "That's what your job is. That's what you're here for."

"You stupid, thick - shit! I'm a scientist, you cretinous bugger, not a bloody maniac philanthropist! If you 've put up with it for two days, you can put up with it until the morning. Now piss off home!"

I pulled open the sliding door to find Max Waters clutching a Thompson's splint and having a crafty smoke.

"Nice one, Robbo," he said. "I knew I could rely on you to be diplomatic."

"Bloody moron," I said.

"I take it you don't want him, then?"

"I'm not having the cretin. You want to give him a bed for the night, you get Pereira to see him."

"I already have," Waters said. "He didn't want him, either."

"Well, I'm off back to bed."

"Yeah - I heard," Waters called after me. "Give her one for me, mate."

As the swing doors banged shut behind me, I could hear O'Malley's offended Celtic tones asking, "And I suppose you call yourself a doctor, do you?"

Divesting myself of my shirt, I gave my breath and my pits a quick olfactory check, and then slipped quietly into bed beside Avalon - a Snow White figure, breathing deeply and noiselessly, so picturesque in the filtered moonlight that my first reaction was that it would be cruel to wake her, but this beautiful relationship of ours has not yet been consummated beyond the stage of a lick, a grope and a promise, and the thing has to be done tonight, otherwise it might never happen. There are times when a man has got to be prepared to sacrifice selfish interests and do what a man's gotta do.

So, where was I, now? "The art of arousal under unusual circumstances". Now the master sidles up behind his quarry, accommodating himself to the convexity of her greyhound-like back like a pair of spoons; now his lips go to work on the ears, fingers count the ribs and then make for the high, perky breasts.

No immediate results, for Avalon is far away in her world of whatever it is that people who *don't believe in experiments on animals* dream about. This is going to take some time.

As I laboured away, I was surprised to find that the Irish question was still troubling me. What was it O'Malley wanted to know? Did I call myself a doctor? OK, then, *did* I call myself a doctor, and, if so, what sort of doctor did I call myself? A pen-pusher, a pill-pusher, a scribbler of notes that nobody but me bothered to read? A performer of menial tasks? A creep who sucked up to his consultant in the hope of getting a decent reference? Yes, I was all of those things. But a doctor? Well now . . .

There was this book - it was called *The Big Citizen.* It sold thirty million copies worldwide. Thirty million and one, if you count Avalon's, for didn't I see a copy sticking out of her tasselled shoulder bag that afternoon at the zoo? The full story of the book is far too tedious to go into, except to say that it concerns one Lucas Devlin, MD (Luke to us) "Healer of the Sick, Comforter of the Aged", who has the hots for this heiress woman. She wants Luke to shack up with her, and let her daddy - who owns Colorado, or somewhere - buy Luke his own breast-enlarging factory. Luke, though, is the kind of four-square guy who gets out of the bath to pee, even when nobody's looking. Because of his terribly high principles, terribly low sex drive, terrible lack of common sense and all the rest of it, Luke feels that his mission in life is to make himself bloody miserable by ministering to the poor and needy of Bolivia. "A moving, wounding, absorbing drama that lays bear a doctor's innermost conflicts" the Sunday Something Or Other called it.

Avalon confessed that she had read that book *three times*. I am convinced that she thinks Luke Devlin, MD is a real live person. I also have a theory that she thinks *I* am Luke Devlin, and that is at least part of the reason that she is in my bed tonight. If so, I am not about to disillusion her - not yet, anyway.

It is hard to believe that anyone could mistake me for Luke Devlin, but Avalon's grasp on medical reality is extremely tenuous: When I first suggested that she might visit me in the Residency this evening, she rather sweetly remarked that she "Hadn't realised I was on night duty", quite clearly under the illusion that housemen clocked off and on for day and night shifts like workers in a car factory. Anyone as naive as that ought to be a sucker for my proper doctor impersonation.

"Oh, hullo," Avalon breathed. "What time is it?"

"Ah - oh, one-ish."

"How is that poor old man with the terrible pain?" she asked. In the gloom, I could make out the furrowing of her brow and the look of genuine compassion on her face. The big red lips were puckered as she asked, "Were you able to do anything for him?"

"Yes - I sorted him out."

"Is he alright now?" Avalon persisted, with a real note of concern in her voice. "I'm not keeping you away from your work, am I?" She gave the word "work" an inflection that was almost Schweizeresque in conception: building a couple of leper colonies, composing an organ sonata or two, that sort of thing, rather than - well - sticking your finger up somebody's bum or any of the other things you were called on to do as a surgical houseman. What an awful lot she had to learn, this girl.

"No, no" I reassured her. "He's fine now. He's in good hands." Which led on nicely to what I now had in my good hands, and the way that Avalon was beginning to respond, making little gurgling noises in the back of her throat as I complimented her - almost entirely truthfully - on some of the delights of her physical attributes.

"Oh yes," she purred, arching her back and stretching her beautiful long limbs. "Oh yes - that's lovely."

Now the master will tease and torment - holding back, delaying the ultimate fulfilment, prolonging the moment into one long, ecstatic fantasy. Avalon is really beginning to enjoy this. I step lightly onto the cold lino beside the bed, shifting my angle of attack, homing in at an acute angle on my target, and Avalon is able to contain herself no longer. Well, who could? The gurgling noises become rapid puffs, the rapid puffs become gasps, the gasps become moans.The moans become -

"My sodding bleep!" I detached Avalon's right thigh from my right ear and swung upright on the side of the bed, dropping the telephone receiver into the gap between the bed and the bedside cabinet. As I groped for it, I could hear a female voice asking, "Dr Fullen?"

"Look - yes, look. Why do you - ?"

"Dr Fullen?"

"Yes, look, why do you go on bleeping me all night? If you know I'm in my room, why don't you just ring the - ?"

"Mr Barrington for you."

"Is that you, Bob? "

"Unn."

"Where the hell have you been, old chap? We've been looking all over for you" Barrington said.

"Did you think of ringing my room? Did you try bleeping me?"

My registrar appeared not to hear any of this. "Can you come up to Ward Five?" he asked, almost as though there was more than one possible answer to that question. "We've got a bit of a flap on."

Chapter 3

"The amazing thing, really," Barrington said, "was the post- mortem result." As he spoke, he tilted his chair forwards and I nodded, noticing with some disquiet the smear of grease - like a giant snail's track - which had been deposited on the X-ray viewing screen by the back of Barrington's head. "Yes, absolutely astounding. Carcinoma of the prostate: carcinoma of the thyroid - well, we'd expected that. But d'you know what had finally finished the old boy off?" Swallowing a yawn, I mimed inquisitive interest, at the same time making a mental resolve to promote Barrington in the batting order of the Stupid Pillocks Team.

"Carcinoma of the bronchus."

"Uh?"

"Yes, carcinoma of the bronchus. The old chap had developed a third, quite separate malignancy, I'm afraid to say."

Thinking what a pity it was that there were not far more things that Barrington was afraid to say, I muttered, "Yes, that's all very interesting, Kush, but I rather wanted to get back to bed as soon as possible. I only had two hours sleep last night, and - "

"Oh yes, of course. I do sympathise," Barrington said, pretending to sympathise. "They really ought to cut down the Surgical Take to twenty four hours. Two sleepless nights on the trot is really a bit much for you chaps." The registrars did one night on call to the houseman's two, which enabled them to say trite, pissy things like that. "Well, let's go and take a look at the old boy."

Gathering up the notes, I followed Barrington out of the office and down the corridor. Why, I asked myself, did someone so obviously Indian by parentage as Barrington have to affect such a god-awful imitation of an English Public School accent? Come to think of it, what was an Indian doing with a name like Barrington, anyway? It was all very sinister. "Have you had any more thoughts about what job you're going to do next?" Barrington asked,

"Not a lot, really."

"Well, you want to get on with it, old chap, get something sorted out. How much longer have you got here with Jimmie? Five - six weeks?"

"Three and a bit."

Barrington gave a low whistle. "My God, that's cutting it a bit fine. Have you asked Jimmie for a reference?"

"Not yet."

"Well I should have a chat with him if I were you," Barrington said. "You've probably gathered that you're not in line for an A-plus houseman's award. I mean, he doesn't regard your time here as an unqualified success."

Thank you so much, Kush Baby. The one thing I didn't need reminding about was the current state of my relationship with my consultant. "Yeah," I said. "Well, I'm not a particularly big fan of his either, come to that."

Barrington simply shook his head and said, "My Dear Chap", then he strode confidently into the side ward and up to the nearer of its two beds. "Mr Pike, is that right?" he asked the old person in occupation, "My name is Barrington - surgical registrar. Dr Leonard spoke to me about you on the telephone."

Pike simply said, "Eh?". There were multi-coloured stains down the front of his thick cotton pyjamas - food, dribble, snot, ear wax, sweat, urine, that sort of stuff. Hair protruded in thick bushes from his ears and his nose, and his mouth had the permanently caved-in look of someone for whom false teeth were too much trouble. He looked so fucked-up that you couldn't imagine him having an independent life - no separate existence as anything but a bed-ridden hospital patient.

I peered over Barrington's shoulder as he scanned the GP's letter. "Family Doctor's Distress Syndrome," I muttered. "Got all the signs and symptoms."

"Dear Dwww," the letter said, "Mwww Abert Pike (aet 78). Thak you for admiting this pwwnt who complwws of abomnal pain. Ywwws Swwwly, H P Lwwwwwd, MB, BS."

"Well, at least he nearly got his age right," I observed. As an example of a GP referral letter, it was pretty average. This, then, was what these men had sacrificed years of their life learning to do - to be able, when confronted with a man complaining of bellyache, to diagnose abdominal pain (if not spell it) and ship him off to the nearest hospital.

"Have you had your bowels open today?" Barrington asked.

"You what?"

"You had your bowels open? Have you been to the toilet today?"

The old person turned appealingly to me. "I don't understand what he means," he said in a tone of justified bafflement, as though an inter-galactic visitor had just tried to communicate with him by tap-dancing.

"Have you been to the bog today?" I translated.

"Look, what is it you're saying? I don't understand what it is you're saying."

"Have - you - had - a - shit - today? Oh, forget it." God give me strength. Opening Pike's notes, I added the words "Not a Cerebral Giant" and left Barrington to get on with it. A copy of the Breckleigh Evening Argus had been left strewn across the cracked green armchair next to the bed. "Dying Widow Turned Away By Hospital" it said. Immediately above this headline there was a photograph of a fat female equestrian, demonstrating just how badly in need of dental treatment she was.

"Put - your - deaf-aid - in!" Barrington was saying in a low, menacing voice.

Now then, could this be a picture of Dying Widow herself and, if so, had she been mounted on a horse at the time admission to hospital had been refused? No. Closer scrutiny of the paper revealed that this was a quite different old person who had won rosettes for something at some local equestrian tomfoolery. The Dying Widow (no relation) had had bellyache for two weeks and when she finally rolled up to Casualty some time after midnight, she had been advised to consult her own doctor the following morning. Sounds fair enough to me: if you're going to have bellyache for two weeks, you should choose some reasonable hour to seek help. Anyway, this one didn't. Died a couple of days later. Oh, so some joker on the Community Health Council thought an inquiry was called for, did he?

"You'd better order about a dozen units of blood," Barrington said, interrupting my perusal of the Births, Marriages and Deaths column. "*Slapton, Richard. Peacefully in hospital*". One of mine.

"Blood?"

"Yes, blood. You know - red stuff. Comes in little plastic bags." He was now probing about in the patient's groins, hunched up over the bed like someone in the advanced throes of constipation.

"Ah, but I thought – ?"

"Yes?"

I flicked through Pike's old hospital notes, searching for inspiration. "He's got a past history of diverticulitis – "

"Not diverticulitis this time though, is it?" Barrington turned his face triumphantly towards me. "Sudden onset of back and abdominal pains in an elderly man," he went on, making the statement sound like a question.

"Oh yes?"

"Well?"

"Well what?" This technique of chipping away my thin veneer of surgical bluff to expose the worm-eaten core of medical ignorance was one that Barrington had picked up from Jimmie Materson. Materson used it simply as a method of humiliating his houseman in public, whereas with Barrington it was more a case of being used as a stooge to show off to himself and to the world in general just how unbelievably sodding brainy he was. "If I told you I couldn't feel his femoral pulses – what would you say then?" Barrington persisted.

An obscene expletive, recommending Barrington's immediate departure suggested itself as the answer to that one. "Don't know," I said.

"Oh, come on, old chap, come on."

"Coronary?"

"Think now – shocked patient – abdominal pain – absent femoral pulses?"

"Oh God, no! Not a sodding aneurysm!"

The patient began to stir, and in the tones of Warrington or somewhere like that, he confided to me, "I just can't understand what this blackie feller says, you know."

"Oh God, yes – a sodding aneurysm."

"Aw! Jesus Christ on a bicycle!" The point is that, while I could cheerfully tell a case of recurrent diverticulitis to take a couple of aspirins and ring me back in the morning, an aortic aneurysm-threatening the imminent rupture of the largest artery in the body-could most decidedly not be treated in a like fashion. "Oh . . . shit!" Rocking back on my heels, I blew out my cheeks while my mind, like an old hand-cranked cash register slowly totted up what this was going to mean to me in terms of hours of lost sleep and, more especially, the other thing.

"So you'd better get a move on with the blood, hadn't you?" Barrington said. "Oh, and while you're at it," he added, "you might give Jimmie a ring. He'll want to be in on this one."

"Can you give me Torrisham Fitzurst 263?"

"Mr Materson's residence? Hold on please."

I looked again at my watch. This is how it adds up: say fifty minutes to get patient to theatre with blood. Allow thirty minutes for Jimmie to drive in, drink his Ribena, get scrubbed up and exchange funny stories with Barrington. Another ten minutes while he bellyaches at the nursing staff, complains about the light and the temperature of the theatre, plus, say, five minutes reminding the anaesthetist what a fucking good emergency surgeon he is and how lucky the patient is to have him. Better say a three-thirty kick off. Add to that the inescapable fact that it will be Jimmie doing the carving. For all his constantly asking to have his teeth kicked in, you had to admit that Barrington could slice people to bits with the best of them. Jimmie, on the other hand, was a fumble-fisted oaf. Of recent years, he had begun to suffer from the shakes, accidentally unthreading needles and so on. It was painful to watch sometimes. Only a week earlier, during a particularly drawn-out gastrectomy, a snickering anaesthetic registrar had remarked, out of Jimmie's hearing, naturally, "If he goes much slower, the patient'll heal up faster than he cuts him."

"Ringing for you."

"Sod you, Barrington," I muttered. The responsibility for calling in a duty consultant lay with the registrar, but there were obvious reasons why this particular registrar did not feel inclined to call in this particular consultant. During daylight hours, Jimmie Materson was the most unreasonable sod you could ever hope to come across. Woken in the middle of the night, though, he plumbed new depths of horribleness. If you asked him to come in, he behaved as though you had personally engineered the whole thing for the express purpose of dragging him from his pit.

"Yurrhs?"

"Mr Materson?" There was a liquid clacking sound. Jimmie had either just put his false teeth in, or else they had fallen out. At any rate, there was a pause. "I'm sorry to disturb you, sir. It's Fullen here." I waited for some sign of recognition, but none came, so I kept talking. "Mr Barrington asked me to ring you, sir. We've got a patient - a Mr, er, Pike - a man of 81."

I stopped again. It was usual at this stage in the proceedings for Jimmie to interrupt with some stupid irrelevant question, like "Is he coloured?", or - in the case of a child - "Are the parents married?". I say irrelevant, but to Jimmie these questions had great importance, since the wrong answer to either automatically disqualified the patient from membership of the human race and the National Health Service. "He's a man with a long history of diverticular disease, and he's got a four hour history of severe lower abdominal pain - "

This time I waited for Jimmie's usual stream of requests for piddlingly trivial information about the patient's medical, social and sexual history - information which I generally supplied from my own imagination, since it was impossible to anticipate the full scope of his inane curiosity. There was a sound like an exasperated sigh, and the clack of false teeth again.

"Mr Barrington's had a look at him, and he thinks he's got a ruptured aneurysm." This was greeted by a snort from the earpiece. "Er, and so, sir, we were wondering if you'd like to - come in - and if you'd - " What else do you want me to say, Mr Flaming Materson? I fought back the urge to shout at the top of my voice "Come on, you stupid old sod, say something!" There I was, pleading for the old man to cast his imitation pearls of wisdom before me, and all he'd managed so far was a series of wheezes and groans like some old asthmatic attempting an uphill run after a heavy breakfast.

"Theatre's all ready, sir," I said, seeing if a quick spot of lying would liven things up a bit. "And we'll have the blood ready by three thirty." How dare this man pretend to be worth his exorbitant salary? Not, as I reflected, that he needed to. Once you'd got yourself into an unassailable position like Jimmie's, you could do just as you bloody well liked, and you didn't have to justify anything you did to any mortal soul. Scratching my top lip brought the fingers of my right hand directly below my nose, and that inevitably reminded me of Avalon. She had promised that this time she wouldn't fall asleep, but would sit up, read her book and wait up for me. That, however, had been her response to my promise that I'd be back in my room within twenty minutes of leaving it. What chance of that now?

"Well, sir," I finally got up the bottle to say, "Whaddaya think?" The false teeth clacked again, and then I could hear slow, steady breathing. "Mister Materson!" Quite suddenly, the pitch of the breath sounds had dropped and I could hear the unmistakable rattle of snoring. "Hello? Hello? Are you still there, Mister Materson?" I swallowed in disbelief. Dismissing my initial reaction of panic as inappropriate - after all, the man was worse than useless in an emergency, anyway - I came to recognise my second reaction as exasperation at the outrageous behaviour of this silly little man. Fall asleep on the phone? Well, he wasn't getting away with a trick like that. Oh no, I would not allow it. I would make the fat bastard get out of his bed tonight, even if I had to walk all the way down to Torrisham Fitzwhatsit and drag him out by the ankles.

"Oi!" I shouted "Wake up!" I tapped the telephone rest experimentally and yodelled "Mis -tah Ma - tah - sun!"

Click. Purr. "You calling?" A woman asked.

"Oh, Christ, you haven't pulled the plug on that call, have you?"

"What call?"

"That call to Mr Materson."

"Oh, I'm sorry, were you still speaking?"

"Yes, I bloody well was."

"Well, it's your own fault if you will jiggle the receiver up and down."

A pudgy red hand suddenly grabbed me by the shoulder, and I spun round to face a big, wild-eyed night sister, puffing like a beached whale and gasping "Cardiac arrest! Quick! Get back in there. He's had an arrest!"

Chapter 4

It looked like a scene from a cut-price horror movie: the yellowish light from the over-bed lamp threw deep shadows everywhere. Pike had been pulled from his bed onto the floor, dragging his bedclothes and his drip set with him. Barrington was perched on his chest like a great vulture, a larded clump of hair flopping across his face as he pummelled with the flat of his hands on the patient's chest. Pike had decided to do away with himself before Jimmie could get his hands on him to do the job for him. Sensible chap. I hung around the doorway for a bit until Barrington spotted me. "Get a tube down him, can't you?" he called.

Trying to look efficient, I stepped over a pile of discarded pillows and stood at the patient's head, looking down on the little black nurse who was operating the oxygen paraphernalia. She was kneeling on the floor, clasping a rubber face mask to the concave, toothless face and blowing great wet raspberries with each squeeze of the Ambu bag. With exaggerated care, I selected a tube from the resuscitation trolley and started buggering about with the bulb in the laryngoscope. There was no hurry. I had no objection to playing my part in the charade, provided nobody decided to take this thing seriously. The main danger was that Barrington or some other fanatic would demonstrate his total lack of compassion and discretion by making a serious attempt to get Pike going again. I would see to it - by physical restraint if necessary - that no such lunatic scheme got off the drawing board.

Death is OK, you see. Nobody minds being dead; it's the dying that they're not looking forward to; the idea that something pretty unpleasant has to happen to you before you can make it over the threshold into oblivion. Pike was in pain, and now he isn't. He was scared stiff, and now he doesn't have a worry in the world: he's already made it over the threshold. If we drag him back, what has he got to look forward to? A lot more pain, a lot more terror, a badly performed surgical operation and - at the best - a slow, painful, lingering death from gangrene and kidney failure. If we resuscitate him, the kindest thing that can happen to him is that he will die under the anaesthetic.

Barrington looked up and saw me hovering. "What are you playing at?"

he demanded. "Get a tube down him!" The physical effort of cardiac massage was beginning to tell on him, and little beads of sweat had appeared on his brow. Muttering to myself, I crouched down and elbowed the nurse to one side. Gingerly, I probed the laryngoscope into the gaping mouth, hunting about for the voice-box. Thick strands of treacley mucus hung from the blue-pink walls of the throat, and I felt my gorge rising. Things like that seriously cut your chances. I mean, can you imagine somebody attempting the kiss-of-life on a character like that?

"Done it?" Barrington wanted to know.

"No; I'm just - Oh, great! Thanks a lot, Goddo!"

"What's happened now?"

"He's just spewed up all down my shirt."

"For God's sake, Bob, give me those things and you take over here," Barrington puffed.

"Alright. Come on, give us it," a voice behind me said. In the gloom, I had no difficulty in recognising the Humberside accent and the strong smell of sweat as the property of Michael Washbrook, the anaesthetic SHO, who had arrived with the other members of the cardiac arrest team. Gradually, the room began to fill up with these people. Like a team of formation clog-dancers, they began to tread on each other's toes in the confused scramble that was their version of the resuscitation procedure. Bits of electrical equipment were being wheeled in, a curtain was pulled in front of the spectator in the next bed, and the objects which I was still holding on to were wrenched from my grasp. I tried to stand my ground and get in the way as much as possible, until I got kicked on the shin for the second time. That was it. Picking my way between the tangle of groping arms and legs and electrical leads, I shuffled off and left them to it.

"No, no, no. It's thump, thump, thump - Squeeze!" I could hear a Celtic voice saying, "Thump, thump, thump - squeeze! For God's sake, laddie, look, thump, thump, thump - squeeze!"

I tell you, when I go, I'm going to glue razor blades on my chest to stop some hairy rugby-playing houseman bouncing up and down on me like that. The valiant never taste of death but once, and I'm not about to have several bites at it, either. I wandered out into the corridor. This thing couldn't succeed, surely? No, for Pike's sake, it had better not succeed, that's all. In five minutes, poor old Pike would be having cotton wool stuffed up his orifices, and in fifteen minutes, Avalon would be having something else stuffed up hers. I did a little shuffle and hissed a tune through my teeth that might have been by Bach or one of those other dead foreigners, but probably wasn't. Life sometimes had this way of sorting itself out.

"Is that blood on the way?" a voice that could only be Barrington's enquired.

"Why? Have they – ?"

"Yes, they've got him going again," Barrington said. "No thanks to you."

Thanks? What was this extraordinary creep trying to imply? That he was in line for some form of gratitude? Was that it? "You're still taking him to theatre, then?" I asked.

Barrington having confirmed that he was indeed still taking him to theatre, I recounted to him the Jimmie-asleep-on-the-phone episode. This did not induce in Barrington anything like the reaction I had hoped for. He seemed to take it all in his stride, as one informed that there might be sunny intervals later in the day. That was unfair. Why was he not moved to berate the old bugger for his indolence, or laugh himself sick at the antics of this fat, red-nosed clown? That confirmed it. They were all in this thing together. You could get away with murder so long as you were who you were.

"You're going to do it yourself, then?" I asked.

"It rather looks as though I'm going to have to, doesn't it?" Barrington said, scarcely able to contain his delight.

"No, not necessarily. Why don't we give him a trial of spontaneous survival? You know, keep an eye on him till the morning, then if he's still alive – " Barrington's pitying gaze was interrupted by the re-emergence of the night sister from the office with the news that Jimmie had broken surface, had managed to divine the reason for his holding on to a dead telephone in his sleep, and had announced his intention of being in the operating theatre at three thirty for the express purpose of setting about the aneurysm with his surgical hardware.

"Ah, great," Barrington actually said.

"Yeah: bloody marvellous." What a greasy pillock this man Barrington was. What could possibly be "great" at three o'clock in the morning that was not connected with being in bed for some purpose or other? I felt like asking him to explain himself. What exactly did he think was so "great"?

What did he mean anyway - "great"? Why did he not take a running jump at himself? Especially that.

Barrington smarmed on. He was going to go down to theatre to "fix things up", in other words, to scrounge scrambled eggs off the night staff - and would I be so good as to inform the Consultant Anaesthetist on call that Jimmie would like to meet him in theatre in an hour or so. Without waiting to hear whether I would be so good or not, he sloped off down the corridor, pausing briefly to stick his head round the door of the side ward and mutter a few words that might have been thanks and encouragement, but could have been a dirty limerick for all I knew or cared.

The cardiac arrest team now began to shamble out in their pyjama jackets and hastily fastened trousers. They were talking away among themselves, and my ears picked out the expression "Eisenmenger complex", which I recognised as something medical that I ought to know something about but didn't. Last out was a nasty bearded Scottish person called McLeod, a medical registrar who was in demand at a certain kind of party for doing tricks like turning his eyelids inside out and leaving them that way. As he passed, he tapped me on the shoulder, "There you go now, Laddie. Now don't go and let old Jimmie cock it up again like he did the last one."

I pulled my chimpanzee face at his back as he swaggered off down the corridor. He must think, then, that he'd done me some kind of favour, must he? I'd had McLeod down as twelfth man for the Stupid Pillocks team. Tonight's performance could well earn him a chance to turn out for the first eleven. I plodded back to the Side Ward. To the left, nurse crouches in pool of vomit, throwing used syringes into plastic bag. To the right, Washbrook - he of the cruddy Fair Isle sweater - is fiddling about with the electrical gismo. Stage centre, Pike, back on his bed, unconscious and breathing jerkily through red rubber tube.

I did not feel like Luke Devlin as I looked down at this crumbling shell of humanity. In these kind of circumstances, Luke is filled with compassion and a dedicated resolve to heal the sick at all costs: "*Quick, nurse, get me adrenaline, ice-packs - the works!*" This is not an occasion for healing the sick; it is an occasion for comforting the aged. Now, I've got nothing against Pike personally. Far from it. Pike had done the decent and sensible thing by having a cardiac arrest - a vote for non- interference, if ever I saw one. And yes,given a choice, I wouldn't be here. I'd much rather be in bed with Avalon, but that has no bearing whatsoever on my decision.

Someone has to protect Pike's interests. I had seen aortic aneurysms before. You spent hours slaving away at them - using up everybody's blood, sweat and tears (especially the first of those) and what happened? The result was always the same. In Jimmie's hands, anyway, the patient never made it, and you can't say fairer than that. What chance, then, for someone who had chucked the towel in before the fight had even begun? To a surgeon, death is the sincerest form of criticism. What was needed here was a slight touch of euthanasia. You could get away with murder so long as you were who you were. Right, then, euthanasia - to "cut short needless suffering". Wasn't that the expression the pamphlets used? And even if Pike wasn't suffering unnecessarily, I certainly was. The sleep deficit of the previous night had caught up on me, and it was now a real effort to put one foot in front of another. That's the really implausible thing about Luke Devlin: no matter how little sleep he gets, he never loses his enthusiasm.

Perhaps the strictly legal way to go about cutting short needless suffering would be for me to get the agreement of my colleagues as to the unkindness of continuing active treatment. That is not as simple as it sounds. For a start, it is not unknown for ruthless buggers like Barrington to operate on hopeless cases just for the practice. The patient's there, so why not cut him up while you've got the chance? Besides, surgery is a fiercely competitive line of work, and a bad reference spells instant death to the career of a registrar like Barrington. Putting some poor sod through unnecessary suffering looks good on your CV: "While I was in Breckleigh, I was enabled to pursue my interest in vascular surgery." A single patient like Pike is such good value for money, too. The time table runs something like this: Day one - graft his aneurysm. Day two - ream out the blocked arteries in his legs. Day four - hack out his sympathetic nerves in a last desperate effort to stop his feet going gangrenous. Day seven - amputate his left foot. Day ten -amputate his right leg below the knee. Day fourteen - amputate his left leg above the knee. And so it goes on, until, day twenty - collect the money for signing the cremation certificate.

Point two is that it is not strictly legal to discontinue treatment, even if your colleagues agree with you. All you need is for one single (usually religious) member of the nursing or medical profession silently to disagree with you. Then he/she goes away and makes a formal complaint, or maybe leaks the story to the press, and you find yourself up Asystole Creek without a defibrillator. No, the buck stops here. We've got to do something to protect Pike from a slow, agonising death. OK, so here's the plan: we stick a finger down the end of his breathing tube. Well, perhaps not. We've got to be subtle about this. With Washbrook and the Staff Nurse still in very visible attendance, a frontal attack - smashing Pike's brains out with an ice pick, say - was out of the question.

"Thou shalt not kill (as some old buffer once put it)/But need'st not strive / Officiously to keep alive." What I intended to do here was not so much what the first bit said you mustn't do as not to do what the second bit said you shouldn't. This is for your own good, Pike. You'll thank me for it later. But how to set about it?

Washbrook wheeled clumsily round to face me. "Another one of your cock-ups, this, was it?" he asked.

"Whaddaya mean - another one of my cock-ups?"

"That bloke with the melaena you over-transfused last month," Washbrook jeered. "Pink froth coming out of his lug holes when he got him down to the ITU."

It was not very kind of Washbrook to remind me of this. It had been a mistake, but a beginner's mistake and, let's face it, I am a beginner. "He survived, didn't he?"

"Yeah, he survived. Only because we managed to keep him away from you, though."

Don't get mad, get even. "Anaesthetised any good stiffs lately?" I asked.

"You what?"

"Nothing."

"What you on about?" Washbrook asked. He came up close to me and peered into my face, almost overpowering me with the rancid smells of armpits and galloping foot-rot.

"You know."

"No I don't. What you on about?"

"It doesn't matter. Forget it."

"No: I won't forget it. Come on: what you talking about?"

Common sense, plus some wise old saw about not throwing stones while dwelling in a frangible domicile, told me to shut my face at this point, but the expression on Washbrook's porcine features was too strong a provocation to resist. "You had a patient dead on the table for ten minutes, and you didn't even notice."

"Oh yeah? You were there, were you?"

"No, but I know somebody who was."

"What - Rossiter?"

"Possibly."

"Rossiter? Get lost. He wasn't there . He'd skived off. Not answering his bloody bleep as usual. Screwing some tart in the linen cupboard on Ward 11 when they finally tracked him down."

"Bollocks. Anyway, what difference does it make?" Secretly, though, I had to admit that it did make a difference. Duggie had assured me that he was standing there watching Washbrook anaesthetise this woman who had died on the table, although Washbrook had not registered this fact until the gynaecology registrar stopped operating, took off his gloves and demonstrated the signs of death to him. That was Duggie's story, anyway. Barring some miracle of gymnastic ability, having it away with some tart in a linen cupboard on Ward 11 at the time of the incident seriously diminished his reliability as a an eye-witness.

"So he knows sod-all about it," Washbrook said. "And anyway, if we're going to talk about cock-ups, who was it - who was it wrote "pupils equal and react to light" in the notes of a bloke with a glass eye?

"Anaesthesia" I said: "The half-asleep watching the half-awake being half-murdered by the half-witted."

"Yeah - "equal and react to light," Washbrook persisted, "and one of his eyes wor made of bloody glass."

"Medd uv bluddy glass, wor it?" I asked, trying to transfer attention to Washbrook's accent - an accent which, combined with some suitable catchphrase such as "Put t'wood in't t'oil" or "Daft as a brush" would have been the livelihood of some northern club-circuit comic, an accent that insisted on not being taken seriously.

"Yeah, it wor made of bloody glass," Washbrook reaffirmed, this time addressing the staff nurse directly. "and he puts down 'pupils equal and react to light'."

"Get knotted."

"And who was it collapsed that bloke's lung with his jugular vein needle?" Washbrook leered, poking me in the ribs with his stubby little fingers.

"Yeah, but at least I recognise a stiff when I see one."

"Oh yeah?" Washbrook asked. I could see he was beginning to enjoy this, which was not good. "And what about that time you tried to put Complan down that bloke's nasal airway?"

"Did I hell as like."

"Yes, you bloody did. Barrington was telling us about it." This last story was pure fiction, but the fact that Barrington thought he could get away with telling such a story was some indication of the reputation I had acquired during my time with Jimmie. "Yeah, you're a useless bastard, you are," Washbrook leered. How to put a stop to this? I'd already tried the funny-voice-imitation angle without success. What next? Should I draw attention to Washbrook's porous nose, perhaps, or his foul complexion, his great fat belly? Should I make insinuations about the cleanliness of his underwear? Should I give him a knuckle sandwich?

"Right wanker, you," Washbrook said flatly. It appeared that he had run out of Fullen cock-up stories, and had moved on to the straightforward name-calling. Good, I could cope with that. Somebody who looked as repulsive as Washbrook ought to know what sort of risk he was running by exchanging personal insults. It was a wonder, looking the way he did, that total strangers did not stop him in the streets to revile him. "Like a dollop of diarrhoea," was how Duggie had described him, "pale, bulky and offensive." So you wanna trade insults, eh, Pig-features?

"Listen, Pig-features - " I began.

"Er - excuse me," the Staff Nurse interrupted. "I think he's stopped again."

"Oh, bloody hell," Washbrook said, waddling back towards the patient and peering at the ECG screen, "He's in asystole." He gave Pike a resounding slap and then started pummelling away on his chest.

I reconnected the Ambu bag to the tube in Pike's mouth but didn't actually start to squeeze it or anything like that. Watching the porker thumping away, I reckoned it was virtually certain that no-one had yet explained the facts of death to him. "Staff nurse, you'd better ring theatre and tell them we'll be bringing the patient down straight away," I said in a stage voice.

Washbrook, right on cue, "Theatre?"

"Yeah, we're going to open this bloke up at half past three."

"Tonight?"

"Yes, oh, and um, Jimmie wants you to get your consultant in," I said slowly.

"Consultant?" Washbrook repeated this word with some difficulty, as though reading it from a foreign phrase book.

"Anaesthetic - consultant - on call. Jimmie's coming in. He's going to chop out this bloke's aneurysm."

"Sorry, Nell." This last, as I took a few seconds to realise, was not an apology, but an oath uttered Humberside style. A subtler or more devious character might have gradually eased up on the cardiac massage with a show of feigned reluctance, but Washbrook just stopped, as though ordered to do so by a man with a gun at his head. "Waste of time, this," he said.

Now I would like to point out that Dr Michael Washbrook is an honourable man, a wonderful, wonderful warm human being, as keen as the next man to do extra, unpaid work. When you've been working non-stop all day, there's nothing you look forward to more than working non-stop all night as well. Of course, as a doctor, you don't actually get paid for doing something like that - you do it for the fun of it, so I would like to make it quite clear that young Mikey's decision was not influenced in any way by the idea that he might have to spend the next five or six hours running errands and carrying out menial tasks on the orders of some captious, bellyaching consultant anaesthetist. No, it was a rational, clinical decision, taken with the best interests of the patient at heart.

"Do you want me to call the arrest team again?" the Staff Nurse asked pointedly.

Washbrook and I exchanged glances. "Ah, no. I don't think so, on the whole," I said.

"You're just going to leave him?"

"Yes, that's just about the size of it," I said. "We're just going to leave him."

"Right," she said, pushing the resuscitation trolley noisily to one side. "If that's what you want." It was then I noticed the badge, in the crude shape of a fish, pinned to her lapel. Jesus Christ.

"That's what we want," Washbrook told her bluntly, but he could see me pulling faces and crossing myself behind her back. His eyes came to rest on the fish badge. "That's – what he want," he repeated, more diplomatically. To be on the safe side, we did a bit more play-acting, feeling the patient's pulse, pretending to look at his pupils and so on. It was all done in the best mock-reverential style. "That's it, he's gone," Washbrook said after what we felt was a decent interval and I pulled the sheet respectfully over Pike's face.

Back in the office, I wrote a brief summary of all this in Pike's notes while Washbrook stoked his face with five or six chocolates from the box on the desk – a gift from bereaved relatives to the night staff. Afterwards, we walked in silence out of the ward and along the corridor to theatre. Watching someone else die is not quite the sobering experience you expect it to be. Like everything else, you get used to it, I'm afraid.

Barrington was in the nurses' sitting room, reading the BMJ. The news that it was all off seemed to come as a real blow to him.

"What: you mean to say he just stopped?" he asked suspiciously through a mouthful of scrambled egg.

"Yep, just stopped. Just like that," I said confidently, daring him to call me a liar. "One minute he was there, the next – poof!"

Barrington thought for a second and then he asked, "Have you told Jimmie yet?"

"No. I rang him last time. Why don't you do it?" Without waiting for a reply, I set off after the waddling figure of Washbrook. I caught up with him in the empty, echoing corridor, and we sauntered off in the direction of Bleak House, side by side, locked in academic debate, like a couple of Oxbridge dons. I put the argument to Washbrook frankly and simply. Doctors are faced, I told him, with a law of diminishing returns: an aging population requiring more and more resources. The result is that we put more and more money and effort into achieving less and less. There should be some set of guide lines, I argued, some cut-off point at which we decided to make the patient comfortable, rather than waste money on cavalier exercises that had no real hope of benefiting the patient.

Washbrook listened to all this in silence, then he turned to me and spoke these words, "Here – that skinny bint dun't half make a racket when you shag her, dun't she?"

Chapter 5

"You'll be Dr Mattinson, then?" the little man asked.

No fear, chum. You won't catch me being Dr Mattinson. "Ah, no, I'm afraid I'm Dr Fullen. I'm his . . . I work for him." I said, even though he could have worked out most of it for himself, if he'd bothered to read my name-badge.

"Oh yes, Dr Fullen." All three of them nodded, as though they'd heard of me. Surely not. "We're Mr Lillicrap's relatives. I'm his brother-in-law, Mr Chapman. This is Mrs Lillicrap, and this is my wife, Mrs Chapman."

Very non-U to refer to yourself as "Mister" - did you know that, Mr Chapman? "Hi," I said, because, well, I'm just a lovable, laid-back, easy-going kind of guy, I guess.

"Sister on the ward said we should have a word with you about how he's getting on, and that."

"We're sorry to come at this time in the morning, only they said you was busy last night, and my sister's going back to Wolverhampton this afternoon," Mrs Lillicrap explained.

"Ah, yes." We were standing in the Hospital Visitor's Room - a shitty anachronism of a place, done out in the worst excesses of Victorian Sanitary Gothic. There was stained glass in the windows and a bomb-proof fireplace of gargantuan proportions, from which life-sized black-marble ladies were flashing their bristols. You were always supposed to interview relatives in this room, because it impressed upon them the tradition and the full majesty of the Breckleigh Royal Infirmary. There was a non-functioning grandfather clock, and oil paintings of bilious eighteenth century surgeons glared down at us from the walls. This arrangement, whatever good it did for public relations, carried the very minor inconvenience that here, a quarter of a mile from the ward in some cases, you couldn't consult the patient's notes. This was doubly inconvenient in a case such as this, where you couldn't remember who the hell Mr Lillicrap was.

"Right then. Mr Lillicrap. Er - How long is it since he had his operation?" I ventured.

"Ooh, that'd be – that'd be a week ago yesterday," Chapman said. "Yes, week ago yesterday. Eight days ago."

That narrowed the field a bit. Lillicrap. Lillicrap? Ah, yes.That's it. Little old bloke in the corner bed. Carcinomatosis from cancer of the prostate. Terminal bronchopneumonia. "Yehhs – Mr Lillicrap." I switched to my undertaker's voice. "Would you like to sit down?"

I'm not too fascinated by all this. All part of the job, I'm afraid. Just one of those things you've got to get through in order to earn an honest crust. I'd much rather talk about Avalon. She was fucking marvellous. She really did keep her promise by staying awake for me – well, almost awake, anyway. She had been reading *The Big Citizen* to wile away the hour, and when I got back, she was full of vicarious doctorly concern for the lives I had been saving, the battle against sickness and disease I had been waging, the sick I had been healing, the aged I had been comforting and all like that. Of course, I had to tell her that Pike had snuffed it, but in some strange way this actually seemed to add to the glamour of the job, a mild aphrodisiac, almost, and I had been able to fall upon her with unbridled whatever it was. It would be an exaggeration to say that we hadn't slept a wink after that, but that was almost it. The surprising thing was, though, that, apart from a slight stiffness in the old genital heft muscles, I really felt remarkably good this morning.

"How long is it since anybody last spoke to you about Mr Lillicrap?" I asked.

"Nobody hasn't told us nothing. Not since the operation, anyway."

What did they want me to say, exactly? Anybody with two neurones to rub together could see that the old buffer had had it. "Well, as you can see, he's a rather sick man." Oh, come on now; don't tell me you hadn't realised. "Yes; he's rather sick. Not at all well, I'm afraid. Now, as you know, he had this growth in his prostate gland, and the growth – "

"Growth?"

"Yes. This growth has – "

"You mean cancer?" the sister-in-law interrupted. She was definitely a brain-cell or two up on the others. I'd put my money on retired school teacher, something like that.

"Well, yes. It's a sort of cancer, and I'm afraid that this growth has spread – "

"We didn't know nothing about him having a growth," Chapman said. "Nobody said nothing about him having a growth."

"Yes, well I'm afraid there's no doubt, you see. Mr Materson took a look with a special instrument, and I'm afraid there's no doubt about it." While I was saying this, I was fighting a running battle with the corners of my mouth, which were trying to strike a compromise between a disarming smile and an appropriately funereal expression of sympathy. The trouble is, you see, that, for them, this is a one off, a great tragedy, even, but for me it's all in a day's work. We've all gotta go sometime. Lillicrap was not in the first flush of youth, and he hadn't spoken a coherent word for the past five days. You can be sympathetic by all means, but you really can't afford to get involved. "We sent a bit off to the laboratory for them to look at, and they say that it is a cancer." The three relatives looked at each other and then stared into space. Finding myself at a loose end, I stared at the marble ladies who stared back as if to say that they had to watch this sort of thing a dozen times a day and were unimpressed. Next, please.

"So it's cancer, then?" The sister-in-law asked, by way of showing that she could comprehend basic conversational English.

"Yes, I'm rather afraid it is."

"Is it a bad cancer, doctor?" the wife asked.

Of the three, she was the one I really did feel sorry for, so I avoided an obvious semantic quibble about what she thought might constitute a good cancer and said, "Well, it's not an early one, I'm afraid."

"Will you be frank with us, doctor?" the sister-in-law asked. "Tell us, straight up, how long has he got?" This line was so obviously lifted from a work of fiction that it was difficult to avoid acting back, to avoid looking like Luke Devlin, MD does when he pronounces the death sentence.

"Yes, well I'm afraid that the growth has spread quite a bit. It's reached the stage where – Well, basically, there's not much more we can do for him now except make him comfortable."

The two women began to bite their lips and sway backwards and forwards in some ritualistic demonstration of grief.

"Nobody told us," the brother-in-law said. "Nobody told us he was going to die." He drew in a breath. "We had no idea."

"I'm sorry," I said. I looked at my watch. "I hate to rush you, but I'm afraid I'm late for – "

"We'll have to let his daughter know," the brother-in-law said." Do you think we could go up and see him?"

"Yes, of course."

"Only we'd no idea, you see. It's all come as a bit of a shock to us."

"Yes, well of course it has. So if you just go and have a word with sister – "

"Yes, we mustn't keep you any longer, doctor."

The very words I was about to use myself. "Yes, well you pop up there, have a word with Sister. She'll see you're alright," I said and, giving the marble ladies a last sneer, I headed for the common room.

"Nice one, Goddo!" Duggie's bleep had gone off as he was pouring his coffee, and he had tripped in walking over to the telephone, half-emptying his cup onto the moulting green carpet. He set down the cup on the telephone shelf, slopping the other half of its contents into the saucer. "Shit, shit, shit!" he hissed mechanically, and began rubbing the carpet with the sole of his shoe, dispersing the steaming white stain into the pile. Abandoning this exercise as being not so much non-beneficial to the carpet as non-profitable to himself, he picked up the phone and began to chew at a loose finger nail. "Yeah, waddaya want?" he asked the voice at the other end. "Oh, fucking hell! Not him again. Alright, put him on." As he lounged back against the wall, he belched softly and began to sniff his pits.

A stranger witnessing this performance might be excused for thinking that Duggie was competing for the title "Dirtiest Doctor Of The Year", but he could do things like that, and much worse besides, without even trying. His nickname, though, referred not so much to these filthy personal habits, (though, God knows, they were bad enough) as to his supposed sexual activities. According to popular legend, the Dirty Doctor had fucked the entire female nursing staff of the hospital, barring the odd lesbian and a few cripples. This claim had once been the subject of a serious late-night debate in the Mess. Some said that, purely on logistic grounds, such an achievement was impossible.

"No chance, my old fruit. Nooo way," he was telling some GP. "We're not here just so you can bog off and play golf, you know."

Settling down behind the Breckleigh Morning News, I pretended not to notice. Ho ho ho. Case of a local family doctor, charged with shoplifting some books from Smith's in the town centre. Consultant neurologist gave evidence that the doctor "might conceivably have suffered some sort of blackout and temporary mental aberration, brought on by bending down." Verdict: not guilty. The doctor left the court without a stain on his character. Well now, we do stick together, don't we? Still, it cuts both ways. I mean, how many of his patients are going to want to think that the old fool on the other end of the syringe suffers from temporary mental aberrations?

"Yes, I know how it is. Want a quiet weekend, eh?" The volume and speed of Duggie's speech had increased to a level at which it was difficult to concentrate on anything else. "Thought you'd off-load her so you don't have to bother looking after her yourself. Right, well you just do that, old son." With that, he slammed down the phone, tipped the contents of the saucer back into the cup and drank with what, in comparison to his earlier performance, was a creditable absence of slurping and gasping noises.

"What was all that?"

"Bloody GP," Duggie said, as if that explained everything.

"Oh."

After a pause, Duggie asked, "You still applying for that job at whatsits, then?"

"Queen Alexandra's? Yeah. I got this this morning." I handed him the inexpertly torn buff envelope from my top pocket. Duggie took out the typewritten note, bearing the scarcely believable heading "Queen Alexandra's Hospital For Consumptives, S.E.28 (Under Royal Patronage)". This wished to inform me that, with reference to my recent application for the post of . . . SHO in Thoracic Surgery . . . I had been selected for interview the following Thursday.

"You must be off your chump," Duggie told me.

"Oh, must I?"

"Yes, you must."

Pigface Washbrook rolled into the room. "Nah then, Fullen, he said, "how's your sex life ?" The smirk that went with this reminded me of something I didn't wish to be reminded of. The anaesthetic on-call room had a door which connected with my room – a hang-over from former times, when a Resident Surgical Officer occupied a suite of rooms in Bleak House. The door had been rendered unopenable, and some sort of pegboard had been glued to it in a gesture towards soundproofing, but even fairly quiet noises from the next room - Washbrook snoring or farting for example - were clearly audible. I would not put it past Washbrook to have been laying awake, listening to all those noises Avalon had let out during three hours of fairly solid nooky. I mean, look at that man, what kind of sex-life can anyone who looks like that have, other than watching other people do it? I suddenly had this revolting mental image of a white, sow-like creature, stretched out on the floor, wanking an extremely tiny sex organ encased in blubber, and trying to peer through the crack under the door.

"Piss off!" I told him." Why must I be off my chump?"

"Chest surgery. There's no money in it. It's just bloody hard graft. You want to get into something soft like skins or eyes."

"Is he applying for a job, then?" Washbrook asked, adding a little coffee to his sugar. "He'll be bloody lucky. You should have heard what Jimmie was telling Winstanley about him last week."

"Look, piss off."

"Hope you haven't asked him for a reference, that's all, kid. He'll bloody fix it for you."

"Have you asked him?" Duggie wanted to know.

"Well, that depends what you mean by asked him. I put his name down on the application form."

"What! Without asking him?"

"Gorr! You're bloody for it, kid!" Washbrook jeered. "He'll fix you. He's still doing his nut about that bloody boat of his. He was telling Winstanley it was all your fault."

"Get lost." Or, alternatively, why didn't I get lost? That might solve quite a few little problems, not the least of which was the matter of the Five Ports Race to which Washbrook had just been referring. Jimmie,you see, had only three interests in life: making money, making more money and sailing. Buggering about in boats constituted a major part of his in-theatre chat. Some months earlier, thinking I might ingratiate myself with my consultant, I let it drop that I had done a bit of sailing in my time. Complete bollocks, of course, but I carried it off OK. Jimmie had even seemed impressed, and my relationship with him had actually taken a turn for the better until the occasion of the Five Ports Race.

This Race was an annual excuse for the rich buggers in Jimmie's Club to rush their consumer durables at high speed up and down the English Channel, sweeping aside anything unfortunate enough to get in their way. Jimmie had a boat called Vodyanoi III, a name so putrid that it made you wonder who the hell could have been bothered to use up the names Vodyanoi I and II. This boat had never won the race, but if financial expenditure and ruthless gamesmanship counted for anything, a win for Jimmie was long overdue.

On the morning before the race, one of Jimmie's crew – a great fat turd of a chartered accountant with a face like a bowl of porridge – turned up at Jimmie's out-patients and announced that his mother had died. Jimmie's response seemed to be based on the premise that the accountant had deliberately put his mother up to it. After a lot of argument, Jimmie had to accept that he was one crew member short and, after a bit of brooding, he went into action. Patients were sent home unseen from that clinic so that Jimmie could bog off and try to find a last minute replacement. People's mothers seemed to be dropping like flies at Jimmie's approach, and eventually Jimmie had to fall back on asking his houseman to fill the gap. No, that's not quite right. He didn't actually ask me. I simply got a message from his secretary that afternoon telling me where I had to report and when.

So this was how it was. Fullen was wearing sandals, brown sweater, blue jeans, saucy American baseball cap, while Jimmie's pals are all identically turned out in shiny blue waterproof gear of the type worn by bearded individuals to advertise codliver oil. First, we sit on a veranda overlooking the sea, sipping gin and tonic, while the least arrogant of Jimmie's cronies tries to talk to me about investments and choosing a public school for my children. But then it's on to the serious stuff. Jimmie sends me up to the pointed end and tells me to lay down flat on what he calls the "deck". I lay there for perhaps three hours, while a north easterly gale shrinks my balls and buckets of English Channel are periodically poured down my neck. Eventually, more out of curiosity than anything else, I raise myself onto my elbows and look back towards the blunt end, only to be asked in a loud voice by Jimmie whether I'd mind keeping my great head down because he is taking this race rather seriously.

The actual event for which I was now apparently being held responsible occurred somewhere near some lighthouse or other. Jimmie had given me the steering wheel to hold while he went downstairs for a crap. My instructions were fairly simple: "Juss keep her going straight, if you think you can manage that". For a beginner, I managed that pretty well until suddenly, from nowhere, there was this loud bang from the back of the boat. The rudder had hit something under the water. With a cry of terror, I fell over backwards as the wheel wrenched itself from my grasp and spun like the middle of a roulette wheel. The boat took a ninety degree swerve. At that precise moment, Jimmie re-appeared on deck, zipping up his flies as he emerged through the hatch. His mouth gaped open as he saw what was happening, but I had no time to utter a warning shout. The boom lunged from one side of the boat to the other, clipping the top of Jimmie's head and sending him sprawling across the floor. I regained control of the wheel and tried to find the brake and the gear lever to put the boat into reverse, but we were now scudding sideways in the direction of some half-submerged rocks. As the distance between the boat and the rocks narrowed, I can remember Jimmie leaning over the side and trying vainly to fend it off – side stepping and grunting like a very bad matador with a very cross bull.

A heavily-bandaged Jimmie had been decidedly cooler in his dealings with me since then, but this was the first time I had heard of a straight declaration by him that it was my fault. How did this affect my chances of getting a decent reference? How did this affect my chances of getting any kind of reference? How did this affect my chances of not actually being beaten up by Jimmie? Should I ring up Queen Alexandra's and tell them not to bother? Should I sign up as a medical missionary in Bolivia? Should I kick Washbrook's teeth down the back of his throat? Perhaps not. The subject had already changed. He and Duggie were discussing some business about the buying and selling of second-hand cars.

The geriatrics housewoman waddled in, so like Washbrook in her appearance that, when she perched herself on the opposite end of the couch from him, it was difficult to believe that they had not been specially paired and placed there as a dreadful warning about the perils of over-indulgence.

"Gawd! I'm absolutely shugged out," she said, lighting up a cigarette and curling up her fat little legs so that we could all throw up at the sight of her elephantine thighs. "If I have to look at another sore buckside today, I shall just scream."

Duggie, meanwhile, was holding forth on the merits of various automobiles for crumpet-catching. "Yeah, that's OK," he was saying,"but you've got to watch yourself on the gear lever when you're getting your leg over."

"Yeah, right," Washbrook nodded, his knowing smile conveying complete familiarity with the problems of getting one's leg over in the particular brand of sports car to which Duggie was referring.

"You still applying for Fountain's SHO job?" I asked Duggie.

"Might do," Duggie said. He was currently doing the pre-registration gynaecology job, which made him, like me, little more than a glorified ward clerk. The next logical step in the hospital promotion ladder was for him to try for the senior house job, which was coming up next month. "Then again, I might not."

"Why? You thinking of retiring?" Washbrook asked.

"I'm thinking of getting out of this crappy business, if that's what you mean."

"Oh, Lord! Here we go," squeaked the geriatrics woman. "Rossiter's getting on his soap-box again."

"Get stuffed."

"Are you volunteering?"

"Christ! I'm not that desperate."

"Oh really? I thought the Dirty Doctor never said no."

"Stupid bag," Duggie said. "You ever worked out how much we get paid in this job?"

"Oh, Lord! Tell us the old, old story."

"Shut your face," Duggie told her, writhing round in his chair and wresting a pay-slip from his hip pocket. "Right: last month, I reckon I worked about four hundred hours. That's how much they paid me. That works out -"

"Don't tell me."

"That works out at about half the rate they pay the oiks in the laundry here."

"Still, it keeps you off street corners, dun'it?" Washbrook suggested.

"Piss off! You know how much they paid the spotty little git of a mechanic when I took my car in last week? Ten times that! And when I complained, the manager told me that he was a skilled man, and he had to pay them that much. Bloody skilled man! He made a complete balls-up of the whole thing. I had to take it back twice. But what about us, if we make a mistake? You know what would happen if we made a cock-up of everything, don't you?"

"Yeah," said Washbrook, "They'd think we were consultants."

"Honestly, Rossiter," the geriatrics woman said, "I don't know what you're grousing about. You chose the job."

"I see. That's alright then. I chose the job, so that makes everything fine. A snotty-nosed, gawky, incompetent, stupid little git of a mechanic gets paid ten times as much as me, but that's alright, because I – "

"I'm not saying that."

"I chose the bloody job, so everything's just fine. It's alright if some little creep, two years out of school with his O level in woodwork, starts pushing the medical staff around, is it?" This was a reference to some bloke who worked in an office somewhere and who had publicly reprimanded Duggie one lunch time for non-payment of telephone bills. "It's alright if I get woken up five or six times a night and get paid bugger-all for the privilege."

"Crikey! However much do you want, Rossiter? It's enough to live on."

"It's enough to live on if deddykins happens to own a chain of knocking-shops and – "

"My father doesn't give me a penny."

" I'll bet he doesn't. And where did the Lotus come from? Taken on a paper-round in your spare time, have you?"

"My father doesn't give me a penny."

"Yeah, I'll bet he doesn't."

"Well he doesn't, so there!"

" I'll bet."

"Dr Rossiter – " The hall porter had entered during this exchange. "Telephone for you outside, Dr Rossiter."

Duggie muttered something under his breath and strode out. The geriatrics woman muttered,"Manners like a pig," and Washbrook added, "Excuse my pig, he's a friend."

"You're not saying much, Fullen."

"He's right though, isn't he?" I said. "You know they take advantage of us, and it's people like you who sit on your backsides and say nothing that lets them get away with it."

"Oh, Christ! Another Trotskyist!"

"Look; why should they get away with it? Why should the O level boys in Administration get more than we do?"

Knocker Lamerton, the gynaecology registrar, stuck his head round the door. "Anybody seen Rossiter?"

"He's gone to ring out a kidney in the john," Washbrook jeered. "He's gone to point percy at the porcelain."

"He's on the phone out in the hall," I told him.

"Look, if you feel so strongly about money, you should have gone in for stock broking or loading ships or something," the geriatrics woman said.

" I feel strongly about money because I haven't got any of it. You can afford not to feel strongly about it because your father's bloody loaded."

"Look, I've already told you, my father – "

"Oh yeah, I believe you. Anyway, that's not the point, is it? The point is that we've been bashing the books for how long? Eight, nine years when you add it all up. That makes us skilled workers. They ought to pay us what we're worth."

"If they paid you what you're worth, you'd end up owing them money," Washbrook smirked.

"Doesn't the job count for anything?" the geriatrics woman asked. "Money isn't all that important."

"Not to you, perhaps, but then we haven't all got parents who're bloody loaded. If I had a – "

"Oh God, how dreary!" she interrupted. "I honestly can't be bothered with people like you."

"I didn't think Rossiter was all that interested in money anyway," Washbrook said. "I thought he had such a sodding big cortical representation of his prick, there wasn't room for anything else."

"Everybody's interested in money except the ones who've got too much of the stuff."

"Oh, do dry up."

"Here, did you see that bird Rossiter was shagging last night?" Washbrook asked. "That scraggy red-haired bint from Dental Outpatients."

"Crikey! Not the Belsen specimen with the bow legs!"

This description of the girl was unjustified, particularly from someone as heavy on the hoof as the geriatrics woman. In comparison to some of the other stuff Duggie had been getting through recently, I would have rated her pretty fuckable, especially in her SEN's uniform, which had the advantage of protecting her from her appallingly unflattering tastes in off-duty clothing. Big tits, too. Emerging from my room at seven-ish that morning, I had seen them on the stairs of Bleak House. Duggie had his arm round, or rather against, her shoulder, pushing, rather than guiding, her at frog-marching pace down the stairs that led, by way of the dustbins, to the back path to the Nurses' Home. The look on their faces was of innocent disinterest, of showing that they had done nothing to be ashamed of, and it did not flicker or falter when they saw me. They had hurried silently past, parting at the front door with a few hoarse words that I could not catch.

"Dead scraggy old boiler," Washbrook said.

"Oh, of course, you're an expert on these things, aren't you?" I asked. "And when did you last get it – from anyone, I mean?"

"I wouldn't want it from that one anyway," Washbrook said. "She's had a dose."

"Who has?"

"That red-haired bit. She's had a dose."

"Has she hell!"

"Yes, she bloody has. Duncan McLeod saw her in the staff clinic. Thought she was pregnant because she was rushing to the bog all the time. Turned out she'd got a dose of Clamydia."

"McLeod told you that did he?"

"Yes, he did."

"Don't I remember reading something somewhere about patient confidentiality?"

"Dun't apply when they're likely to give *you* the clap though, does it?" Washbrook opined. "Get your priorities right."

"That'll give the Dirty Doctor something to think about," the geriatrics woman giggled. "Dirty great sprirochaets crawling up his drainpipe."

"The clap, woman, not the pox."

"Yeah, wouldn't like to be Rossiter tomorrow," Washbrook leered. "Pissing razor blades." He did an impression of a man with severe dysuria, and began to sing:

"*Oh how the penicillin stings*

These foolish things

Remind me of you"

The geriatrics woman was laughing rather too much at all this, a white scum of coffee clinging to the moustache on her upper lip. That was enough for me. I settled down behind my newspaper while the conversation drifted from Duggie's genitals, through the doings of the Royal Family and on to how much the geriatrics woman was making out of signing cremation forms, or "ash cash", as she insisted on calling it in a crowing tone which implied that she had not only invented the alliteration, but had introduced its component words into the English language.

At last, with a groan of relief from the springs, they both got up from the couch and started to demonstrate how much nastier they looked waddling as a herd than as a pair of static bookends. As she came past me, the geriatrics woman turned to me with something she had been working on, something terribly witty and devastating, the final word on the subject of doctor's pay and conditions.

"Of course, the trouble with your sort is – " she said, but before she could tell me what the trouble with my sort was, the door opened sharply, catching her squarely on the shoulder and knocking her staggering back against the wall.

Duggie stormed in, ignoring her injunction not to "mind" her, as she pushed a length of heavily-lacquered hair back into place and went out, uttering beautifully enunciated swearwords to the corridor outside. The Dirty Doctor fumed for a moment in the middle of the room, staring hard out of the window.

"I'll bloody murder that bastard Fountain!" he croaked between clenched teeth.

"Alright, what's he done now?"

"That rat-bag McAllister tried to palm some stupid old cow onto me."

McAllister was a local GP with an Irish Surgical Fellowship and a temper to match. He seemed to think that the Fellowship entitled him to a sort of honorary hospital consultancy. "She's had vaginal bleeding on and off for six months, but she rings him up when he's about to bugger off for the weekend, so instead of going out to see her, he rings me up and tries to send her in."

"To which you reply 'piss off'."

"To which I reply 'piss off', so he rings up Fountain, and Fountain says, 'Yes, Dr McAllister. No, Dr McAllister. Kiss your backside for your, Dr McAllister."

"So he's sent her in?"

"Yeah, but I'm buggered if I'm going to clerk her. If he's so keen on Dr Bloody McAllister, he can bloody well see her himself." Giving a roar of frustration, he kicked out wildly at the arm of the chair next to him and then, seizing a handful of darts, hurled them with all his strength in the direction of the dartboard.

"I - will - bloody - murder - the bastard!" he shouted.

"Shouldn't if I were you," Washbrook said. "It might not look good on your job-application form."

"Honestly, Duggie, you want to be a bit careful. You're going to be asking him for a reference, even if you don't want his SHO job."

"He's got you by the testimonials" Washbrook added.

"He can stuff that," Duggie said. "Soon as this job's over, I'm chucking all this in. You know what all that was about, don't you?"

"All what?"

"All that licking of arseholes. Private practice. McAllister sends Fountain a lot of private work, and if he doesn't keep him buttered up, he knows he'll send it all to Willie Morgan. The whole system makes you bloody puke."

"So you're giving it all up, are you?"

"Don't think I'm bloody joking, mate, because I'm not."

"Bullshit."

"You just bloody wait and see, then."

"Yeah, biggest bloody bullshitter out, you," Washbrook said, with his hand on the doorknob. "Anyway, I'll see ya."

"Not if I see you first," Duggie said quietly, lighting up a cigarette which he produced, bent and flaccid, from his top pocket. He thumbed through one of the tabloids, dwelling a while over the tit pictures and then embarked on a coughing fit, gathered a great gelatinous gob of mucus in the back of this throat and spat it out, with all the appropriate noises, into the wastepaper basket.

"God, you really are a filthy bastard. I don't know what the birds see in you: I really don't," I said.

"Gets you does it? The crumpet-pulling?"

"Oh yeah. Dead jealous. Some of the stringy old boilers you've been through." I said this without conviction. You automatically tended to assume that it was easier to pull a stringy old boiler than a bedworthy, but was it? The only one of Duggie's cast-offs I had ever tried to fuck was a woman from the switchboard - a bit smelly and at least thirty years old. I had felt quite noble and self-sacrificing about it - doing my best to comfort the aged and what have you - but when it got to the point where I told her to get them off, she refused. Nor was this some shallow demonstration of maidenly dignity, some hard-to-get, I'm-not-that-sort-of-girl ploy. She genuinely didn't want to. Yet Duggie assured me that this particular one had laid down on her back and screamed for it. Wouldn't leave him alone, kept ringing him up, buying him underpants, refusing to put through personal calls to him from other women. Could it really be that he had been there, and with such apparent lack of effort? Did he really have to hold them back, the way he said he did? If so, credit where credit is due, a score was a score, whoever she was, and the Dirty Doctor was scoring consistently where some of us were not even getting to the wicket. Pouring himself another cup of coffee, Duggie was expounding just that line of argument by reciting, in his wool town politician's voice, that old proverb about not looking at the mantlepiece while one is poking the fire.

"Ay, lad, but tha mun be mooer careful wheer thee sticks thi poker."

"What does ta mean, lad?"

"Nay, yon lass thi wor laiking wi' last neet."

"Oh, ay?"

"No, seriously, Duggie. That bird I saw you with. She's had a dose, recently."

"Has she hell!"

"Alright, have it your own way, but McLeod saw her in staff clinic and he said she'd got the clap."

"Balls."

"OK, don't believe me. It's your urethra. I can see you ending up in Jimmie's sounds clinic with ten inches of stainless steel up your shaft."

Duggie seemed to contemplate his genitals for a second. "Yeah, well it's better than leprosy, I suppose. Anyway, last night was strictly a one-nighter. No, don't snigger. Look, seriously, Bob, that's one particular bearded clam I didn't plan on spearing again, anyway." He sipped his coffee and then asked "How'd you get on with that posh tart?"

"Who? Avalon?"

"Is that what she's called?" This piece of information seemed to impress Duggie. "Don't remember seeing her around here before. Which department does she work in?"

"Why d'you always assume that the Hospital is only here to provide you with cock-fodder?"

"In other words, she doesn't work in the hospital?"

"Right. She doesn't work in the hospital."

"Great legs," Duggie said.

"Nnn." The Dirty Doctor clearly thought that I was about to be mug enough to tell him where he could accidentally bump into Avalon. The Dirty Doctor was wrong.

"Did she fuck you?" he wanted to know.

"What's that to you?"

"I always tell you."

"Yeah, I know you always tell me, even when I don't want to know."

"So she didn't fuck, eh? Could have told you she wouldn't."

"I'm not saying anything."

"This isn't true love, by any chance, is it?"

"Look, I'm quite fond of her. That's all I'm saying."

"No, seriously, does she fuck?"

"Oh, you wicked little trickster," I said. "Trying to worm information out of me with your deviously subtle little questions."

"No, I really – reckoned her, that's all," Duggie said.

The telephone behind me rang and I picked it up. "For you," I said. "Get your blunt instrument ready. It's Fountain."

Duggie took the phone and turned to face the wall, so I couldn't read his facial expression. There followed a fairly long harangue from the other end of the line, during which Duggie began to thread the telephone lead in and out of his fingers, clenching and unclenching his fist. "Yes, well the point is, sir – Yes, I know that – I realise that – No, but he hadn't actually – He hadn't actually been out to see her himse- Well yes, I know. No, but the story he gave me – No, I realise that, sir – Yes, sir – Yes, OK, sir – Well, if you – Yes, sir – Right, thank you, sir."

He threw the receiver back at its rest, missing the target by several feet, so that it rebounded into the accumulated fluff beneath the shelf. "I hate you, God, you bloody disgusting old bastard!" He kicked the chair next to him several more times, grunting with effort. "You disgusting, horrible, filthy old shit! God! I hate your guts, you cruddy, bearded old clown!" He began to punch the back of the chair with almost a sob in his voice, and from the telephone receiver came the parrot-like voice of the switchboard supervisor.

"Is that you, Dr Rossiter? Please replace the receiver correctly. I've asked you before about this, Dr Rossiter. Please replace the receiver corr- "

I picked the thing up and dropped it back on its rest. "That's what you call murdering him, was it ? Yes,sir – no, sir – please, sir?"

Duggie spun round and struck me a glancing blow with the flat of his hand on the back of my neck. "Shut your fucking face, you bastard!" he shouted. A typical Dirty Doctor embarrassment-covering manoeuvre, that. He was such a flaming big sod – unjustifiably tall with shoulders even a bit too broad in comparison – that a token show of violence was generally enough to settle any argument. He raised his coffee cup to his lips and drained it, distributing a fair proportion of its contents down the front of his shirt and tie. "Bugger you again, you old bastard!" he grunted. "I'll get even with you for that!" And, pitching the cup at the armchair, he stomped out of the room.

Chapter 6

"Front Hall? Ward Five, Sister. We've got a body for you." Sister MacGregor flicked a length of cigarette ash expertly into the empty cigarette packet on the desk. "No, half an hour won't do. We've got the lunches to get out. Well, call him back. I want it shifted now."

Perched respectfully at the far end of what she insisted was her desk, I certified that James Livingstone, aged 78, had died of: I. Bronchopneumonia, due or as a consequence of Ia. Carcinomatosis, due to Ib. Carcinoma of the prostate. Other predisposing factors: II. Congenital stupidity? No, better not risk it.

"Yes, and listen, we've still got some bacteriology specimens that have been sitting on the shelf here since 9.30. No, don't send him, for God's sake. He's hopeless: Can't even read his own name, never mind anyone else's."

I closed the long orange death certificate book, pushed it a couple of inches closer to her on the desk and walked out onto the ward. There were one or two things that had to be seen to before Jimmie's afternoon ward round. I got out the notes of some geezer who had been found at operation to have a perforated stomach ulcer – a diagnosis that hadn't occurred to me when I'd admitted him.

At the end of his notes, I had written "?cholecystitis." With a thick-nibbed pen, I obliterated this line and wrote underneath "I think this is almost certainly a perforated peptic ulcer." It looked pretty convincing, but what exactly did I think I was achieving by all this? Would anybody bother to read it and, if they did, would it change their opinion of me in any way? Highly improbable, but at least it didn't cost anything.

I waved the notes around briefly to dry the ink, and I was just about to replace them in the notes trolley when I noticed Livingstone's relatives half-way down the ward. They seemed to be deep in conversation, arranged around the bed of this old cockney geezer with glasses. That was odd. Why were they doing that? Livingstone. Livingstone? No! Lillicrap. Oh, my God, no! Lillicrap! Hell's teeth! I'd got the name wrong.

James Livingstone was the bloke in the corner bed, the stiff whose removal from the ward was currently being negotiated by Sister McGregor.

Lillicrap - Fred, or Harry or Walter or something - was the other bloke, the one they were talking to, and therefore presumably belonged to. Why hadn't I realised it before when I was signing the death certificate? I'd gone and told them that it was Lillicrap who was going to snuff it.

Frank. That's it. Frank Lillicrap. Now I remembered. He was the bloke we'd admitted a couple of weeks earlier for investigation of rectal bleeding. Jimmie had consistently claimed that he could feel a lump in his abdomen that nobody else could feel, so the poor old bugger went under the knife. After a bloody and butcherly laparotomy, the original diagnosis of bleeding piles had been confirmed, and Lillicrap was now recovering from a totally unnecessary operation. Tough luck, but the chances of his being so obliging as to drop dead within a decent time span approximated to my chances of being elected Pope, so it rather looked as though I was going to have to go down and arrange some sort of retraction of the death sentence.

But what was I going to say to them? Should I go down and get them to laugh it all off as an amusing case of mistaken identity? "Get so many of 'em in here, Madam. Can't expect me to remember all their names, can you?" Not too likely. That's the sort of thing that gets you a mention in the Breckleigh Evening Argus, alongside "*Dying Widow Turned Away By Hospital*" and "*Family Doctor's Blackout In Store- Claim*".

Whatever I was going to do, speed, as the saying goes, was of the essence, not least because a patient called Halfhide was now bearing down on me. This joker ran one of those shops that sold trusses, incontinence devices and dirty books. He thought that this gave him some sort of special relationship with the medical profession, an impression which no amount of sarcasm or bloody-minded rudeness had managed to shift. Jimmie had settled his hash by chopping out half his bladder, and his mobility had been cut down for a few days by anchoring him to a water-butt with a length of firehose. Unfortunately, he had now regained the use of his legs, and he was proving this by shuffling towards me with the whole plumbing system in his arms, like a prisoner with a ball and chain.

"Ah! Good morning, Doctor. Looking a lot clearer today, don't you think?"

Dutifully, I looked at the pink-tinged piss in the bottle. "Yeah, great, Mr Halfhide."

"Course, you know what they say about the bladder, don't you, doctor? They say it's ay - they say it's an, um - ay, ah, very deep-seated organ in the body's constitution."

Piss off. Piss off. Piss off. "Yeah. Deep-seated. Great."

"What was it St Augustine said? 'Oh Lord, do not take me through the bladder'?"

"Yeah. Well look, Mr Halfhide, I haven't got time to talk just now."

"The Ancients, they knew that the, ah -They knew that the bladder – "

"Look, Mr Halfhide, d'you think we could talk about this some other time?" He'd been giving me this herbal remedy stuff ever since he got here. Didn't stop him getting a socking great bladder cancer, did it? "Excuse me: if you don't mind – " I pushed him to one side, as being the only method of getting away from my position against the wall, short of vaulting over the notes trolley or hopping through the window and shinning down the drainpipe.

I stepped over his drainage tube and headed off down the ward, with his voice still droning on, "Yes, well I think, ah, doctor, that what you in the, ah, medical profession refer to as, ah, what you like to call – fringe medicine – is ay, um is ay , ah – "

Around Lillicrap's death bed, the conversation was of various brands of washing powder, demonstrating, just in case anybody needed it demonstrating, that what people talked about when you were dying was no more earth-shattering and poetic than what they talked about when you were dead. I bent down and took the temperature chart from the bed, knitting my brow to extract the maximum possible from the medical mystique angle. The conversation died away.

"Here he is," said Lillicrap. "This is the man. Dr Dracula we call him. Always after you for a bit of blood." You were always expected to laugh at that one, but, under these circumstances, I figured it was safer not to.

"Um – I wonder if I can steal your visitors away from you for a few minutes, Mr Lillicrap?" I asked.

"After their blood too, are you?" he croaked. "He's a lad, always after you with a needle."

"Oh yes. Good. I was just wondering, though, if I might have a word with you all for a minute."

"Why? What is it?" Lillicrap asked. "What's up, Doc ?"

"Something new's just come up. I wonder if you'd mind all just stepping down to the – "

"What - us, you mean?" Mrs Chapman asked, stopping short of peering under the bed to exclude the possibility that I might be addressing a crowd of mute, crouching midgets.

"Yes, you, please. Thank you so much. If you'd all just come down to the er - "

"Whatcher mean, doc?" Lillicrap wanted to know. "Whatcher mean 'something noo'? You mean I got plague or water-on-the-brain or someink?"

"No, nothing like that. Honestly. It's just that I'd like another word." I grabbed the back of the wife's chair and jerked it backwards, forcing her to stand up. The others rose untidily to their feet and followed me in single file down to the Side Ward. I arranged them on the edge of the empty bed where Pike had breathed his last, gave them all my very best smile and then I said, "Good news, I'm pleased to say." This seemed to confuse them, rather than reassure them, so I dropped the grin and went straight on to say, "We've got the result of a special blood test, you see? It's a test to show the health of the prostate gland. A bit technical, so I won't go into it. Anyway, the result of this test is very good. It shows, in fact, that Mr Lillicrap's prostate is very healthy." No response, except from Chapman, who was darting his gaze around the room in search of an ashtray. "So that's - very good, you see. We weren't really expecting that. So - er - his prostate is, in actual fact, extremely healthy."

"You're telling us now it's not his prostrate?" Mrs Chapman asked.

"That's right. So that's absolutely terrific news. His prostate gland is very healthy, and there's a very good chance that this trouble of his might clear up altogether."

"What about his cancer then, doctor?" Mrs Lillicrap wanted to know.

"Well now, I think that the word "cancer" is rather a strong word to use here. I don't really think we could call this condition of your husband's a cancer. You see - "

"But that's what you said," interrupted Mrs Chapman. "You said yourself he had a cancer."

"Well I think it's awfully important," I bullshitted, "to understand the difference between what the man in the street calls a cancer, and what we in the - er - profession call a cancer. When I used this word 'cancer', I didn't mean, well a malignant growth - not an actual malignant tumour."

"Then what did you mean?" she persisted. God, she was an ugly woman. But, worse than that, there was something about the line of her mouth, the angle of her shoulders, that seemed to spell trouble. I had underestimated her. I suddenly realised that what I had here was a Guardian reader, a card-carrying member of the Liberal Party, someone who didn't take kindly to being pissed about. This was going to be more difficult than I thought.

"Well, you see, the word 'cancer' has many meanings. It's a Latin word – cancer, the crab. Well, this so-called 'cancer' of Mr Lillicrap's, this tumour – Tumor, another Latin word. Tumor, tumoris, a lump, a protrusion, a swelling. That's just a rather technical name for a lump in the back passage. What you would call haemorrhoids, or piles, if you like."

"Oh," said Mrs Lillicrap. Chapman was gazing into space, exhaling smoke through his nose and nodding very sagely.

"So he's not going to die?" Mrs Chapman asked.

"Well, no. Not immediately, anyway."

"But we understood he was going to die."

"Oh dear me, no, he's not going to die. I don't know what gave you that idea."

"You did. You said he was going to die."

"Well now, I don't think I actually said that. I don't recall actually using the word die."

"Yes, he told us he was going to die, didn't he?"

"Ah yes, well when I used the word 'die' there, I didn't mean – you know – die. Not die in the sense of – I didn't mean he was going to, you know, pass away – "

"Shuffle off his mortal coil," Chapman volunteered, socking me in the ear with an expression which, coming from him, sounded as forced and improbable as an impromptu exposition of Newton's Third Law of Motion.

"Yes, that's it. Quite. No, what I meant – what I said, if you remember, was that Mr Lillicrap was a very sick man."

"Yes. You said he was very sick and he was going to die."

"Really, Mrs – er. You must get these morbid ideas out of your head. Morbid ideas about death and dying. As I said, there's no chance at all that he's going to die."

Even Mrs Chapman seemed half-convinced now. "Yess - well," she said.

"Anyway, I'm pleased I had chance to have another little chat with you."

"So he'll be coming out of hospital soon?"

"Yes, I should think so. Another few days. It really depends on - you know. OK? Well now, if you'll excuse me - "

"Yes, of course, doctor. We know how busy you are," said the brother. "Thank you for all you've done."

I nodded diffidently, but the sister-in-law had had time to sift through the flotsam and jetsam of our two conversations. "Here, just a minute," she said. "You told us the laboratory had had a look at a bit of the cancer."

"No, I don't actually think - "

"Come on, Grace. The doctor's a busy man."

"Everything's fine now," I assured her. "It'll all clear up in no time."

Mrs Chapman drew herself up to her full height and started to fiddle with her coat buttons. "It still doesn't make sense," she said.

"Well, I hope everything goes well," I said. "And if there's anything else you want to know, don't hesitate to ask."

As Chapman ushered the other two from the room, I could hear his wife muttering something to the effect that if there was anything she wanted to know, she wouldn't ask that young twerp, anyway. She still sounded unconvinced. Could she still make trouble for me? How? I hadn't put anything down on paper. Their word against mine. Who would they believe? I got out a cigarette and I was just about to light up when there was a knock on the door and Chapman shuffled back in.

"I'd just like to say, doctor," he began, "You know, about Grace just then. I know she sounded a bit disrespectful and all that, but she didn't mean it. She's just a bit upset about Frank's condition and all."

"That's alright, Mr -er - "

"No, see, what I mean is - Ethel and me, we know how hard you young doctors work." He grasped my spare hand in his, and clung to it, limpet-like. "See, we appreciate all you done for Frank." There were tears in his eyes, and for a moment I felt like a real shit. Should I come straight out with the truth, tell him everything? Yes, everything, including what Jimmie had put poor old Frank through for absolutely sod-all? Should I hell as like.

"I'd just like you to know that we're very grateful." He stopped and looked up at me expectantly. What was he expecting me to do, precisely? Cry? Grab him in a Neapolitan embrace? Break into song?

"Well that's very nice of you, Mr –er – But I mean, that's what we're here for." From outside in the corridor, I could hear the metallic rumbling of the mortuary trolley, and Mr Fred, or Frank or James Lillywhite or Livingstone or Lillicrap or Liversedge or something could be seen passing the door in a tin box, the top of which was thinly disguised with a stained cream blanket and a pillow, a device which might just about persuade a myopic cretin that this was not a mortuary trolley at all, but just an ordinary, innocent, empty hospital trolley.

"I've no idea what they pay you, but in my opinion, whatever they pay you, it's not enough," Mr Chapman was saying. "It may be nothing to you, doctor, it may be nothing to you. But to me and Ethel, it's more than we can ever repay, and I'd just like you to know that we're deeply and truly grateful."

Chapter 7

"And you haven't even mentioned it to him, you say?" Barrington asked, polishing the lenses of his spectacles on the tail of his white coat. There were dirty great pink dents in his nose where his gold, round-rimmed glasses normally sat. Somehow, without them, he looked even more Indian than usual. At other times, his slightly owlish appearance was deceptive: at a distance he could easily have passed for a studious, sun-tanned Dago. What really gave him away when you got up close was the acrid breath.

"No. Well, I was going to, but you now how it is, he always gives you the impression that he's got something more important to think about."

"What about when he's operating? Don't tell me you never get a spare moment when he's – "

"Have you ever tried to talk to him when he's operating? About anything other than surgery or boats, I mean?"

"Yes, I suppose you've got a point there." We were walking back down the ward after our sorting-out round, a kind of dress-rehearsal before Jimmie's official Friday afternoon Round of the Men's Ward. By catching up on most of the notes I hadn't written up, the X-rays I hadn't ordered, the bloods I hadn't taken, we usually managed to reduce the level of Jimmie's bellyaching to a point where it was just about bearable.

"Well, you'd better make sure you ask him this afternoon," Barrington insisted.

"Yeah, sure." I didn't really need to be told this. Unless I could get in there somehow this afternoon and discuss my application to Queen Alexandra's, Jimmie was likely to answer an unheralded request for a reference with something resembling a poison pen letter. We had stopped near the desk, and Barrington replaced his glasses, squinting through them critically at the thin sunlight. "Anyway, why chest surgery, of all things?" he asked.

If anybody else asks me that, I thought, I shall bloody well scream. Why not chest surgery? Why not pox medicine? Why not diseases of the lowland gorilla, if I felt like it? What was it to them?

I mumbled a mouthful of platitudes about chest surgery being an interesting and challenging field of this and that, and Barrington replied with some pseudo-encouraging remarks of semi-agreement. His bleep went off, and as he made his way down to the office to answer it, I looked around the ward and began to plan the best time to make my approach to Jimmie. The patients had been ordered into their beds, where they lay looking apprehensive, phased-out or just plain bored. Know how you feel, I could have said. Jimmie always made a Big Thing out of his ward round – Man With The Golden Hands, that sort of stuff, but, when you get down to it, what is the man? A butcher? A plumber? Nah, nothing as skillful as that. With plumbing, you have to join things up properly first time; with surgery, you only have to get it approximately right and the old healing process does the rest. If Jimmie were to drop dead, things would go on pretty much as they always did. If we all dropped dead, it would be no big deal. Some patients had come here to live, others to die, and in the long run, our intervention made very little difference. Medicine is ultimately a futile occupation because eventually everybody dies, and saving lives isn't too big a part of the job description, I'm afraid. Still, mustn't get morbid. Think positive. Say the round goes OK, and I approach Jimmie while he's having his tea, so that his blood sugar's high. Yeah, good thinking. Who knows, there might even be a chance that he'd be prepared to overlook past unpleasantness. He might even be prepared to give me a good reference, just to get rid of me. Then I remembered that, of course, he didn't have to get rid of me. After six months, I had to go, like it or not: and where I went made no difference to him.

Where was the old swine, anyway? It was ten minutes past three. Even if the man showed negligible concern for the feelings and interests of others, he didn't normally add unpunctuality to his vices. Just as I was beginning to hope that he might have been flattened by a number 7A bus, I saw Barrington and MacGregor leap to their feet and make for the office door, and characteristically loud footsteps became audible down the corridor.

James McFee Materson, MS, FRCS, had obviously had a profitable morning at his rooms because he was humming some kraut tune or other as he strutted into the ward. At first glance, he looked curiously out of place: a short, fat, red-faced man with a nose ridiculously over-ornamented with scrolls and whorls that could never be taken seriously as an organ for shifting air through. Standing there, looking round the ward, slowly wringing his hands, he looked like an corner greengrocer about to extol the merits of a particular brand of potato.

"Afternoon, Sister, Barrington, Fowler, slurp." The man was in his manic phase. Good.

Barrington promptly soured things up by telling Jimmie that he had to go and see a patient of Grosvenor's on the Kid's Ward. That was not so good. Jimmie looked at Barrington over his half-glasses. "Yess, well I suppose you'd bedder go, slurp," he said. Jimmie had this way of talking that made his tongue seem too big for his mouth. Come to think of it, his tongue was too big for his mouth. You rarely saw him with his lips together. There was always this tag of redundant pink flesh hanging out. Perhaps this had something to do with the fact that he had obviously been born with a hair lip and that his parents should have asked for their money back from whoever it was that had tried to fix him up. Since the day I met him, I had been trying to work out whether the sparse gingery hairs on his top lip were simply an unsuccessful attempt to hide the white Y-shaped scar there, whether they wanted to be taken seriously as a moustache, or whether he simply found shaving in that area too uncomfortable. At any rate, the poor old bugger had the tonguey speech of a cleft palate sufferer and this, together with the fact that he tended to slobber a lot, made it difficult to understand what he was saying.

Barrington skipped off, and Jimmie turned on the louring silence, but this was just as quickly turned off again, and after a bit he brightened up. "Lovely afternoon," he said. "Remind me, slurp, tell you funny story later on. Vair funny. Vair amusing."

"Righto, sir. I'll look forward to that," I said brightly, trying to look as though I was looking forward to that. "Um, by the way, I hope you didn't mind, uh – "

"Eh? Whassat?"

"Well, you know, sir, last night – "

"Last night?"

"You know, sir, when I rang you up about – "

"No, I doan know, Fowler. What you trying to say?"

"Well, um, nothing,sir. I just – " So much for the telephone incident. As far as he was concerned, the incident had never happened, an automatic cut-out in the memory department of a mentality that never entertained the faintest possibility of being in the wrong. Jimmie shook his head, tutting slowly, and we moved off down the ward, followed by MacGregor, the notes trolley, a couple of student nurses and a woman with a mop and bucket. It was the best show the hospital could manage under the circumstances, and it clearly did not please Jimmie.

"Mr Roache," I said. Livingstone's place in the corner chute bed, nearest the mortuary, had already been taken by another equally-shaky looking old geezer, his mortal coil already on the shuffle.

"What wass name, slurp, that chap who was here before?"

"Er – Livingstone, sir," I looked at Sister to check that I hadn't made another gaffe of the Lillicrap variety.

"What happened t'him?"

Lowering my voice, I said, "Well, sir, I'm rather afraid he – "

"Fell off the perch, eh? Slurp. Thought as much. Right. Who's this?"

"Mr Roache," I repeated. "Admitted yesterday afternoon. Acute retention."

"Ernie preeby mumbles tree unit rubble?" Jimmie asked.

I inclined my head towards him, grinning inanely. "I beg your pardon, sir?"

"An-y pre-vi-ous his-tor-y ur-in-ar-y troub-le?" Jimmie hissed.

"Er – no, sir, no."

He grunted, cast his eyes over the GP's letter and gave Roache the benefit of his tobacco-stained dentures. "Alright?" he asked. "Quite comfortable now?"

Roache, becoming aware of our presence for the first time, lifted his gaze from the blankets and croaked, "Nurse!"

"Right. Next," said Jimmie. We made our way swiftly and reasonably uneventfully around the ward, Jimmie laying on the healing hand and beaming genially. "Yew well this Arthur Noon, mumble Lillicrap?"

"Ooh, not too bad, thanks, Doc."

"Yewparse whim sins apraise yawn?"

"Eh?"

"Yewparse winter day?"

"You'll have to speak up, doc. I'm a bit deaf."

"Have – you – passed – wind?" Jimmie demanded at the top of his voice.

"Nah, not me, doc," Lillicrap said cheerfully. "It must be one of you lot."

Steam appeared to issue from Jimmie's ears while he explained to Lillicrap the purpose of his question. At the end of this period, Lillicrap looked none the wiser. "Anyway, I was pleased to hear about the prostrate gland," he said eventually.

"Whassat?"

Lillicrap stopped chewing his gum for a second. "I said I was pleased to hear about the prostrate gland. Doctor - er - here was telling my wife about them tests on the prostrate gland and that."

Jimmie lifted his eyes from the treatment chart and looked at me with an expression of belligerent bafflement, but I was looking straight ahead, stroking my chin and avoiding eye contact. "Yehhs . . . well, slurp. Glad to see you mumble better."

"What you think's causing these headaches I been getting, Doc?"

"Fowler?"

First I'd heard about his bloody headaches, so I bullshitted. "Nothing much, sir. Mainly functional, I think."

"Nothing serious, mumble. Nothin' you slurp worry 'bout."

"OK, Doc."

"Yoojuzz slurp mumble mumble mumble."

"Whassat, Doc?"

"Izedd yoojuzz slurp mumble mumble mumble."

"Sorry. Come again, Doc?"

"You just take things QUIETLY!" Jimmie bellowed, his short red neck swelling and reddening.

"Oh yes, thank you, Dr Mattinson."

Jimmie slammed the temperature chart back on the bottom of the bed and huffily led the little procession back to the office for the Ceremony of the Hot Ribena. Jimmie had this crank idea that tea and coffee caused bladder cancer, so all the theatres and surgical wards had to lay in a stock of blackcurrant juice, in bottles marked "Mr Materson only". It was rumoured that one departing antipodean SHO had shown his contempt for Jimmie by peeing into a half-full bottle, and that Jimmie had contentedly worked his way through the cocktail over the ensuing few weeks. If so, all I can say is "Good on yer, sport."

This beverage had to be mixed to Jimmie's very precise crackpot instructions before the rest of the company were allowed to expose themselves to the imbibed carcinogens. While Sister MacGregor busied herself with this, Jimmie started wading into the toast and strawberry jam, spitting out a mixture of crumbs and the odd name from his little black book, punctiliously labelled "J. Materson, FRCS: Patients for Admission".

"You got all that down, Fowler?"

"Yessir."

"Juss see if there's anything here, slurp," he said, and he put his hand in his inside pocket, drawing out a bundle of hospital mail, held together with a rubber band. He fanned the things out like a bridge hand and began to sort them like a true professional. Six or seven of them bore the logos of drug firms or medical publishing houses, and these he deposited, unopened, in the wastepaper basket. That left three envelopes, none of which, I was relieved to note, exhorted him to Come Nursing At Queen Alexandra's. He swiped the jam from his knife onto the side of the plate and used it to rip open the first envelope with an impatient jerking action.

Taking a deep breath, I began "Ah: um, sir: I was wondering whether . . . "

Jimmie was squinting at the letter, and for a few seconds he appeared not to have heard me. Eventually the half-moon glasses turned towards me, "Wha'?" he asked.

"Well, sir: I've been thinking about what I was – er – going to do now that – um – "

"D'you remember Pepper?" Jimmie asked, half-turning towards MacGregor.

"Pepper!" MacGregor laughed. "Yes, I remember him alright!"

"Yehhs!" said Jimmie, and they began nodding and grinning at the secret shared joke. " 's written to ask if I'll put in a word for him when he puts in for the radiology registrar job down here, slurp."

"Not seriously!" MacGregor laughed, and they looked craftily at each other again, Jimmie beginning to laugh aloud with a deep bass ahur-ahur which sprayed us all with fine saliva.

"D'you remember the time he gave the wrong blood to that coloured man?"

"Yehhs!" smirked Jimmie. "Yes, I remember that." And then, by way of sharing the joke, he explained to me, "Chap came in to have a hernia done and ended up quadraplegic on a ventilator."

I looked at his face to see what sort of emotion I was supposed to register at this story. Shock? Disgust? Surprise? Nausea? Jimmie's face broke into a ghastly grin and he began to cackle. So that was it. It was a funny story. I forced a smile and began to nod my head and hunch my shoulders as a signal that I could see the funny side of it. Some poor bastard paralysed for life, that's all, but you have to laugh.

"Yehhs. Came walking in off the street, fit as a fiddle, juss to have his hernia done. Ended up - slurp - quadraplegic on a ventilator."

Raising my eyebrows to indicate a sufficient degree of professional interest, I managed to hold on to the fixed grin which showed that, underneath it all, we were all lads together, taking the piss out of some poor sod who had once sat where I now sat. At the same time, a sick feeling in the pit of my stomach told me that the names Pepper and Fullen were freely interchangeable, and in a few years time, stories about Fullen would be providing the cabaret at some other Ribena and strawberry jam matinee.

"Yehhs, well," Jimmie said, giving the letter one final read-through before returning it to its envelope. "I doan think Dr Pepper's goin', slurp, get an awful lot of help from me."

"Wasn't he the chap that rammed your yacht with his motor cruiser?" MacGregor asked, not so much from a desire for information as from a desire to keep this line of conversation going.

Now, in a court of poetic justice, the penalty for anyone even hinting at the subject of bloody boats while I was in the process of asking for a reference was death - death by the most horrible method imaginable. I controlled my anger by picturing MacGregor in various stages of torment. Kicked to death by a horde of pregnant black ladies? Strangled to death by a chimpanzee with hallitosis?

"Yehhs, thass the chap," Jimmie said, nodding his head in pseudo-laughter, pretending it had all been forgiven and forgotten. So my worst suspicions were confirmed, eh? Jimmie was perfectly capable of nurturing and acting on a grudge, even years after the event, and nothing was more certain to provoke a grudge than an attack on his property. Killing off the odd black man was excusable – desirable, even, since it replenished his stock of funny stories – but it was not for that crime that Pepper's hospital career was about to come to a premature end. Pepper had committed the unforgivable sin: he had assaulted the only love of Jimmie's life. "Yehhs...middle of the day, bright sunlight," Jimmie continued, his face twitching with suppressed rage. "He wasn' properly insured, of course."

He helped himself to another cup of Ribena and I realised that, boats or no bloody boats, I was committed to going forwards now. As he tore open his second letter, I began, "Yes, well, I wondered if I might ask you, sir about a job that I've – "

Jimmie had switched off again, opening out the letter on the desk. It was a bill, bearing the letterhead of a boatyard in Plymouth, and in the paragraph on the left, the words "Repairs to Hull" had been underlined in red. The right hand column was a jumble of figures, but I could see that the pounds column extended to four figures. Jimmie had stopped in mid-swallow and was sitting with his cup only inches from his face, staring open-mouthed at the document on the desk.

"Um, it's a job at, er – " My voice trailed away as I saw his nostrils flare and the twitch returned to his face. He brought the bill nearer to his spectacles and read it again, apparently unable to believe what he saw, and then he looked straight ahead at the wall, and I could see that he was talking to himself under his breath.

I realised that now was not the time to bring up the question of references. Any time but now. Some other time when the subject of bloody boats had been forgotten or at least pushed from the forefront of Jimmie's mind. Could I get away with changing my subject in mid-sentence, so that when Jimmie's hearing came back into focus on his surroundings, his memory of what I had already said would be falsified? The trouble was that I couldn't think of any topic of conversation that could possibly interest Jimmie, and I was left lamely muttering, "And he said that ah – "

"Wha' ? Whassat you said?" asked Jimmie, folding away the bill with sudden decision.

"Nothing really, sir. I was just – "

"Something about a job, you said." Obviously he wasn't as deaf, blind or stupid as he pretended to be. He could hear perfectly well what other people said. It was just that he generally chose to ignore them.

"Well, yes, it's a *sort* of job. I wondered if I could talk to you about it."

"Wha' sort of job, slurp?"

"It's just a job I saw advertised in the BMJ. It's at – er – "

"Will you 'scuse me?" he said. "I mus' jus' make a phone call." He had opened his third letter and had started to read it during this last bit with a facial grimace approximating to a smile. " 'scuse me," he repeated.

He asked for his number, and within half a minute he was deep in conversation with someone he addressed as "Wallo". This person obviously had a vast fund of whatever it was that made Jimmie laugh, because he soon had Jimmie chortling away like a drain. "Yehhs, quite right, Wallo. Wad I always say is – Wad? – Yehhs! – Wad I always say is – That's the operation that separates the men from the boys. Wad? – Yehhs. The boys – The boys are the ones that can do it! Wad? – ahur,ahur – I said: the boys are the ones that can do it. Wassat? – ahur,ahur – Righto. Give my regards to Alice. Yes, you do that. Ahur,ahur – slurp – wad? ahur,ahur – Goobye, Wallo. Yehhs, I will – ahur,ahur – Goobye – slurp – Goobye!"

He put down the phone and picked up his conversation with me as though there had been no interruption. "Yehhs, well I haven' got time to discuss it with you now, Fowler, slurp. You'd bedder come 'n' see me in theatre on Monday morning, slurp. I've god a meeting to go to."

"OK, sir" After all, what's the hurry? It's not your career we're talking about, is it, Mr Materson?

Jimmie brushed the bread crumbs from the lapels of his pinstripe with a business-like flick of the cuffs and rose to leave. "Well, thank you vair much, sister, slurp. Vair nice."

I walked with him down the corridor, while he went droning on to MacGregor at the far side, and all I could catch was the odd slurp and mumble. In the front hall, MacGregor left us, and I stood in an embarrassing silence with Jimmie. "By the way, sir," I said, "you asked me to remind you to tell me that funny story."

Jimmie looked at me in silence for a second. "I've just been telling it to you," he said.

Chapter 8

I didn't actually spend Sunday in church, but I did the next worst thing. I spent Sunday in a real-live vicarage, talking to a real-live vicar. Avalon took me home to meet daddy. I didn't know that vicars got Sunday off. This one did, anyway.

"And what precisely do you intend to specialise in?" Mrs Death asked, sounding like somebody with a clipboard. The lady had unbelievably hairy legs and a face that looked as though it needed a hot iron running over it. It had therefore come as a considerable relief to me when it came up in conversation that this was Mrs Death Mark II, and therefore no blood relation of Avalon. Balancing a ginger biscuit in my blue and white saucer, I said, "Well, things are a bit fluid at the moment. I have one or two possibilities in mind."

"He's thinking of taking up heart surgery," Avalon volunteered, giving my hand a possessive squeeze. This piece of intelligence seemed to impress the Death family. Guinevere stopped playing with her fingernails and gave me an eyeball re-assessment. Even the humourless, owl-faced Merlin looked at me through his granny specs with renewed respect.

"Heart surgery?" The Reverend Arthur Death wanted to know. "Frightfully interesting, of course, but won't the training for that take rather a long time?" Old Man Death and his now wife even sounded like vicars and their wives are supposed to sound - even using the pronunciation "rather a long tame". There was no other discernible accent, and I wondered if he had started off foreign - an Australian or a South African, say - and had been taught to speak English as a foreign language by an elocution teacher. That might explain where Avalon had got it from.

"All the hospital specialties are pretty hard graft," I told him. Queen Alexandra's, incidentally, didn't do heart surgery, but "lung surgery" somehow didn't have quite the same impact.

"So you'll be studying for quite a long time to come, then?" Mrs Death wanted to know. I had started off badly with her, taking her by the ring-encrusted hand and saying, "Pleased to meet you, Mrs Deth".

Gwendoline looked down her considerable nose at me and replied, "Day-ath."

"Sorry?" I muttered, looking for help towards Avalon, who was giggling. Some laugh. Had she perhaps forgotten to mention that her mother was an immigrant who could speak only Albanian?

"It's pronounced Day-ath. It's a Belgian name."

"Oh, right." Well, how was I to know? I had seen Avalon's surname written in various places - she wore a name-badge when working at the gallery, for example - but I had had no call to pronounce it. Moreover, it wasn't the sort of thing you liked to mention, was it? Even having a surname like Fullen was bad enough - you went through life being called either Fuller or Pullen - but if I'd been saddled with a surname such as Smellie, Crapper, Phallick or, to take one glorious recent example, Mrs Ophelia Balls, self-preservation would have driven me to change the thing. There had even been one old geezer who'd had his prostate frozen by Jimmie and who rejoiced in the name of Mr John Thomas Frosdick.

"Fifteen years or so," I told Gwendoline, guessing wildly. After all, I was applying for a chest surgery job just so I could pay the bills. Any long-term aim, such as ending up one day as a thoracic version of Jimmie Paterson hadn't occurred to me.

"I expect there are lots of exams and things," Gwendoline ventured.

"Something like that."

"Still, it must be wonderful to be able to help people the way you do."

Was she taking the piss, or what? No, the Death family were all managing to keep a straight face, and Avalon said, "They work him terribly hard at that hospital. He works all day, and then they call him up two or three times at night."

"Well, not every night," I said, modestly.

"Oh, come on now," Avalon said. "You hardly got to bed at all on Thursday night, and last night you got called up to see that Jehovah's Witness man." I felt myself colouring slightly. Avalon was betraying an awfully detailed knowledge about my sleeping arrangements. Surely some member of this family would put two and two together. It would not be long before the vicar would rise to his feet and scream: "You mean to say you've been fucking my daughter?"

"And there was that child on Friday night. You were up for four hours with him," Avalon said. "You were absolutely shattered when you got back. Lay there snoring and talking in your sleep, jabbering on about a boat or something." Why stop at that, Avalon, I wondered? Why not go the whole hog and tell your family all about the hilarious episode with the over-lubricated vibrator? I stole a sly glance at the Reverend Arthur. He didn't look as though he was preparing to kick me in the balls or anything.

"Don't you ever get nights off?" he preferred to ask, sounding genuinely concerned for my well-being.

"Well, two or three nights a week," I said cagily, "but it's a bit uneven. Some weeks work out worse than others."

"Perhaps you should have gone into the Church, instead, like Merlin here," Gwendoline said brightly. Under the cover of the heavy green tablecloth, Avalon took my hand and guided it up her skirt - over the slightly catchy surface of her stocking tops, up the long silky pathway of her thighs, to the frizzy Brillo pad of pubic hair. Just one of her little ways. I couldn't help thinking of something Washbrook had once said, "You can always tell when they're not wearing knickers . . . They've got dandruff in their socks."

"The money's better in your line though, I would have thought," Merlin said. I felt the stirrings inside my jockey shorts, and realised for the first time why Avalon had deposited my overnight bag in the same bedroom as hers. An invitation to spend a night as a guest in a vicarage had conjured up an image of a cold, abstinent, solitary bed under the leaking eaves with a Gideon's Bible as the only permissable aid to masturbation. The Reverend Death's invitation had clearly also included an implicit invitation to enjoy his daughter as well. This gave a whole new slant to my view of Christian charity.

"But surely, I'd have to believe in God to do something like that," I said.

"Good Lord, no, " the Reverend Arthur said. "I mean, think of the people you work with in medicine. You think they've all taken it up because they want to do something to help humanity?"

Careful here. We are in the presence of someone who reads Luke Devlin books. "Well, not all of them, of course, but there has to be a fairly strong element of – "

"Vocation?" asked the vicar. "Surely you can't believe that? A desire to serve one's fellow men? No. Bollocks, if you'll pardon the expression."

I was not going to pick an argument with someone who was not only about to let me fuck his daughter, but was going to provide me with a room to do it in, so I said "Well, perhaps not."

"I'm damn well certain not," Arthur Death said. "People choose their jobs for a lot of reasons, but in general they're pretty selfish reasons. What is it that medicine offers, after all?"

I began to count them: insomnia, indigestion, faecal glossitis, a permanent fear of litigation, a certain amount of gratuitous sex -

"Job security for one," Merlin volunteered. "People are never going to give up getting ill. Plus the job offers a certain amount of kudos, and the money's not too bad once you get there."

"Right," Arthur nodded, sucking on his empty pipe. "In the same way, why do you imagine people go into the Church?"

They like the uniform? Free wine and biscuits? Plenty of opportunities to meet choirboys?

"For very much the same sort of reasons," Arthur said, answering his own question. "Though no one in his right mind would go into it for the money, of course." The Death family, even the mute Guedoline, all gave a hollow laugh at that, and Arthur went on, "No; the point is, you see, that human beings are all basically bloody selfish. It's part of their make-up. It's how they survive, how they got where they are today, you know, Darwin and all the rest of it. Any caveman who stopped to help his neighbour would have been eaten up by a sabre-toothed tiger. The tendency towards altruism has been selectively bred out of us."

I had read a book somewhere that discounted that idea. "You're trying to tell me you don't believe in God?" I asked.

The family Death had a little chuckle at that old chestnut. "Well, that rather depends what you mean by God," Merlin explained. "Do you mean do we believe in a basic pattern to existence, the answer is yes, but if you're thinking in terms of the old picture-book idea of a bearded old man sitting on a cloud – "

"Surely no one believes in him any more?" Gwendoline suggested.

"I know someone who does."

"Who's that?"

"A friend of mine at the hospital, Duggie Rossiter."

Avalon laughed out loud at this. "Oh, surely not," she said. "He spends all his time shouting at God."

"Yes, well perhaps it's not quite the conventional idea of God that he's got. I think he pictures God as a masked sadist with a big whip who lays in wait for him all the time."

"Now that's a view I can sympathise with," chuckled the trendy Reverend Arthur.

His elder daughter, meanwhile, had silently unzipped my flies and was starting to warm her hands on my unfolding genitals. "We ought to go upstairs soon and unpack our things," she said softly.

"The way I like to see it," Merlin said," is that a clergymen is a second-hand car salesmen with a dog-collar on."

"Precisely," said Arthur. "Just as, in the same way, we might regard a doctor as a double-glazing salesmen with a stethoscope."

I was not in much of a condition to say anything to that, instead concentrating on keeping my breathing slow and regular as Gwendoline asked, "But this place you're going to - the place Avalon was telling us about. It's in London, isn't it?"

"Queen Alexandra's? Yeah, it's - it's in Catford or somewhere."

"So that means you'll be leaving Breckleigh, perhaps for good?"

"Well, yes, I suppose it does."

"Won't you mind that?"

Three days ago, I would have answered "You kidding?", but somehow it wasn't like that any more. Avalon's pressed her thigh up against mine, my nose was filled by her nice, musky, understated perfume and I suddenly realised that I would mind that very much.

"There are some things about the place I would miss," I said, and I think it was at that point that I realised for the first time that things were beginning to get serious.

Chapter 9

Jimmie normally passed his Monday mornings by peering into people's bladders, an experience which, because of the essentially monocular nature of the cystoscope, he was unable to share with those around him. This was clearly a disappointment to him. If it had been at all possible to split the bladder wide open and take a coach party on a conducted tour round the thing, Jimmie would have done it. The next best thing was to have someone sitting at his shoulder, taking down dictation while he described the scenery as he saw it. My Monday morning function was therefore to sit behind him as he crouched between the towelled legs, and to jot down whatever part of his rambling commentary sounded relevant to the patient's welfare.

This was no easy job. Apart from having to edit out all the bits about the bloody light's not working and the patient's coughing and the water's stopped now sister and get your great head out of my way, it was necessary to understand what the man was actually saying. As if his normal speech-impediment were not bad enough, he insisted on trying to talk with his mouth almost occluded by his rubber-gloved hands.

Almost anything was better than that. Almost any excuse was worth engineering, but today that hadn't been necessary. Just before the start of Jimmie's list, Jehovah had decided to call his Witness back to that great Kingdom Hall in the sky, and I had taken the opportunity to skive off as part of the cardiac arrest team.

This Witness character had appeared, vomiting blood, on the Grosvenor Take on Friday night, and had graciously allowed Arthur Grosvenor to hack out half his stomach on the understanding that no blood should be given - an act of naive optimism equivalent to agreeing to get into the lifeboat, so long as the bottom was knocked out first. That morning, his last remaining red-cell having got lost somewhere in his salt-water circulation, his heart had chucked in the towel, and who could blame it? Only McLeod had managed to work up any enthusiasm for the idea of keeping this biological preparation going - no doubt so that he could write a letter to the Lancet telling everybody what a sodding clever bastard he was. Fortunately, this had had no effect on the outcome, but McLeod's efforts did have the beneficial effect of prolonging my absence from Jimmie's list, and when I finally appeared in theatre, Jimmie was in a rare old temper, his little green hat bobbing about as he mumbled unintelligible gobbledygook to the staff nurse who had been drafted in to fulfil my usual function.

"Erm - trays are, erm, no, wader bit - yerrs - trays are tribulation."

"Sorry? What sir?"

"Eh? Oh, er - slurp trays are mumble tribulation."

"Sorry? I didn't quite catch that last bit, sir."

"Trace of trabeculation!" Jimmie bellowed.

Something else was wrong. Normally, irrigating water ran from a plastic reservoir, through a tube to the cystoscope, then out of a side port onto Jimmie's long rubberised apron and finally down into a bucket placed between his feet. I noticed almost at once that the apron was shorter than normal, but the full significance of this did not strike me for a few minutes. Then I realised that the normal sound of trickling water was absent, because the shortened apron was emptying, not into the bucket, but into Jimmie's big white rubber boots, which were consequently being very slowly filled up with a dilute solution of pee.

That put paid to Duggie's image of God. If ever anything tended to support the idea of a just deity with a sense of humour, it was this predisposition of Jimmie's to incidents and accidents that showed him up for the great clumsy, pompous buffoon he really was. Falling asleep on the phone, for example, and then there had been that other Monday morning when an over-keen student nurse had removed Jimmie's stool before the end of the operation. The great clown had fallen flat on his backside and put up a three minute display of temper before realising just how bloody ridiculous he looked and had tried, much too late, to pretend that he could see the funny side of it.

Peeing in his boots, eh? Good. That was so exactly the sort of thing I had been wishing on him all weekend, it seemed a pity to put a stop to it, but at some point I had to approach him about my future career, and there was no point in making him any more bloody-minded than was absolutely necessary.

"Mr Materson," I called.

"Juss a minute. Juss a minute."

"Sir, your - er - apron - "

"Wha' ? Uh, whassat?"

"Sir, the water."

"Oh, s'you, Fowler. Where slurp been?"

"Um, sir, your apron has been – The water from the – "

He looked down and saw the straw-coloured liquid running into his boots. After a stupefied second, he leapt to his feet, knocking his stool over backwards and jerking the cystoscope from the patient's urethra. "Who slurp bloody hell?" he demanded. "What bloody half-brained cretin – ?" He held the shortened apron up and stomped round the theatre in his squelching boots. "Which stupid moron slurp took it into his head t' castrate my bloody apron?"

"Somebody in the sewing room," the theatre sister ventured. "Somebody must have . . ."

Jimmie prised off his wellies and displayed his wringing wet green and yellow socks, padding around, leaving great wet footprints everywhere. "Look!" he shouted, lifting his left leg to show off the sole of his foot. "Sopping bloody wet! Which cretin castrated my apron?"

As usual, once he started swearing, every syllable of Jimmie's outburst had become clearly discernible. You felt that, in some ways, it would be better if he talked like that all the time. Indeed, Jimmie had long ago earned the right to swear as much as he liked in theatre. Once, a long time ago, a fairly junior sister had made an official complaint about Jimmie's language. Jimmie had had to suffer the indignity of giving evidence to a committee of inquiry, but he got his own back by striding into theatre next morning shouting, "If anyone in here objects to my language, they can fuck off right now."

"Look at it!" he was shouting. "Look at it! Perfectly alright before. Which stupid moron's gone and castrated – ?"

"Circumcised, sir."

"Eh? Whassat, sister?"

"Just circumcised, sir," the sister repeated. "The apron's been circumcised." Now when this particular theatre sister spoke, Jimmie paid attention. It was the hospital's worst kept secret that the two of them had been *at it* for years. Gruesome to contemplate, I agree, and I would hate to describe them as lovers, but the relationship was so well documented, you had to believe it was true. There was even one famous occasion when

Jimmie took her with him to a surgical conference in Brighton, of all places, only to find that the conference organisers had booked them into two single hotel rooms. "Bloody idiot!" Jimmie had thundered at the man behind the desk, "When I said I was bringing my sister, obviously I meant my *theatre* sister."

"Whassat you said, sister?"

"The apron's been circumcised, sir. Had it's end chopped off."

Jimmie stopped ranting and a smile came to his face. So that was how you made the old bastard laugh, was it? "Circumcised, eh? Yes - ahur, ahur - Good. Circumcised. Yes, slurp, thass very good."

He took the hem of the garment and gave it a mighty wrench, undoing the process that someone in the sewing room must have considered it worthwhile spending time doing. "There you are, sister," he said. "You're wrong, you see. Circumcision is an entirely irreversible process - ahur ahur!"

Sensing that this was a joke, and sensing also that Jimmie's mood had now altered sufficiently to allow audible acknowledgement of the fact that this was a joke, people began to laugh. "Look, you see?" Jimmie asked, holding the thing out to me. "Circumcision is an entirely irreversible process. Nothing irreversible slurp 'bout that, eh?"

"Oh no, sir!" I creeped.

He picked up the boots and inverted them, pouring the small amount of residual fluid into the bucket. "Pra'cilly finished, anyway, slurp. Mumble mumble. Less have an H.M.D." (hot milky drink - all clever stuff.)

The anaesthetist was brought out of the rest room, where he had retired to touch up the nurses. "What? Finished already, have you, Jim? " He turned off the gas taps like a housewife finishing off Sunday lunch. "That was a bit quick."

"Yehhs" Jimmie said. "Cystoscopies are the operations that separate the men from the boys. The boys are the ones that can do them - ahur ahur!"

"So you've said before, Jim."

"Nurse, go and make Mr Materson's Ribena" Sister said.

I followed Jimmie out of theatre and along the sterile corridor. "Juss have a quick word with the patients," he explained. Jimmie loved playing the Eminent Surgeon for the benefit of the poor sods he had just been carving up, and he now waddled off into the Recovery Ward where a row of four patients lay on their beds in varying stages of arousal from anaesthesia. Approaching the first bed, Jimmie threw aside the bedclothes and then hoisted up the operating gown of a wide-awake youth with ear-rings and tattoos. "That looks vair' good - slurp," he said, feasting his eyes on the youth's genital organs.

"You what?" the youth asked defensively.

"Vair' nice, vair' satisfactory - slurp," Jimmie repeated.

"How d'you mean?" The youth wanted to know.

The Recovery Sister stepped forward and primly tugged down the youth's night-shirt. "Mr Materson," she announced, "this is the patient from Theatre Three. He's just had his wisdom teeth out."

In the rest room, Barrington was arguing with some medical rep about a chunk of medical ironmongery the man was trying to sell him. As I came in, he was saying something that began with, "I have it on the authority of Professor MacTaggert in Cardiff - " The sort of phrase you could imagine issuing only from the mouth of someone like Barrington.

The rep appeared to be as impressed by this as only a rep could appear to be, and then countered it with another hunk of glib sales-talk, which Barrington tried to interrupt with phrases like "Give me your references, old chap," and "Yes, but Simpson and Wellbeloved showed - ", all of which, I was pleased to see, the representative talked through without batting an eyelid.

Jimmie came in, sipping his hot Ribena. "Yehhs, Barrington, slurp - Cystoscopies separate the men from the boy. The boys can do them."

"Ah, yes, very good that, sir."

"Um, sir, I wondered if I might - "

"Oh yes, Fowler," Jimmie said. "Been thinking it's about time we had a little chat. Go through into the, er - " he said, guiding me out of the rest room and into the adjoining locker room. He put one foot up on the tiled surround of the shower and leaned against the laundry basket with his great paunch sagging over the pyjama cord of his operating trousers. Because of the ill fit of this garment, I was treated to an unsolicited view of his voluminous underpants which bore a motif depicting Wines Of The World, no less.

"Lessee now, how much longer've you got with me?"

"Three weeks, sir. I finish on the thirtieth."

"Oh yes, thass right. You had any thoughts about what you want to do next?" This was an obvious formula, a pre-formed phrase that he had trotted out time and time again to a long line of housemen.

"Well, I – "

"Done your medical housejob, haven' you?"

"Yes sir I – I did Dr Medmay's job." Get off that tack. I felt sure that Jimmie had still not forgiven Medmay for recommending me to him. "I had thought about doing chests, sir."

"Wha? Chest medicine?"

"Er, no. I was thinking about applying for the Chest Surgery job at Queen Alexandra's."

"Wha? Chest surgery?"

"Yes, sir."

"With wha' aim, slurp ?"

"Well, sir, I thought I'd have a crack at Primary."

"You goin' try slurp for Surgical Fellowship?" he asked with a note of incredulity in his voice.

"Er – Yes, sir."

"Waddever for?"

I resisted the temptation to scream "Why the hell d'you think, you stupid bastard – so I can spend the rest of my life flogging double-glazing?" and instead mumbled, "Do surgery, sir."

"Wha'? Slurp, you plannin' t'do surgery?"

"Yes, sir. I was going to ask you what you thought about the idea."

Jimmie blinked and gave a nervous little cough. "You ever thought 'bout general practice?" he asked.

Chapter 10

So what's a nice boy like me doing in a job like this? I'm bad at it, that's why. Lots of people choose their jobs for precisely that reason, but the way I came to be a doctor was a bit more tortuous than most. You see, at school I used to come near the top in English, History, French and Latin, and near the bottom in Chemistry and Physics, so naturally I chose to do sciences. In the science stream, there was a group of us who played a really vicious card game called Sloppy Liz. The game, which often ends in physical violence, needs four players, and every spare minute of our time was taken up by it.

The first day in the Remove Form - yes we were posh at my school- old Bumf, the Biology master, walked in to the crowded science class and asked all those wishing to do Biology rather than Maths to put their hand up. Only six hands went up out of forty odd, so I decided to stick with the majority. Then, just as Bumf closed his book, it dawned on me that three of my fellow Sloppy Liz players had opted to do Biology. There simply wouldn't be a Sloppy Liz quorum in the Maths stream. I put my hand up. "Sir, I want to do Biology as well."

Bumf stared at me. "Make your mind up, boy."

"Yes, sir, I do, sir."

Grudgingly, Bumf re-opened his book and wrote down my name. "Right" he said, "I want all the biologists to come along the corridor with me."

We followed him down to the Biology lab, where he seated us around a bench and said, "I want you to tell me what career you're planning, so I know why you've elected to do Biology."

My ears started to burn. I had no idea what I wanted to do with my life, and I couldn't think of a single acceptable reason why I should have chosen Biology. Fortunately, my name was bottom of the list. The chosen careers of the others were - and I can ever. remember the order of them to this day - Medicine, Medicine, Forestry, Medicine, Medicine and Medicine. Bumf looked in my direction and grunted. "Medicine, sir," I said. And here I am. Incidentally, the pupil who said Forestry was one

Rossiter, D. W. Form Remove Bio.

It was this same Rossiter, D W who was in the Mess Common Room the following Friday afternoon. As I came through the door, he was on the telephone, hacking bits of tartar off his teeth and talking between mouthfuls of screwdriver. "Yes, I know iss long dissunce," he appeared to say. "You will hell send me a bill. Iss hospissal call. Right well get flaming supervisor."

He thrust an empty cup and saucer in my direction. Taking this as an unspoken request to recharge it with tea, rather than hawk into it, I filled it for him and walked over to my pigeon hole. There were two letters waiting for me: one, a final demand for meal bills, which I slipped into my pocket with no intention of doing much about, and the other bearing the postal franking of Queen Alexandra's Hospital. Well, bugger that. I screwed it up into a ball and heaved it at the wastepaper basket, then, realising that it might relate to travelling expenses, I grovelled on the floor to retrieve it, smooth it out and open it. No such luck, just a mass-produced form thanking me for my interest in the job vacancy, which had now been filled. I checked the date on the envelope. It had been posted the day before the interview. Well well, how very subtle of them.

I screwed the letter into an even tighter ball, blew my nose on it for luck and succeeded in hitting the wastepaper basket with it this time. I couldn't work up enough enthusiasm to feel angry about the way those buggers had wasted my time like that. It had been obvious at the interview that the job was already lined up for some chinless public school bastard from one of the right-wing London teaching hospitals. This man had not only rowed a boat for Cambridge University, thus increasing his abilities as a thoracic surgery houseman out of all reckoning, but he had gone to all the bother of marrying one of the awful daughters of one of the awful surgeons at Queen Alexandra's.

Against Division One creeping like that, Jimmie's grudgingly-given lines of apathetic semi-recommendation and Medmay's confused and amnesic ramblings had counted for nothing. I had been brought along, together with a couple of blokes from the Indian sub-continent, to make it look good. Not that it worried me all that much. Queen Alexandra's had turned out not too unlike Duggie's classification of it as a right shit-hole. Even the Breckleigh Royal Infirmary, nasty as it was, seemed homely and familiar by comparison. Besides, I was coming more and more to realise that what really mattered was that Breckleigh was where Avalon was, and the only thing going right for me at the moment was my sex-life.

"Listen, Mrs Thingy, I want a London number," Duggie was now growling. "I want St Augustine's Hospital, Harlesden. The number is – Whaddaya mean? Listen to me, misses – "

Duggie had finally admitted to me – on the Tuesday evening – that he had applied for the gynaecology SHO job at St Augustine's, and that his interview was on the same day as mine. He responded with uncharacteristic reluctance to my suggestion that we could fiddle our travelling expenses by sharing a car. Only later did I discover the motive for his reluctance. With typical Dirty Doctor frugality he had already made other arrangements – travelling up to London the night before and combining his expenses-paid trip with a dirty night in a cheap Paddington hotel with the wife of a local GP. Fucking on the National Health. So now you know. "Right you are. Thank you so much. Now get the flaming number for me, will you?"

"What's up then?"

"Wanker's wrist" Duggie said, wriggling his right forearm about.

"No, not that. What happened about the job?"

"Don't even ask me."

"Did you get it?

Duggie covered his face with his hand and sighed. "Have you got any idea what sort of a dump St Disgusting's Hospital is?" he asked.

"I had heard rumours to that effect."

"Well, it's ten times worse than you can possibly imagine. There was only me and a couple of bints in saris interviewing." Duggie said this in a simple, matter-of-fact way. He is no racist, isn't Duggie. He will screw any woman, whatever colour she is.

"And so you got the job?"

"Yeah, course I did. I tried not to. Tried to pretend I was pissed, and all the rest of it. Even told them I was a flaming Catholic, can you believe?"

"Catholic?"

"Yeah. Makes them think they'll have to do all your abortions for you. They didn't seem interested. I ended up practically wiping my nose on this bloke's tie. Nobody seemed to notice. They must be bloody desperate. Haven't seen a white face there for ages. I felt like walking in and saying 'Dr Livingstone, I presume'."

"Why didn't you just tell them you'd changed your mind?"

Duggie considered this in silence for a few seconds, as though telling the truth was a revolutionary alternative that had never occurred to him. "Nah," he said eventually. "Don't talk daft. You don't get your expenses if you turn the job down, do you? Besides, they were bloody desperate. So keen to have me - Hello? Oh, come on, woman, for Christ's sake."

It was an obvious question to ask, but I asked it anyway. "So why did you apply if you didn't want the job?"

"I'd got no idea what sort of a dump it was, had I? I don't want to be stuck out in the wilds of British West Harlesden - Yeah, hello. Can I speak to, er, Mr Martin, is it? Yeah, medical staffing. Thanks."

I watched Duggie lean back in the creaking chair, crossing his legs and fiddling with the bleep in the top pocket of his white coat, and I thought what the hell is it that women see in characters like that? Crumpled trousers with undefinable stains near the flies, yellowing shirt, hair uncombed, the stubble on his chin congregating in little patches, so as to dispel any doubts that this might be some sort of fashion effect he was deliberately cultivating. Too sodding mean to buy new razor blades, that's all that is. "You didn't accept the job, did you?" I asked.

"Well I had to. I kept trying to think up objections, but they kept on being so bloody accommodating - Hello? Mr Martin? My name's Rossiter."

"Who?" The man Martin had a penetrating North London costermonger voice that carried to the other side of the room.

"Doctor Rossiter, you remember? I interviewed for the gynaecology job yesterday? Look, I'm afraid something's come up." He drew in a deep breath, as he always did when he was about to drop the big one. "You remember I said I'd be able to start on the eighth? Well, I've spoken to my present consultant, and he insists that I can't take terminal leave. I've got to work right up to the end of the month, you see." After a pause he said, "July - I won't actually finish till August the fourth. That means a four week delay, you see, and in the circumstances, I don't really think it's fair to keep you waiting. And so, well - " he was waving his hand around, as though trying to grasp even bigger lies from the air. "In the circumstances, I think the only fair thing would be for me to withdraw my application."

Duggie clutched the receiver to his chest, lifted his eyes in supplication and muttered. "I don't want your stinking job. Can't you see that?"

"Why don't you just tell him?" I suggested. Duggie gave me an impatient

V-sign and farted. If I were a woman, I wouldn't let something like that within half a mile of me. Yet Rossiter is by no means unique. In any street anywhere there are women without obvious physical or mental deformity walking along in the company of tattooed gorillas, hooligans, freaks, you name it, apparently perfectly content not only to be in their company, but not minding being seen in their company. The only conclusion you can reach from this is that Women Have No Taste.

Duggie was back on the phone, saying, "Yes, look, it's very kind of you, but I can't put her to all that trouble." I could see that he was really suffering now, and I was enjoying it on several counts, partly because it showed that I wasn't the only one who only wanted what he couldn't have, partly because it made up for the embarrassment I was going to suffer when I told him that I hadn't got the job at Queen Alexandra's, but mainly because it was good to watch the Dirty Doctor being given a hard time by somebody he couldn't simply dismiss with a thump behind the ear. To put the cherry on top, it would be nice to learn that the GP's wife had been put out of action by a sudden attack of vaginismus, but perhaps that was asking too much.

"Much the simplest thing would be if I just withdrew - No, really, I - Yes, but you see, the fact is that I've been offered another job down here when my present one finishes. - Yes, yes, I appreciate that, but you see I've got all my things down here. I'd like to do Miss Fairbrother's job, honestly, but it would be much more convenient for me if I could - " There was another pause, and then he said, "Ah, but I didn't actually sign anything, did I? You've got nothing down on paper to prove that I accepted. I mean, it's only your word against - Hello, Miss Fairbrother - Yes, yes. I understand that. I realise that." Duggie's face which, up to then had become progressively suffused, blanched visibly at the voice of his would-be employer. "Yes, I realise that I've caused a lot of trouble and inconvenience, and I'm very sorry - Yes, well when I accepted, I didn't realise that I could have a job down here, you see. Yes, well can't you get one of the other applicants? Yes, I'm sorry. No, really, I'm very truly and deeply -Yes, well look, I'm very sorry about it, but I didn't - Hello?" He slammed the receiver down. "Bastards!" he screamed at the phone. "I don't want your piddling job! "

"You're a silly bugger, Duggie. You get yourself into these situations."

"Yeah, you're bloody clever, aren't you? What happened to your Christian Frigging Barnard act down at - where was it?"

"Queen Alexandra's. I didn't get it."

"I knew you wouldn't. You're a useless cunt."

"I'll get myself fixed up, don't you worry."

"Oh yeah? Well let me know when you do. I need a laugh occasionally." He leapt to his feet and stomped out, slamming the door behind him, and I was left thinking oh no you won't though, will you, Fullen? The essential feature of any career move was that it should leave me in a geographical location where I could go on fucking Avalon, which meant that I had to get a job somewhere in Breckleigh, and jobs in Breckleigh were not easy to come by. The dole queue was only a fortnight away, and what did I think they would offer me down at the Job Centre? "I see that you have experience in your last employment of dealing with piss and shit: have you ever considered lavatory attendantship, I wonder?"

Pay and conditions would be better, of course, but I had Avalon to consider. The sex thing with her was just getting better and better. Why, I was walking around in a daze with a lazy half-erection, simply waiting for the next time she showed up in my room. If I'm not there, she lets herself in, undresses, gets into bed and keeps it warm for me. No more dull moments, either, sitting in the car waiting for traffic lights to change - not while Avalon's got a spare hand, anyway. There have been times when it has become physically impossible to drive straight, times when I have had to head for the nearest bit of cover so that we could fall upon each other like ravenous beats.

Last Wednesday afternoon, we went to this trendy secondhand bookshop not far from the gallery. Avalon had expressed an interest in - what was it? - Victorian illustrated children's books, which were kept in a little alcove on the second floor. There was a wooden table there, and Avalon simply hoisted up her skirt, set her pert little bum down on the polished mahogany and within a few minutes there we were, silently at it like knives, separated from the browsing bibliophiles only by - I think - Topography and The History of Religion. Yep, Avalon is a walking wet dream, alright. Randy, I think you'd call her, a woman with the precipitate sexual urges of a man. Even the smallest thing can set her off, and suddenly she is uncontrollable, demanding, and on occasions practically insatiable.

Who wouldn't want to swap places with me? Duggie certainly would. I have read the silent envy on his face as Avalon crosses her legs or walks her gazelle-like walk with those high, unfettered breasts of hers moving tantalisingly beneath the starched white blouse. He, of course, cannot understand what she sees in me and, being Duggie, he told me so. "You mean you can't understand anyone wanting me when you're available?" I suggested.

"She's only after you for one thing" Duggie said.

I smiled a lecherous sort of smile. "Yeah, I know. Good, in'it?"

"No, I'll tell you what she is - a medical groupie."

"A what?"

"A medical groupie. Got a thing about doctors."

"Bollocks."

"Listen, mate, I know what I'm talking about. If you weren't a doctor, she wouldn't give you the time of day."

"Oh yeah?"

"Yeah." Yeah, well maybe he was right. And how did medical groupies feel about *unemployed* doctors, I wondered? I didn't really want to have the chance to find out, either, which is why I decided I'd give Charlie Winters another ring. The previous Monday Max Waters had caused a minor sensation by abandoning his unsavoury wife, his two snotty-nosed brats and his job in Casualty to run off somewhere with a big-knockered Casualty Staff Nurse. This had been on the cards for some time. Only recently he had been asked by the Domestic Supervisor to refrain from besmirching the sheets in the Casualty on-call room with a blood-coloured liquid - obviously menstrual fluid. Instead of relying on the dubious discretion of the domestic staff, Waters had characteristically made a public argument out of it, pleading repeated nose bleeds - a highly unlikely explanation unless Antipodeans made a habit of sleeping upside down, curled up into a ball.

Water's sudden co-habitational reorganisation had caught the Casualty department on the hop. Following Water's hasty departure - in the middle of a minor operations list - I had nipped straight in to see Charlie Winters, the senior Casualty officer, to offer my services as a replacement. Winters had said that he would let me know, something which, after four days, he had not done.

"Is Mr Winters there?" I asked.

"Who wants him?"

"My name's Fullen. I'm a surgical houseman."

"Oh, yes, well, I'm afraid you've missed him. He's gone."

"Gone?"

"For the weekend. He left a couple of hours ago." I looked at my watch. Quarter to four. So that was what senior casualty officers did on Friday afternoons, was it? "Do you want to leave a message or anything?"

"Nah, it's alright. Forget it." Shit. What next then? Even as I thought this, my eye came to rest on a part of the notice board where a new-looking postcard nestled among yellowing advertisements for second-hand motorbikes and Christian Union house parties.

Assistant Required by Single-handed Practitioner. Underneath this, some wit who owned a red biro had already scrawled "Why, where did he lose his other one?" *Urban practice. Possible View to Partnership.* The address underneath was familiar enough to me: *Dr A G Chaucer, The White House, Crosshills, Breckleigh.*

Chaucer. I'd never met the man, but I had read large numbers of his almost-illegible letters, often of the type beginning with the dreaded words "Dear Doctor, This old man lives alone and –" the classic opening to a grot-off-loading letter, designed to get your sympathy for some revolting old creature with nothing much wrong with him that soap and water wouldn't cure.

Casting a quick glance around me, I unpinned the postcard from the board and stuck it into my coat pocket. Medical school had always taught me that general practice was the scrap heap - a place where ignorant, skiving, overpaid, opinionated egotists went to practice witch-doctory on an even more ignorant, skiving population. On the other hand, Crosshills was in Breckleigh, which meant Avalon and lots more where that came from. It also meant no more interviews or London SE 28. Besides, being skiving, ignorant and all the rest of it was OK, so long as you were *overpaid,* ignorant, skiving, opinionated and all the rest of it.

The coincidence was almost uncanny. Was this postcard, perhaps, a supernatural sign of the type that Merlin had told me about? No need to believe in God or anything irrational like that, he had told me, in order to believe in things like pre-ordination and supernatural intervention in human life. Stroll on, Merl. The problem with getting a supernatural phone call, though, was that, if you didn't understand it, there was no way you could ask for the message to be repeated.

On the other hand, if Goddo were not on hand to give personal advice, there were other God-like figures around who might serve the purpose, and one of these - one who had earlier, on a ward round, offered his advice - was now audible in the corridor outside.

"Doan know why they thought I was goin' t'put up with thadd," he was saying when I got out there. "Arfer all, I am slurp senior surgeon."

"Yes, absolutely right, Jim. You're absolutely right." The man doing all the agreeing was George Winstanley, the Convenor of the Breckleigh Gas Company, a mob of tight-fisted anaesthetists who controlled the private practice in Breckleigh with a ruthlessness that would have shocked the Cosa Nostra into issuing pleas for leniency.

Jimmie did not seem to register my presence, embarking now on a three minute diatribe against whoever it was that had thought that the senior surgeon was going to put up with whatever they'd wanted putting up with. This address was notable chiefly for the fact that, by continuing to talk even during inspiration, Jimmie prevented anyone from interjecting any word of his own, of agreement or otherwise.

"That's just it, Jim," Winstanley finally managed to say. "That's it in a nutshell."

"Erm, Mr Materson, I wondered if – "

"I'll tell you something else, Jim. I had to go down to Whitewater last week. External assessor for the new anaesthetic job down there."

"Din come across Patrick Harcourt while you were there, did you?"

"Sorry, Patrick who, Jim?"

"Harcourt. You know. Yousser be my registrar years ago."

"Don't remember him, sorry." Tactical error on Winstanley's part, because Jimmie now launched off into another three minute monologue, this time describing the appearance and life-history of the man Harcourt in so much detail that I began to suspect that Jimmie must keep secret files somewhere, containing everything - including nail-clippings and finger prints - relating to all his past employees. Even this did not stir Winstanley's memory, and he said so.

"Good chap, Patrick. His mother was Lord Mangell's daughter, you know."

"Should think he must be, Jim. Anyway, there were four applicants for the job, and you know what?" Jimmie didn't know what. "All blacks."

"Goo' lord!"

"Four applicants for the job - consultant job, this is, and every one of them was a black. Not one white face among 'em."

Jimmie shook his head in disbelief at this, as though informed that the Pope's Easter message had been a plea for easier abortions and an end to World Peace. "Goo' lord!" he kept saying.

"Not one white face among 'em. All blacks."

"Yehhs, well there you are," Jimmie said, appearing to come to terms with the inevitable.

"Couldn't believe it. All bloody wogs. Not one white chap had even applied." I wondered how many guineas this learned conversation would be costing if these two gentlemen had been applying the combined might of their intellects to the problems of some poor bastard of a private patient.

"Yehhs, well tha'ss the way idd is nowadays, issnit? What you want, Fowler?"

"Sir, I wondered if I could ask - ?"

"Course, we get a lot of 'em doing anaesthetics nowadays," Winstanley said. "Harry Smith was saying they've just appointed one to the staff at the Western."

"Goo' lord! Have they really?

"Apparently, he's not a bad little anaesthetist, this chap. Mother's English. He can speak the lingo, unlike - "

"Oh, yurrs! Ahur, ahur! Tha' chap Qureshi," Jimmie guffawed. "Heard any more about the business with - ?"

"Fingers crossed, Jim, fingers crossed. Heard from the MDS that the relatives might be dropping the case."

"Well there's a bit of luck."

"I wondered if you had any information, sir, about - "

"Yehhs, yehhs, jussa minute, Fowler. Go on, George."

"Well, I heard from a source not a million miles from the Region that they've agreed to settle out of court, provided Qureshi gets off back home."

"Not before time, eh George? Not before time. Ahur, ahur."

"Just what I said, Jim."

"Yehhs, well," Jimmie withdrew from his waistcoat pocket a gold watch on a chain festooned with so many medals and gongs that he looked like a South American general at a garden party. He peered inexpertly at its dial and said "Must dash off now, George." He started to back toward the door. "Yehhs, now whaddisit, Fowler?"

"I was thinking of applying for a job, sir, and I wondered if you knew anything about – "

"Jussa minute. Oh, George, can we make it slurp ten o'clock sharp on Wednesday?"

"Yes, OK, Jim."

"Only the Yacht Club wants me to meet some people for lunch, slurp, 'n I'll have to be away by twelve."

"OK, Jim, knife to skin at ten."

Jimmie got his watch out and looked at it again. "Goo' lord, is that the time?" he asked. No, you old buffoon, it's the barometric pressure. "Now what you want to see me about, Fowler?"

"I just wondered if I could quickly – "

"Yes, come, come on, I'm in a bidduva hurry."

Thank you so bloody much, Mr Bloody Materson. Come and ask my advice any time, Fowler. Just how did he think I was going to do that? Run alongside his car with my head through the window? Shout at him through a loud hailer from a passing yacht? "OK, I'll leave it for now. It wasn't important." Only my whole flaming life, you bastard, but what's that to you?

"Alright, slurp. Have a good weekend."

Well, well, well. There's one for the diary. Even if he hadn't registered the fact that I worked alternate weekends, of which this was one, he had at least recognised that I did have weekends like other human beings, and that I was in the market for being wished a good one.

"Try 'n get there on time on Monday morning, if you can." He waddled out to his Daimler and drove off, narrowly missing a traffic bollard and an old buffer on crutches.

The idea of ringing old Medmay momentarily occurred to me as something that I might as well not bother wasting time on. Medmay was now sixty five but looked and acted twice that. It was only six months since I had finished doing his housejob, yet whenever I came across him, he insisted on calling me "Miller". This was not because, like Jimmie, he couldn't be bothered to learn my proper name but because he genuinely believed that I was someone else who had done his housejob ten years earlier. The chances that Medmay might have anything useful to say about Chaucer - always provided, of course, he realised that I wasn't talking about another Chaucer who used to write a bit - were so slight that I might as well save the wear on my ears while Medmay ummed and ahed his way through establishing, a) who I was, b) who Chaucer was, c) why (a) might possibly want to know something about (b), and d) what he might then have to offer (a) by way of useful information about (b).

It was too much to ask - a) would be better off getting onto b) directly. That, on the face of it, seemed simple enough. The telephone number was typed under the practice address, and three minutes later I was back in the Common Room, counting the number of times the telephone rang. After seven, unlikely to answer. After thirteen, certainly won't answer.

"Dr Chaucer's Residence." Middle-aged, lower middle class Celtic female. A Taff or a Jock, something like that.

"Could I speak to Dr Chaucer, please?"

"I'm afraid the doctor is out this afternoon. You can obtain emergency advice on Breckleigh 716 - "

"I don't want emergency advice. It's Dr Fullen here."

"I'm sorry. It's a bad line."

"Full - en. Doctor Fullen. I work at the hospital."

"Oh, I see. What was it about, Dr Fullen?"

"I was wanting to enquire about the advertisement."

"Advertisement?" she asked, almost in disbelief.

"Yes, the assistantship."

A silence from the other end of the line. Come on, Blodwyn, surely it can't be all that staggering? Then, as if on a sudden realisation that it was not a total loony she was speaking to, "Oh, that advertisement! You know, you had me worried there, for a minute I'd almost forgotten about that, we've been advertising for so long." She gave a vulgar sort of smoker's laugh. "Can you tell me where you saw it - was it the BMJ or Pulse?"

"Well neither, actually." I wasn't the sort who read medical journals, and it seemed odd that she should think that the sort that did read them would be applying for the sort of job this obviously was. "No, I - er - saw the postcard at the hospital."

"Oh, the postcard. Yes, I suggested that. Dr Chaucer said no, but I told him, you never know your luck, do you?"

"When will Dr Chaucer be back?"

"Well, confidentially, now I know who you are, I might as well tell you. He's gone away for a few days. He won't be back till Tuesday or Wednesday, if you ask me. Dr Parfin covers for him."

"Dr Parfin?" God, that's encouraging. None other than our friend of "*Family Doctor's Blackout In Store - Claim,*" and much more besides. When I was doing my medical housejobs, Parfin had achieved a similarly miraculous acquittal on a drink driving charge, on the grounds that his blood alcohol level at the time of the accident was theoretically incompatible with life. "It must be obvious," the judge had instructed the jury, "that some sort of error crept into the laboratory estimation, and it would therefore be unsafe to convict on this evidence alone." The man must lead a charmed life, but it was not that, nor even his obvious incompetence that had made the most lasting impression on me. It was his close attention to financial detail. I had once come across him in the hospital pharmacy, a bent-backed, hatchet faced little Scotsman, trying to scrounge a length of second-hand bunsen burner tubing to shore up his archaic, perished stethoscope. Rather than go to the expense of buying notepaper, he would send his patients into casualty with a few lines, usually of the "Dear Doctor, please see this patient. ?Feet" variety, scrawled on bits of cardboard and used envelopes.

So Parfin was tied in with this lot, eh? Well, I was desperate, but not that desperate. "Well, look," I said, "if Dr Chaucer's away, I'd better leave it, because I wanted to know one way or the other before the weekend. I've got one or two other jobs lined up, and - "

"I shouldn't think there'd be much difficulty. It's an urban practice. Two surgeries a day, except Wednesdays. No obstetrics, and there's - "

"Oh dear! Well that's shot it, then, because I was actually looking for a practice with obstetrics."

"That's no problem. I dare say we could sort something out. Alternate nights on call, and two weekends in three. Oh, and you get petrol and oil, of course."

"Well that sounds fine, Mrs – er – but as it happens, I do have this other practice in mind, so I really wanted a decision before the weekend. I think I'd better leave it for now."

"No need to bother about that. If I say it's alright, Dr Chaucer will agree. He'll fall in with any arrangements I make."

"That's very kind of you, but really – "

"No, it's no trouble. We can sort this out here and now."

Time for a bit of Duggie-style lying. "No, look," I said, "I've already got myself fixed up with a job in – Gateshead, as it happens, so I'll – "

"Gateshead?" she echoed. "My dear, have you any idea what Gateshead is like? You don't know when you're well off. You stay down here."

The problem now was how to get out of this without embarrassment. She knew my name. I couldn't just hang up on her. "No, look, thanks. I just rang up out of idle curiosity, really. And anyway, I don't think I'd really be suitable."

"Not suitable?" She gave another of her throaty laughs. "Just answer me a couple of questions, love. You are registered, aren't you?"

"Well, yes."

"And you're not – er – foreign, by any chance, are you?"

"You mean black?"

"Yes."

"No."

"No you are, or no you aren't?"

At this point,I realise that I had missed the boat. Too late now to put on a Darjeeling accent. "No: I'm not."

"There you are then" she said triumphantly. I obviously fulfilled the stringent requirements for the job, and I hadn't even been asked if my parents were married. "The job's yours. Start on July the first – alright?"

"Ah, no. Can't, I'm sorry. I've arranged to go on an overland safari trek across Africa for the whole of July, so I'm afraid I'll have to call the whole thing off."

"August the first."

"Er – Well, I don't know, really. How much, precisely, is the salary going to be?"

"You'll have to talk to Dr Chaucer about that. Meanwhile, I'll make all the arrangements. Bye for now!" and she rang off before I could tell her where to stick her job.

Chapter 11

Over the weekend, Avalon was the perfect girlfriend. She came round to the Hospital when I rang her, bogged off without being told whenever she sensed I was harassed. She was witty, charming, intelligent, considerate, screwed like a rattlesnake and even managed to prepare one or two nice bits of vegetation to eat in the kitchen museum of Bleak House. On Sunday, it was warm enough to sunbathe, and we sat out in deck chairs behind the mortuary and talked to an extremely queer pathology registrar and his live-in boyfriend. I have to say that I felt a warm glow of ownership - proud to be seen in public as the proprietor of such a splendid piece of crumpet. Even the pathology registrar told me what a "fine-looking" girl she was. Well, I certainly fancy her more than I do yours I almost told him, but the whole thing felt so right , so pleasant, so comfortable, that I couldn't feel any nastiness towards anyone. Whatever turns you on, baby, I almost said, when the two woofters made an excuse and left, and it was then that Avalon told me that Merlin was also of the bent persuasion.

A pre-requisite for the job, I would have thought, but I kept a straight face and expressed concern. Oh no, Avalon assured me. He was very happy that way. He had found himself a permanent companion, and old man Death regularly loaned the two of them a room in the Vicarage where they could do unspeakable things to each other. Duggie appeared at this point, sat on the grass trying to look up Avalon's skirt and made one or two sexist remarks before getting bleeped. His presence seemed to disturb Avalon, and somehow, once he had gone, the atmosphere of relaxed bonhomie, of goodwill to all mankind, had evaporated.

Monday was - well, just Monday, except Charlie Winters rang up and offered me the Casualty job, or as good as. No Avalon to share the news with, since she was away at an auction in Bath, and didn't get back till late, and Tuesday morning was Outpatients and Sounds Clinic. I was normally spared this ordeal, so a summons to attend, delivered third or fourth hand by Sister MacGregor, filled me with a sense of foreboding. This could mean only one, or possibly two of three things: either Jimmie was going to tell me to do some extra (unpaid) work of some kind, or he was going to dismiss me summarily for some offence - real or imaginary - or else I was going to be asked to contribute generously towards a subscription in aid of that putrid boat of his.

I edged my way, squeaky-toed into the main consulting room, where Jimmie was taking a history from some stupid-looking berk. "Oh, yurrs - Come in 'n' siddown, Fowler." He turned back to the patient, "When you get this trouble, d'you still get an emission?"

"You what, doctor ?"

"I say - d'you still get 'n emission, d'you still reach slurp climax ?"

"Um - "

Jimmie inclined his head and smiled craftily over his glasses at the staff nurse, a lady who had once been had rotten by the Dirty Doctor. She had recently changed her hair style, but she was easily identifiable by her oreasts, which were remarkable not so much for their overall size as their extreme mobility on perambulation. It seemed unlikely that a girl who had been through what she must have been through would be upset by anything Jimmie might say, but she bowed to his Olde Worlde prudery by nodding weakly and heading for the door. "Right, now then, do - you - *come off*?" Jimmie demanded.

"Oh, yes, yes, doctor."

"Right. Now we're gedding somewhere. Go'n get undressed next door and we'll come through and see you." Tutting and shaking his head, Jimmie wrote up his notes, then he turned to me. "What're you doing here, Fowler?"

"You asked me to come, sir."

"Oh, yes, thass right. Well look, I'm juss goin' through to do some sounds, so you may as well help while you're here."

I smiled as though this was going to give me real pleasure. "Right, sir." I said and I followed him through into the treatment room, where he slipped on a rubber apron, rolled up his sleeves and scrubbed up. There were three couches in the room, all within three feet of each other. On each couch lay a little old man, fully clothed from the waist up, but with his shirt pulled up and his trousers and pants round his ankles. Jimmie took a stainless steel bladder sound, rubbed it in lubricant and then, without any sort of ceremony or even an introduction, grabbed the penis of the nearest patient and rammed the curved steel rod firmly up his urethra. Conditioned by years of this sort of thing, the little man uttered no protest, except to jerk convulsively and let out a pained "Ooaarh!"

Jimmie, without taking his eyes from the window, muttered, "Same again. Three weeks." While he went to wash his hands, the little man was helped from the couch by an aging, abject-looking male staff nurse. As this shabby pair hobbled towards one door, an almost identical little man came shuffling through the other door with his trousers round his knees and began to shuffle himself onto the vacated couch.

"Well now, Fowler, slurp," Jimmie said, lubricating another sound and making for the second couch. "Wass this I hear 'bout you applying for a job in Casualty?"

I realised now that I had been hopelessly naive in thinking I could do a thing like that without Jimmie sticking his great bulbous nose in. "Well, yes, sir, I've always been interested in Casualty, you see, and I thought it would be a useful step towards – "

"Keep still!" Jimmie bellowed at his second patient, who was groaning and wriggling as the sound was jammed further and further into his unyielding urethra. All the while, Jimmie had this sort of fixed grimace on his face. You could tell that he really enjoyed hurting these patients – regarding himself as an instrument of divine retribution against dirty old buggers who had contracted the clap.

" – doing the Primary Fellowship – "

"Yes, well you see, Fowler, slurp. Bit tight that one. See him again next week. See, the thing is slurp 's not my place to tell you what you should or should not do – Where the hell's my towel? I can't stand these damn paper things."

"Um, no, sir. I understand."

"No, 's not my place to do that." We were now approaching the third couch. "What's this chap have last time?"

"Er – 14 to 18, sir."

"Yehhs, well, you see. I've given you my opinion. I've told you what I think about you doing Primary." He sank the sound in up to the hilt and left it there, tilting his head back to look at me through his half-glasses. "Iss your career, an' iss not my place to tell you what to do, slurp, but I doan think iss a very good idea, you doing Casualty."

"No, sir." Think what you bloody well like, you old bastard, I'm still going to do it.

"Right. See this chap in a month, slurp – So I hope you woan take this the wrong way, but I've asked Mr Winters not to give you the Casualty job after all."

"But he's already promised me – "

"No he din', Fowler. He tol' you he couldn' see any reason why you shouldn' have the job. Well now I've given him a few reasons why you shouldn', and he's decided to take my advice.

"Why?" I demanded. "Why did you do that?"

"Why did I do that? Because I doan think you ought to do Casualty, thass why!"

"But it's nothing to do with you, sir. You said yourself it wasn't your place to interfere."

"I din' say it wassen my place to interfere. I said it wassen my place to tell you what to do. Two quite differen' things, slurp."

"But it's none of your business, sir. I don't see why you had to go and do a thing like that."

"Yehhs, well you see, Fowler, I doan have to justify it to you. I doan really think there's any place for someone like you in surgery, slurp – 'n fact, I doan think there's any place at all for you in the hospital service. Good day to you."

"But why did you have to do it, sir?"

"Good day, Fowler, slurp."

"Just tell me why you did it, sir."

"Keep still!" Jimmie bellowed. "How c'n you expect me to get the damn thing in when you're darting about like a blue-arse fly?"

Chapter 12

"Hullo – yes?" an Irish voice asked.

"Is that Breckleigh 27477 ?"

"What is it you want ?"

"I wanted Breckleigh 27477. Is that Dr Chaucer's residence?"

"Who d'you want ?"

"I wanted to speak to Dr Chaucer, please."

"He's not here at the moment."

"Oh, I see."

"Alright?"

"Yes, well in that case, I wonder if I could leave a message for him ?"

"I suppose so, what is it?"

"Could you tell him that Dr Fullen rang."

"Who ?"

"Dr Fullen, from the hospital."

"I see. You're Fullen, are you?"

"Yes, that's right."

"Oh, well – er – This is, um, Andrew Chaucer speaking, actually." Chaucer had suddenly dropped his stage-Irish accent. Now he sounded more like someone doing a very bad impersonation of a retired army colonel. I was just about to tell him that I liked his other funny voice better, when a thought struck me: perhaps he couldn't help it, Perhaps he usually talked like that.

"Sorry about all that, old boy. Thought you must be a patient, you see. You've got to be careful, otherwise they ring you up all hours of the day and night. Mmm. Yes, well – Hullo, how are you? Nice to hear from you at last."

"I was just ringing to say that I've thought it over, and I would like the job, if that's alright."

"My dear chap, I didn't realise there was any doubt about it. It's all been arranged. I thought our Mrs Clode had fixed it all up with you."

"Yes, well there was this slight problem about a safari trip to Afghanistan that I'd – "

"Mrs Clode said Africa."

"Sorry. Yes. Africa. The thing is that the trip's now been called off, so – "

"Oh dear. Bad luck."

"So I wondered if it was possible for me to start on the first of July, as we originally planned."

"Let me have a quick look. Yyyyes – That would be absolutely first rate. Look, I'll tell you what I'd like you to do for me. There's something I especially wanted to go to that weekend, so I wonder if you'd mind awfully much managing by yourself for a couple of days – till the Wednesday, shall we say ?"

"Well, normally I wouldn't mind, but the thing is that I've never done any general – "

"No, no. Don't you worry about that. Our Mrs Clode will show you where things are, and all the rest of it. So can I pencil you in for that, then, can I ? You'll do the surgeries and the rest of it, starting on the – Monday, and I'll be back – what ? – Thursday or so ?"

"It's just that I'd like to come over some time and discuss one or two things with you, if that's at all possible."

"Yes, of course you would. Of course you would. There is a bit of a problem here in that this is a bad week for me, and next week – well!"

"How about now? Could I possibly come – ?"

"Well, unfortunately not, old chap, because I'm actually just on my way out. I'll tell you what – you give Mrs Clode a ring – shall we say – Friday? Then I'll let her know my whereabouts for the next week or so, and we can fix up a time and place to meet. How does that sound ?"

"Yes, that would be fine, Dr Chaucer, except that before I start, I'd really – "

"Fine, then, fine. Let's leave it like that, shall we? I very much look forward to meeting you and having our little chat - Oh dear me, there goes the doorbell. So I'd better say cheerio for now, and see you a week next Thursday. Hope the first couple of days work out for you."

"Um, yes, but the thing is that I haven't even been told yet how much my salary is going to - Hello? - Hello, Dr Chaucer, are you still there?"

Chapter 13

"Hi, sorry I'm late."

"Hello, Pigface," Avalon said, giving my hand a squeeze. "What kept you, then?"

"One of Jimmie's private patients, would you believe? Jimmie wondered if I'd mind popping up and putting a new drip up on him."

"Does he pay you for looking after his private patients?"

"What? Jimmie? You've got to be joking."

"Why don't you just tell him what he can do with his private patients, then?" Avalon suggested. "You don't owe him anything, and besides, he's not in a position to do you any more harm than he's already done, is he?" The girl learns fast. A month ago, she would have been more concerned about the welfare of the poor rich bastard, but it had been several weeks since she had made any comments of a Luke Devlin-like nature.

"You're adorable, you know that?" I put an arm around her beautiful waist and pulled Avalon gently towards me, planting a kiss on the big, soft lips. "And you're looking absolutely gorgeous," I added. Avalon coloured a little but didn't answer. It's difficult to say why she looked gorgeous, because nobody I had ever known dressed quite like Avalon dressed. She was such an amazingly beautiful girl, and she exuded such confidence and panache that you sometimes forgot that she had almost no money. One day, in a rash moment, while bemoaning the lot of the Poor Houseman, I told her how much I earned. With no outward sign of censure, she told me how much Ivor, the proprietor of the art gallery, paid her for her services. I am ashamed to say that I could almost have paid her to work for me.

Today she was wearing lilac coloured sweater, pink chiffon scarf, blue skirt, black possibly tights, perhaps stockings, and the sort of little brown shoes nurses wear. All of this had an air of being good quality stuff that had seen better days and didn't quite go together. Miss Death's costumes by Oxfam. I had once made this remark, in jest, and Avalon had replied, in all seriousness, that that was indeed where the stuff had come from. She also bought things from jumble sales.

The overall effect today was of Cinderella before the Fairy Godmother bit. Poor little poor girl. Dated, slightly bizarre and - heartbreakingly beautiful. More than that, it was far more endearing than any expensive clobber could possibly have been. This had the effect of making me feel soppy and protective towards her. Standing there in a busy shopping street, I was overwhelmed by affection for her, and I immediately lost any doubts about what I had intended to do next. "For you," I said.

"Ooh, an old brown paper bag. Just what I've always wanted."

"Well go on, open it."

"No, let me guess what's in it." Avalon took the parcel and kneaded it with those long white fingers of hers. "It's - It's your dirty washing."

"Nope."

"A hospital suet pudding?"

"Nope."

"It's a - one of those things you stick under doors to stop draughts."

"Nope."

"What is it, then?""

"Why don't you open it and find out?"

"Spoil sport." Avalon gave me a peck on the cheek and started to unwrap the thing with great care, as though she intended to save the wrapping for further use.

"That's what it is."

"Aw, Bob, how sweet."

"He's called Bonzo" I told her. What it was was a stuffed toy dog - a felt and leather creation, resembling - somewhat loosely - a member of the beagle species.

"Bonzo?" Avalon asked doubtfully.

"Yeah, well we couldn't really call him - what was it?"

"Bleoberis?"

"Er, yeah, that." This was the name of the Death Family's beagle. Not for old man Death a dog called Towzer or Fido. Highly individual, of course, but, let's be honest, not a lot of use as a name. "Walkies, Bleoboris. Don't shit in that man's garden, Bleoberis." If the dog had sported a name that sounded like a name, rather than like some sort of tropical disease, I might have felt more confidence when I tried to dissuade old Bleoberis from falling in love with my left trouser leg on my first visit to the vicarage. The dog had taken it into his head to consummate this touching relationship right there in the kitchen while Avalon prepared some cups of herbal tea. As it was, I tried a few silent dislodging manoeuvres with my foot and then had to settle for pretending not to mind. Avalon had laughed a lot and whispered something in my ear about knowing what it felt like now.

Avalon kissed the toy on the nose and said "No. I'm going to call him Palomedes."

"Dare one ask why?"

"Wel, he looks like Palomedes," Avalon said, and then, as though she didn't really need to explain that, she added. "The beagle we used to have before Bleoberis."

"Oh yeah, of course." Why didn't I think of that?

Avalon hooked her arm through mine and kissed me warmly on the lips. "Thank you, Bob. You're very sweet," she said. "He's lovely."

I felt my genitals stirring at the wonderful, clean, minty, familiar taste of her mouth. "I hope you're not going to do this with our children," I said. Avalon looked blank. "You know, give them names like that. I was rather banking on an Oliver or a Victoria or something like that, to start off with, anyway."

I had never officially got down on one knee and asked Avalon to be my lawful wedded whassname, but it must have been blindingly clear to her now where I thought this relationship of ours was heading. She had never said anything to indicate where she thought it was heading, but pseudo-matrimonial banter along those sort of lines had always been OK between us so far. Today, though, Avalon's response was not quite what I had expected. The smile was just a fraction late, and when it arrived it was not the usual wholehearted and affectionate grin that left you feeling limp and exhausted.

"Nnn," Avalon said. "What time are we supposed to be seeing this man?"

"Mrs Palmer? More likely to be a woman with a name like that, don't you think? I told her three o'clock. We're a bit late already. It's not far down here."

We walked fairly briskly, still arm in arm, past a row of shops until number 74, Gertrude Road came into view. This property formed the end of a terrace on a busy street corner, and as we approached, we could see that the ground floor was divided into a ladies' hairdressers on one side and a small general store on the other. Between these shops was a common entrance, and it was outside this doorway that a Junoesque figure in a paisley dress was standing with a plastic document case under one arm as she checked an oversized timepiece on her other wrist.

"Mr Fullen?" she asked.

"Yeah. Hi there" I said. "Sorry we're late. I got tied up." The woman didn't look too convinced by this excuse, so I added, "At the hospital, you know. I had to attend to an emergency." That always got them. You could get away with parking on double yellow lines and things if you used the old "Let me through, I'm a doctor" routine. Duggie had told me - and I believed him - that he had once been caught by an irate husband with his cock quite a long way down a young lady's throat. When this gentleman asked Duggie what he thought he was doing to his wife, Duggie had calmly explained that he was a doctor, and the man seemed to accept this as a perfectly reasonable explanation.

"Oh, I see. You're a nurse, are you?" the woman asked.

"No, a doctor, actually."

The woman looked quizzically at Palomedes, then at the bit of paper balanced on her briefcase. "So that should be Doctor Fullen then, should it?"

"Well, yes. Not that it - "

"Or is it Mister with you hospital doctors? I'm never sure."

"No, just plain old Doctor will be fine." You could tell that this quite pleased her, and she scribbled this new piece of information down on her bit of paper. Our agency deals with many professional people, you know, doctors, businessmen, those classes of persons. Avalon smiled possessively at me, gave my arm a squeeze and brought herself close enough for me to be able to smell her perfume. It has to be said that, now that I had had time to think about it, Duggie's definition of Avalon as a medical groupie no longer seemed like total bollocks. Avalon definitely regarded a medical degree as a mild aphrodisiac.

"Right then, doctor," the woman said, shaking my hand. "I'm Rosalind

Palmer. I'll take you straight up to see the flat now, if you like."

"Wonderful."

Roz led the way into the front hall, past a half-closed doorway, with its smell of whatever it is that ladies' hairdressers always smell of, and unlocked a door at the far end. This led straight onto a narrow staircase. Avalon gestured for me to go in front of her up the steps. At first, I thought this was a ploy to stop me sticking a hand up her skirt as we mounted the stairs, but to my delight she was ahead of me on that one. Her cool little hand went unerringly up between my thighs and grabbed playfully at the tumescence in front of my crotch. My cock leapt to attention in her hands. Avalon took two stairs at a time until she was level with me and whispered in my ear. "Ask her if we can have half an hour to look round the place on our own."

"The central concourse," Rosalind said, pivoting on her heels and gesturing expansively with her free arm at what was, let's face it, a common or garden landing. "All of the rooms lead off this, and there's a staircase here that leads up on to the roof."

Avalon nodded appreciatively and apparently attentively as Roz started to tell us about the arrangements for heating water. Roz then said that she'd get the geyser in the kitchen going.

"You do that," Avalon breathed in my ear, "while I get the geezer out here going."

Roz didn't seem to mind that we had not followed her into the kitchen, and, without a sound, Avalon took me by the hand and led me in a business-like fashion into the room opposite, which turned out to be the dining room. Avalon knew what she wanted, and she wasted no time in getting it. She parked Palomedes on the dining table and, after a second's thought, covered his eyes with the brown paper. As she spun round to face me, she was breathing deeply and had a wide, sexy smile on her lips. Then she leaned back against the table with her bottom on its edge and parted her legs just *so* much.

I didn't need to be told what to do. In a flash, the reliable old left arm was round her shoulder and I was kissing her urgently but lightly on her slightly parted lips. Her eyes were closed now and she let out a little gasp of pleasure and - surely not surprise - as my right hand began to run up the valley between her parted thighs. Smooth silky stockings and then the long expanse of creamy, soft thighs. Half way up this bit, my finger tips encountered the first traces of dampness, then the undisguised wetness coming from above. The silky material of her french knickers was soaked in the wonderful stuff, and I peeled these gently from her crotch.

Her labia were spread wide, and my fingers skated smoothly over the glistening surface. A sharp intake of breath from Avalon as two fingers carried out a brief internal inspection, then darted off, probing for the hard, jutting clitoris. In its erect state, Avalon's clitoris would give plenty of men penis-envy. Not me, of course. Hell, no, I got no worries on that score. As if to confirm this, Avalon's hand came down briefly to apprise my bulging trouser-front, and she let out a low groan from deep down in her throat. I tell you, at that point, I was sweating semen.

"Get rid of her," Avalon moaned, eyes closed. "Just get rid of her."

Reluctantly, I withdrew my hand and, covering the front of my trousers with an accommodation agency handout, I left Avalon performing gentle self-abuse and headed for the kitchen. Roz looked a bit quizzical. "Doesn't your wife – ?" she asked.

"She's just – looking at the dining room," I said. "Look, I wonder if we could possibly – "

"I'll just show you how to operate the gas meter, because it can be a bit tricky," Roz said, bending down to open the cupboard under the sink. She was a bit on the chubby side, was our Roz, but she'd not got bad legs. Definitely wouldn't put it past her to have a sex-life of her own, and I wondered whether she'd understand if I asked her if she'd excuse me for a couple of minutes while I fucked Avalon. Come on – I am a bona fide client, after all. Or how about some kind of doctorly excuse? "You'll have to excuse me: but my wife appears to have lost a tampon," or "I have to do this to her every two or three hours, otherwise her blood sugar falls."

Roz spent two or three minutes explaining about when you had to turn the key thing left and when you had to turn the key thing right. By now, my cock was really painful and the poor, confused thing was leaking little spurts of stuff into my boxer shorts. Would this lecture never end?

An idea struck me. "Look, I wonder if you could excuse me for a few minutes," I said. "My wife acts as my secretary, you see, and it just occurred to me that I forgot to ask her – "

"Well, actually, doctor," Roz said, consulting her watch again, "I was just going to ask you the same thing. We're a bit behind time, you see. I have to see some other clients later, and I really ought to call the office. Would you excuse me for a few minutes while I pop down to the call-box?"

"No, no, please feel free," I said. "I – I'll just – "

"I won't be too long, but I'd better shut the door behind me, to stop the cats getting in. When I get back, I'll ring the doorbell."

"Er – fine" I managed to say above the sound of the blood pounding through my ears.

Roz started to make for the door, then she stopped and said "Oh, I didn't show you where the immersion heater switch is."

Just bog off, Roz, will you? "I'll zeeorlthadwhenyergedbag" I heard myself blurt out.

"Oh, alright then." Roz walked much too slowly out onto the concourse and started to descend the stairs. "Just popping out for a couple of minutes, Mrs Fullen," she called to Avalon. "Won't be long."

A strangled cry came from the direction of the dining room. I didn't even wait for Roz to reach the bottom of the stairs before I threw off my jacket, ripped open my trousers and staggered back into the dining room. "The bedroom," I gasped, taking Avalon by the hand. "I think it's the one over in the – "

"No," Avalon gasped. "Please don't tease me. I can't wait. Here. Now. I want to – you know – astride you on a chair."

I grabbed a dining chair from under the table and sat on it, facing Avalon, who now had her skirt pulled up around her waist and was already advancing on me with one suspender detached from the top of the black stockings and swinging bawdily in a way that just about summed up the wonderful heady mixture of dissipation and wantonness. In two willowy strides, she had straddled me and was holding the leg hole of the french knickers open, guiding me into the heavenly depths of her wet, warm, secret bits.

"Oh – God! That's wonderful!" Avalon moaned. Couldn't have put it better myself. Men admire long-leggedness in women because, to achieve this effect with a short-arse, you'd have to be practically bent double, crouching down on a pixie's toadstool or something. With the gazelle-like Avalon, you simply sit comfortably at your ease and let her bring the whole thing to you. I looked down admiringly at the long, slim legs that reached easily to the floor on each side of the chair, then back up to Avalon's flushed cheeks and the wide open mouth as she threw her long hair about her shoulders and continued to moan deeply in time to her own urgent thrust.

The view from here was *magnificent*, but the problem with situations like this is that they can become just a teeny bit too exciting. When your loved one is completely abandoned to the joys of the flesh, when she is relying on you for a bit of carnal gratification at its most basic, when you most want to perform like a superstud, that is the very time that her enthusiasm becomes infectious, and suddenly all those advertisements about premature ejaculation don't seem quite as funny as they did. It's at times like this that you realise one of the big advantages nature has handed out to women in the sexual stakes. They can abandon themselves - let themselves go completely from start to finish - while the man has to hold part of himself back until the very end. Not to worry, though: I've had quite a bit of practice at this sort of thing. The trick is not to think about it. Difficult, I concede, with a girl as beautiful as Avalon gyrating like a naked go-go dancer around your maypole. Close your eyes. Don't watch. Just concentrate on - just think about -

"Oh, Christ, Baby!" I moaned, cupping her neat little buttocks in my hands. "Slow down, or I'll - "

"My nipples," Avalon muttered, not apparently paying any attention to this. "Suck my nipples."

Together, we hoisted the lilac sweater up over the streamlined rib cage, until the gratifyingly large breasts bounced jauntily into view. The disproportionately wide nipples were rudely erect and Avalon presented the right breast to me, almost forcing the nipple between my lips as her fingers got to work on the left one. Avalon's bouncing action changed to a slower, more concentrated, circular motion and she began to let out low pitched obscenities from the back of her throat. This was the way she liked it best - on top and in command, grinding the bloated mini-penis against me, so that she was, in every sense of the words, fucking well in charge.

The slower motion took the heat off my pulsating organ, which had just been about to explode, and suddenly I knew - It's OK. You're in expert hands here. Relax and enjoy it. You can handle this. No problem.

"Oh, darling," Avalon confided to me softly, "I'm coming."

"Yes, come on, baby, come on!" I just about managed to enunciate around a mouthful of areola.

Avalon did just what she had promised, panting rapidly as she arched her back and then going all soft and compliant with her arms around my neck as I felt the muscular twitches of her pelvic floor. The grinding action slowed to a gentle rocking action. "Oh, sweetheart," Avalon breathed, kissing me repeatedly on the forehead. "That was lovely. Thank you - Thank you."

We stayed like that for a bit, Avalon using her lips on my neck, while I went to work on her nipples, setting off a series of mini-orgasms and causing her body to jerk like someone being given a series of mild electric shocks. Eventually she went limp again and clung to my shoulders, burying my face in a mass of heavenly-scented black hair. "You want a rest, sweetheart?" I asked, not entirely selflessly. "Or can you manage some more?"

"Just a minute or two's rest," Avalon whispered, starting up a gentle fidget with her buttocks on my naked thighs. I could feel her juices staring to soak into my pubic hair. It felt terrific. "And then I'd like some more."

By now, I was pretty blase. Putting off the first urge to ejaculate gives you a sort of second wind. I began to think of ways to have Avalon next. On her back across the dining table? Doggy fashion kneeling on this same creaking dining-chair? Stick old whassname - old Palomedes - under those beautiful buttocks and roger her on the red-plastic work surface in the kitchen?

Merely thinking about this sent a muscular impulse along the length of my cock. Avalon sensed it and wriggled encouragingly. "Ooh, yes," she muttered. "That's nice. I think I can manage some more - now - please."

I slipped a hand under each of her thighs and stood up with Avalon still impaled. She had her arms wrapped around my neck, her knees wrapped around my back, and there was no weight there to speak of. It was the easiest thing in the world to carry her, still giving her the occasional thrust - out onto the central concourse, and then to back down the stairs until she was at a level where I could lay her on the floor of the landing. Stretching luxuriously, I began to use the full length of my organ to penetrate her so deeply that a little bulge appeared intermittently in the white flatness of her belly. Avalon looked down at this, giggled and said, "Oh, aren't you clever? You're so - big!"

Now that I was on top, I had a chance to show off some real sexual gymnastics - fucking Avalon with a sort of millstone motion that rolled her clitoris like a roll of plasticine between our pubic symphises. Avalon really liked that. The overall effect was to get

Avalon red-faced and talking dirty again.

What she said was principally a sort of eulogy about the size of my sex-organ. If nothing else, a big cock gives you something to talk about at times like this. Saves you from all that embarrassing no-honestly-it-doesn't-matter-darling-really sort of crap. But while it is a jolly useful thing for lots of other things in bed, outside bed, it has no practical sexual merit. Most other physical characteristics - hairy forearms, non-hairy forearms, broad shoulders, weedy shoulders, big bums, little bums - all of those things can be sexual signals that will appeal to some sort of bird or other. But if you've got a big cock, how does anybody find out about it until it's too late? No practical form of clothing will show the thing off and, in any case, the thing packs away far too neatly for travelling. There are actually laws against getting the thing out and showing it to people, and the only alternative - telling people about it - is a form of verbal flashing that would turn anybody off.

"Oooh - yesss," Avalon was saying now. "That's how I like it." Then, opening her eyes, and with a cheeky grin on her face, she told me plainly in a few four-letter words what she wanted me to do next. I wouldn't betray her confidence so far as to tell you what words she used, for it was, in essence, an incitement to commit a criminal act, against the crown and dignity of our Sovereign Lady, by the Grace of God, Elizabeth, the Second of that name. Hoping that old Liz wasn't actually watching what was going on, I gasped. "The stuff. Have we got any stuff?"

Naturally enough, Avalon had. Her tasselled handbag was lying there near the top step. She reached over, pulled the bag to her and withdrew from its side pocket an almost empty blue, white and red tube. Sexual toothpaste. Avalon never travels anywhere without it.

"Here, honey. Let me do it for you," Avalon said.

I withdrew and watched, lost in wonder, as Avalon anointed me with a squirt of clear jelly and then emptied the tube with a delightful wet farting noise onto my finger so that I could do the same for her. While I was enjoying the erotic sensation this gave my finger a thought struck me. "Here, is that the new tube I gave you last week?" I panted. Well, I say *I* gave her. It was a sort of gift from the Health Authority, really.

"Mmm," Avalon nodded.

"Where's it all gone?" I asked. "It was full last Friday."

"We - used it all, " Avalon smiled. "We didn't waste any of it - don't worry." The new angle she had adopted on the top step left no doubt that she didn't want me to waste this last bit, either, and with tears in my eyes I gently and patiently waited for her to relax so that I could commit the felony she had suggested. Avalon's moaning took on a new degree of urgency. "Oh - baby!" she kept moaning. "Oh, yes, yes. That feels so good!"

I supported the weight of her legs and looked down on this beautiful woman as she lay back on what Roz's handout led me to believe was called a deep textured-pile carpet. Avalon's big eyes were moist, too, reminding us both that what we were doing was doomed to ephemerality and therefore tinged with a sense of sadness, but the porcelain skin of her face was coloured by the rouge-like arousal blushes of her cheeks and she smiled broadly up at me as she lazily used one hand for her nipples and the other for her clitoris. The sheer intimacy of it all was the ultimate act of mutual trust. This be the reason, y'see, why H.M. made the act illegal, so as to add a bit of spice to it, so as you'd appreciate it properly. Not that she needed to have gone to all that trouble on my behalf. For me, it was special enough in itself, the breaking down of the final taboo, of the final barrier that separates one individual from another. It's not really a physical act at all. It's an emotional one, and simply agreeing to do it made Avalon and me physiologically and emotionally one person.

The expression on Avalon's face was one of absolute trust. It's the face that's the sexiest organ of them all. She had handed over control of her body to me in the knowledge that I wouldn't hurt or abuse it. It was an expression of hedonistic abandonment, of a totally self-confident sexual animal who knows precisely how each bit of her body works, and how to get the very best result out of it. I smiled back at her, and turned my head slowly from side to side. "Isn't this fucking marvellous?" I asked in all seriousness.

"Wonderful," she breathed. "Wonderful!"

"Avalon - ?"

"What?"

"I love you," I told a woman, for the very first time in my life. That's why this thing - undignified and unspiritual though it may appear - is called love-making: because it makes you love the person you're doing it with. Trouble is, if you're not careful, you sometimes end up letting her in on your secret.

Avalon simply closed her eyes, nodded and smiled. With each stroke, I seemed to be penetrating deeper, and the pace of things began to hot up. The noise she was making now might just have passed for a groan of agony, but I was pretty sure it wasn't, especially when she added. "Oh, that's it! Come on baby. Deeper! Harder!"

Her cool little fingers came up between my thighs and began to fondle my balls, ever so gently.

"Oh, Christ, Baby," I grunted. "I just can't help it if you do that. I can't hold back. I'll . . . "

"Yes, that's it, come on!" Avalon puffed. "I want you to. Oh, come on, baby, come on! Do it!"

I was now grunting noisily and emitting staccato obscenities, while Avalon lay there wriggling, kitten-like, encouraging me. I felt the old seminal vesicles stick a bullet in the breech. That certain tingle started to creep up between my balls, and then –

There was an urgent knocking on the glass in the door six feet below us.

"Dr Fullen?" Roz was asking.

"Come on, honey. Come on! Now!" Avalon gasped. "Don't stop!"

"Dr Fullen, are you in there? Can you open the door please?"

"Jeezus Christ!"

"Don't mind her" Avalon panted. "Come on! Please. Do it!"

"I can't, love." I said. The spell was broken. "She's bloody well spoilt it."

"Dr Fullen? What's going on in there?"

Avalon planted a kiss on my nose. "Alright. Later," she said. I withdrew and she began to console my drooling, member with her nice cool hands. "Not too much later, though, eh?"

The doorknob downstairs began to rattle. "Hello? Hello? Are you still in there, Dr Fullen?"

"Not now, I'm not," I muttered. "Look, honey, can you let her in? I'm not going to be able to get my trousers closed."

Avalon giggled at this, stood up and hastily smoothed down her skirt. "Yes: go on, off you go. Try not to look too guilty," she said.

I struggled into the kitchen with my boxer shorts round my knees and heard Avalon opening the outside door. "Oh, hello, Mrs – er – Palmer.

Sorry, I think the door bell must be broken or something."

Roz did not sound altogether convinced by this. I could hear her pushing past Avalon on the stairs, probably scanning the things for pubic hairs and wet bits as she went. "Where is your husband?" I heard her ask.

"Oh, in the - er - dining room, I think" Avalon said smoothly. "We were just admiring the dining chairs."

I could hear Roz making for the bedroom. Tough luck, Roz Baby. You gotta be a bit more imaginative than that to work out what Avalon gets up to.

I could hear Roz skipping through the bedroom, opening wardrobe doors. Avalon appeared at the kitchen door, her face still flushed, her pupils dilated, and her chest heaving. She raised her eyebrows, patted her chest and gave a mock whistle of relief. Between her fingers, she was waggling the crumpled blue, white and red tube which she had just scooped off the carpet. She beamed conspiratorially at me. "Ah, no, here he is, in the kitchen," she called.

Roz strode in. I had not yet succeeded in getting my zip to close, and I was standing in the doorway to a sort of broom cupboard, wearing only one shoe, my shirt open to the waist, gazing intently at a tin of Vim. Avalon saw my problem and stepped between us. "And how, precisely, do we settle the electricity bills?" she asked in her best Art Gallery voice. "Do we pay them quarterly or what?"

"Have you thought over what I asked you?" I said.

"What was that?" Oh come on, sweetheart, don't give me that rubbish. I haven't been able to sleep for three nights, waiting for your answer.

"You know."

"What? About going on holiday together?" She paused. "It's very - difficult," Avalon whispered.

"Why? What's difficult about it? We just buy a couple of tickets. We get on the plane, and three hours later, there we are - on holiday together."

"Not quite as simple as that though, is it?"

"I'm sorry, I don't see what's - "

"Well, it's a big step forwards in our relationship. I've never been on holiday with any of my boyfriends before."

I didn't want to hear this. She must have had plenty of boyfriends before me, obviously, but I didn't want to think about them. The idea of Avalon yielding up her secret places to anyone else made me flush with rage and jealousy. Still, yer can't make an omelette without breaking eggs, and yer can't get a girl as good in bed as Avalon without letting her practise, I suppose. The idea that she hadn't been on holiday with any of them ought to have been something of an encouragement, but for some reason it wasn't.

"Look, I love you, you know," I said, just like that.

"Do you?" Avalon asked.

I took her hand in mine and looked her straight in the eyes. "Yes, Avalon, I do."

Avalon lowered her long eyelashes. "Please, honey," she said, "don't talk like that. Not now."

"Why not now?"

"Because things are very - difficult for me just at the moment."

"In what way?"

"Oh, just work and - things."

"What sort of things?"

"Please - I don't want to talk about it."

"Why not? I'd tell you anything. I'd share anything with you. I've got no secrets from you. I love you." Avalon smiled. "What's so funny?" I asked her.

"Here - you see that couple over there in the rowing boat?"

"Mmm."

"They've just been over to that island to have a crafty bit."

"How can you tell?"

"He's got grass stains on his knees. Look."

"Oh yeah, so he has." We were laying on a grass bank sloping down to a river at the back of a pub, where we had gone not to get drunk but to get something to eat. After telling Roz that we'd think about the flat, we had stormed back to Bleak House and pounded the hell out of the bed springs.

Oh, it was enjoyable enough, but somehow it didn't have that extra something - that bit of excitement that comes from fucking where you're not supposed to. After her third - or possibly fourth - orgasm, Avalon had rolled onto her back and declared, not I love you, I love you, My Darling, but "God! I feel so hungry. I'm absolutely ravenous."

So here I was, provider of her needs at both ends, and she now lay, contented and sated, looking radiant and wonderful. And grateful? Well, not really. But then, why should she be? If I didn't want the job, there'd be no shortage of applicants for the vacancy.

"You watch," Avalon said, nodding excitedly. "I bet you five pounds she's not his wife."

We watched as the man brought the boat inexpertly into land, and over-solicitously helped the girl onto the landing stage. The sun glinted briefly on a gold band on her wedding finger.

"There you are. look at the way he's looking after her," Avalon said. "Those two are never married to each other."

"Where d'you think they've been, then?"

"There's a place on the island. It's dry and sheltered and - surrounded by bushes and things. Nobody can see you - even from the river."

I didn't dare to ask how Avalon knew all this. We watched in silence as the couple strolled, red-faced and a bit sweaty but otherwise apparently unconcerned - not even holding hands - as far as the car-park. After the briefest of goodbyes, he got into a Volvo Estate with child seat, she into a Red Mini, and they went their separate ways.

"Looks like that's five pounds you owe me." Avalon giggled.

I inhaled deeply and felt an involuntary catch, almost a sob, as I recognised the vunerability of my situation. I had nothing to bargain with. Women who look like Avalon can do more or less as they bloody well like. For them, it's a seller's market all their life. When half the population of the world wants to fuck you, you just lay there and take your pick. Hey, you there, Big Boy. Yes: *you*.

Besides, no woman was ever wooed and won who didn't want to be. Women don't love you for what you are, or what you do, or anything as logical as that. No. It's something inside them. They either want you or they don't, and that decision has got precious little to do with any merits or demerits you happen to have. It's a mental process the woman does for herself, and you can do sod-all to affect it.

If you happen to be in the right place at the right time, she will do the wooing. Ignoring your glaring faults, she is the one who will send the cards and the poems and the presents. You simply can't lose. But if she loses interest in you, or she simply doesn't fancy you, give up. You're banging your head against a brick wall. Even if you shoved your head up your arse to show how much you love her, it would make no difference. She simply wouldn't care, and nothing you can do will make her care.

I suppose I ought to have been grateful for what I'd got. After all, Avalon still enjoyed fucking me, which was fine.What am I talking about? It was unbelievable. Here was this beautiful creature that got my juices flowing so copiously and so effortlessly that I could think of nothing else except the next time I got my fingers round the elastic of her drawers. And not only does she not mind me doing those things to her, she actually wants it as much as I do. All the same, in all the time I had known her, Avalon had never so much as once offered to die of love for me.

Since Avalon's return from the Bleak House bathroom there was something about the way she had been talking to me. She was friendly enough, she laughed a lot, made jokes, even gave me a quick hand-job in the car but somehow something was missing. It was as though there was someone else sitting beside us on the river bank at the moment, somebody invisible, watching our every move.

Chapter 14

Tapping my front teeth lightly with a biro, I took my seat again. "The heart tracing," I repeated neutrally, "was completely normal."

The patient – a dirty old person called Peacock – readjusted his position on the creased leather of the examination couch and paused in the act of fastening a shirt button. "See, what it is, Doc. Sometimes I only gotta climb a few stairs – I stop. Then all of a sudden – " His arms were gorilla-length and covered with the sort of skin you could read. He now crossed one of them over his chest and slapped it rapidly with the other hand in an imitation of what he had already described as the jibbers. "Just like that," he said.

"Yes, but as I say, the tests you had at the hospital were all fine. The heart tracing was normal. There was nothing in the blood tests to suggest – "

"Then sometimes, I'm lying in bed," Peacock went on, apparently also suffering from cloth ears or from the ability to recognise the sounds I had just uttered as human speech. "I sit up, then all of a sudden – "

I sighed inwardly and stared blankly ahead, focussing my attention on the ideas of coffee (which I had been promised some of as soon as I could give this specimen the push) and sex (which I hoped to have some of that evening, provided Avalon kept her promise to ring me back). Peacock was still talking but I now realised that I need pay no attention to what he was saying. Nodding and umming at intervals, I settled back into the creaking swivel chair and looked around the room.

I was in a sort of glorified corridor with a very high ceiling that went in and out a lot and seemed to have collected more than its fair share of muck. The place was dark, despite the french window at the far end which opened (or more probably didn't open) onto a small garden where there was an ornamental pond containing a lot of dead plants and animals. Although it was a warmish morning, a gothic gas fire, its clay burners cracked and derelict, hissed and spluttered away in one corner, and in the opposite corner there was an old weighing machine that worked (or more probably didn't work) by suspending horseshoe-shaped weights from one end of its beam. It looked filthy and rusty, and its possibly once green paint was scabbing off everywhere.

"But then Dr Chaucer, he put me on this new medicine for the bronchitis. He told me it's got a lot of like ingreedyants in it. My feeling is – and you'd know a lot more about this than I do – my feeling is that it's ingreedyants that I need. I mean to say – "

On one of the patchy bits of wall over the couch there was a mouldering photograph in its black-painted frame. Two young snots in knife-edge collars and overbig homburgs were standing in front of an aerodynamically-unsound antique car, clutching a pair of Music Hall doctor bags. On the smudgy cardboard surround, somebody with very bad handwriting had written "Teddy and Andrew". Chaucer and partner in the first flush of qualification. The smug expressions on the unrealistically-smooth faces said it all, that they were doctors, now, thank you so much, and they knew everything there was to know about it. Looking at them again, I wondered what it was they thought they knew a lot about.

So far this morning, all I had done was to listen to a load of boring old rubbish about trivial ailments, and then hand out prescriptions for things that were at best cheap and useless, and at worst expensive and dangerous. "Primum Non Nocere – First, do no harm." It was alright for bloody old Hippocrates. He didn't have to hold Monday morning surgeries in British West Crosshills.

My other function was to put my name on the bottom of various forms and certificates, the truth of which I did not necessarily believe in, and this I now did for Peacock, signing the work-shy bum off for another two weeks.

"Well, as you may know, Doctor," Peacock said suddenly. "I'm what you call a religious man. I like to think I'm among the followers of the Lord Jesus Christ, a good Christian. You follow my meaning?" He walked over and parked his great smelly backside on the desk, waiting for the nod of approval.

Managing a half-smile, I said, "Ah yes, good, good."

"I try to live my life according to God's Holy Word."

Wondering what the hell this had to do with me, I said, "Hmm."

"I believe that prayer is our first defence against disease and iniquity, you see. But I also believe that the Lord wants us to make use of your skill and art too, Doctor."

"Yeah, right."

"Yes, you are God's gift to us, aren't you? That's what the Lord put you on earth for. To heal the sick – "

"And to, ah, comfort the aged," I suggested.

"Yes, to comfort the aged," Peacock said. "After all, in the Holy Gospels, does it not say – "

Looking at my watch, I said, "Yes, Mr Peacock, but I've got to be – "

"Of course, doctor, of course. I know how busy you must be." He got down from his perch, looking genuinely hurt, picked up his certificate from the desk and read it, his lips moving as he did so. "Hard Doses?" he asked.

"Sorry. That says 'heart disease'."

" Heart disease? Dr Chaucer usually puts 'bronchitis'."

"Well, I'll give you one saying 'bronchitis' if you like."

"No, no, this'll be alright," Peacock said. "Tell you something though, doctor."

"What's that?"

"This bronchitis of mine, you know where I got it from?" Harrods? Selfridges? Go on, surprise me. "Swimmin', " Peacock said proudly.

"You what ?"

"Swimmin'. Swimmin' in water where the bad air had got to it."

"I'm not sure what you mean by – "

"Dr Chaucer, he told me. He said your bronchitis – your bronchitis, he said, is due to the fact that when you was a lad, you went swimmin' in water where the bad air had got to it. Not a word of a lie," he suddenly added, as if I had challenged him. "When I was a lad, I used to go swimmin' up by the metal works at Hebworth. It was the bad air from the works done it for me. Give me this bronchitis, see? Dr Chaucer, he told me that. You hadn't been swimming up there, he told me, you'd be running round now like a boy of twenty."

Oh yeah? I looked at the filthy brown cigarette stains on his fingers. This story was so preposterous that it cried out to be ridiculed just for its own sake, but the thing that was really annoying was the forelock-tugging way this old fool was quoting an even bigger old fool for his authority. Already this morning, five patients had told me that Chaucer was treating them for "low blood pressure", and it was galling to realise how much better Chaucer was at conning people.

"Mm, yes:, well, frankly, I find that a bit hard to believe. Mr – er – " I said "I think what Dr Chaucer must've meant was that you – "

"That's what he told me," Peacock persisted. "It was the bad air what'd – "

" I'm afraid that's not very likely. You see, chronic bronchitis is a – "

"You believe what you like, boy," Peacock shouted. "I was there! I know what happened! You believe what you like!" At this, he turned and stamped out of the room, swinging his gorilla arms and revealing a previously-hidden tattoo which said that he preferred Death to Dishonour. Well, who knows ? Some day I might be able to oblige him.

The door from the file room opened and the manic old drab I now knew as Mrs Vera Clode stuck her head round the door. "Don't ring for anybody else" she chirped. "I've got some things for you to sign."

"Right you are." I scribbled the date and the words "Cert. two weeks" on Peacock's card (this being the full extent of the sort of medical records Chaucer kept), muttered "Silly prat" (meaning Peacock) and reflected that even if youth had been wasted on the young, at least common sense and open-mindedness had not been wasted on the old. I yawned, stretched, did a silent belch and wondered whether I ought give Avalon another bell. No. She had sounded distant and preoccupied when I rang the gallery just after nine. She was, she said, "tied up" with some customers. She had even been a little tetchy. Did I think it was an awfully good idea for me to keep ringing her at work the way I did?

Right, that's the way you want it. Up yours, darling, I would normally have said to something like that, but the truth is that I am besotted with the woman. This is getting very serious. Last week, I went out and bought her some flowers, of all things. The occasion was the Grand Gala Opening of my new apartment. I finally got up the balls to ring Roz and told her that Dr and Mrs Fullen had decided against her flat. No. Wouldn't do at all. The stair carpet had played hell with my kneecaps, and you should just see the state of my wife's buttocks. After a search through the Slight Seconds department of her little book, Roz came up with this bachelor penthouse – well, actually a couple of attic rooms and a half-share in a bog – in Hogdown, which is left at the scrapyard, straight on towards the gasworks, and fork left at the abattoir. I could see the disbelief beginning to register on Avalon's face as I drove her down there, but once inside the door, things perked up enormously and we christened the double-bed with a vigour and enthusiasm that delighted and exhausted us both.

Afterwards, I shyly presented her with the flowers, and put the proposition to her as delicately and diplomatically as I could. How's about you and me shacking up together, I asked? Avalon was a bit evasive on that one. There were her present flat mates to consider, she said, a matter of a three-year lease, and there would be problems with the business. Dealers were in the habit of ringing her up at home - and oh dear, that feels wonderful, no, no, please don't stop.

"There you are then," Mrs Clode said, slapping a thickish wad of EC 10's on the desk in front of me. "Sign those and I'll get you a cup of coffee."

I appended my schoolboy signature to the repeat prescriptions that had been dashed off in Mrs Clode's fluent and confident handwriting, and settled down to explore the only two drawers in Chaucer's ink-stained desk that I hadn't yet been through.

The first of these was difficult to open and contained a lot of dust, four paper clips, a tennis ball with teeth marks (probably a dog's, but possibly even Chaucer's), a piece of sealing wax and a folded sheet of paper slightly superior in quality to the nastier sort of continental toilet roll. On one side of this, there was a child's pencil drawing of some giant gooseberries with legs discharging firearms at a heavily-armoured prune with caterpillar tracks. There were also a few ill-written words in ballpoint: "Darren's shoe's are black waynes shoe's are brown swade." It was the sort of stationery that would have done justice to one of J. Parfin's "Dear Dr please see" letters, or even to a shopping list, which is what it turned out to be. On its other side, written in blunt, friable pencil and with an assortment of upper- and lower-case letters, it probably said :

> deaR doKTuR pLeaSe caN I haVe sum mooR TabLiTS fouR my sTomiCK aLSo leGs theY aRe PLayaN Up somThinG oWFuL alSo caN mauReen somTHinG fouR THrowT wicH HaVE BiN SaW faTHeR neeD moRe OynTmenT fouR his baCK iT geTTiN nO beTTar aLso baBBy haVe biN SiCK anD paiN in STomicK tO daYs caN We StuFF fouR THiS aLso raSH oN buM pLeaSe OBLiGe thaNk yoU D RamSToNe (MrS) 7b weLLinGToN fLaTs

Hey bloody ho. The bottom drawer on the left looked relatively dust-free, and appeared at first sight to contain only a five-year-old copy of Country Life. When I lifted the front edge of this publication, though, I came upon the drawer's real purpose (and probably the only object in the entire desk that got any regular sort of use). It was a green glass bottle, three quarters full of air, one quarter full of clear liquid, and bearing the label of an old- established London distillery.

"You found that already, did you?" Mrs Clode said, looking over my shoulder. "He thinks I don't know it's there if he keeps it covered up like that." This was said purely as a matter of information. There was no note of censure in her voice, just as, earlier on, she had told me quite simply about the times Chaucer had been physically unable to get out of bed to answer night calls, and how, on more than one occasion, she had had to go out for him. The reason for his inability to get out of bed was now more apparent.

"Yes, he's very partial to the Gordon's Dry," she said. "Can't get through his evening surgeries without it nowadays. Mother's ruin. Good job he's given up doing ante-natal work, otherwise it'd have ruined quite a few mothers round here." She shuffled off into the file room and immediately re-appeared with a cup of milky coffee half slopped into its rose-encrusted, non-matching saucer."You've been getting on alright, have you ?" she asked, the intonation rather than any discernible accent betraying her Swansea origins.

"Yeah, well it's – er – "

"Not quite what you expected, though, I dare say."

"Takes a bit of getting used to."

"Well of course it does. Usually we get quite a crowd in here on a Monday, but you heard, I suppose. A lot of them left when they heard Andrew Chaucer wasn't going to be here. Well, of course, you must have done. You mustn't take that to heart, love. They were exactly the same with a young lad we had down here last year, doing the locum." She looked at me as though I ought to be taking it a lot more personally than I was doing. "Coffee alright for you, is it?"

Burnt underpants and treacle. I said, "Mmm" and handed back the sheaf of completed EC 10's. "Will those do?"

She leafed through them without enthusiasm. "Yes, they'll be alright." After a pause, she said, "Course, they all love Dr Chaucer, you know, I mean – you know what he's like, don't you?"

"Well, no, I don't actually."

"Oh, no, of course. I was forgetting." I now realised that the principal of the practice – for reasons best known to himself, but now becoming very apparent to me – had never intended to have the "little chat" he had talked about on the phone. I had spent a large part of the previous week trying to drop in on him unannounced, only to be out-manoeuvred and out-evaded by a past master of the art.

This was no joke. For a single-handed practice, this one spent a large part of its time being a no-handed practice, with Chaucer not only unavailable for personal consultation, but uncontactable in any form, and with total ignorance on the part of Mrs Clode and Chaucer's wife as to his whereabouts.

"Yes, he's a lovely old chap, is Dr Chaucer. You'll like him."

Not if he's pissed out of his mind during evening surgery and makes me do all his night calls, I won't, missus. "Yes, well, I'll look forward to – "

"Oh, hello, Mrs Midgely. Want to see doctor, do you?" A figure like an anthropomorphic female bulldog was standing with her hand on the door-handle. "Come in, dear. This is our new doctor, Dr Fullen. Want a word with him, do you?" The woman looked me up and down distrustingly and edged forwards towards the desk.

"I'll get you Mrs Midgely's card," Vera Clode said.

"Would you like to take a seat?" The woman let herself down onto the patient chair, wiped an overflow of snot onto a crumpled lilac tissue, sniffed, coughed a couple of times and then sat gaping open-mouthed at the only other wall decoration in the room – a sepia photograph of some mutton-chopped geezer – presumably even more ancient than Chaucer – who had just finished looking into a brass microscope on the table in front of him. From the look on his face, he had been using it to study microfilm transparencies depicting scenes of a frank sexual nature.

"Right then.What's the trouble been ?"

"Um – I don't hardly know where to begin."

"Take your time and tell me how it all started."

That was a big mistake. Starting off with a halting and stumbling account of her mother's funeral five months earlier, her narrative gradually increased in speed and fluidity until she was reciting every last snivelling gripe and petty grievance that had been building up over the years of her snotty, shabby life. I could cope with that sort of thing in small doses, but the problem with a full-blown performance like this was how to tell the performer to shut her face without appearing to do just that. In hospital, the standard escape from this situation was to interrupt in mid-sentence with, "Yes, well I should go and see your own doctor about that, if I were you", a device which was obviously illogical here, unless I could persuade her that Chaucer was the bloke she really wanted.

"Just a minute," I said, seizing on the only real physical complaint in her narrative, "You were saying just then about your ears – "

"Ears?"

"Yes, you said that at night, your ears get very – "

"Oh – tight."

"Tight. OK, so I think the first thing we have to do is have a look in your ears, don't you? Which ear was it, in particular?"

The dirty old hag was in the process of trying to identify some "nerve tablets" which she said Chaucer had put her on. Chaucer's notes – naturally enough – did not bother to record trivial details like that, and the woman had at first tried to describe the things to me, and had then made several not at all accurate attempts to reproduce the sound of their name. Finally, she had emptied the contents of her vile handbag onto the desk, and was sorting through part-used snot rags, bunches of keys, nit-infested hair combs and cigarette butts of varying lengths and degrees of soiling.

"They was called Leganish – Liganish – something like that," she said. "I know I've got them in here somewhere."

"Yeah, well, look, never mind about the tablets for the time being. Which ear was it that was giving you trouble ?"

While she set her few remaining brain cells to work on that problem, I walked over to the glass case next to the weighing machine. "I think it was – um – no, wait, it must have been – " The door knob on the glass case refused to turn either way, but the door shuddered open of its own accord. "I think it was this one."

For practical purposes, it didn't really matter which of her ghastly orifices it was. Perhaps I ought to be grateful that I wasn't going to be called upon to stick an instrument into something even nastier.

Still, if you were ever stuck for something to stick somewhere, this glass case was the place to find it. The dust-powdered shelves groaned with corroded metal objects, the function of which could only be guessed at. A device for squeezing boils in the region of the buttocks, perhaps? Something over there for inserting ring-pessaries in female elephants? And what was that thing at the bottom for – the one with all those rubber bladder things – if not for administering colonic lavage to six persons at a single sitting?

"Right. Can you turn and face the wall over there?" She managed this at only the third attempt, having first turned her back on the wall indicated, and then stood up and bent over backwards. It was at this point I discovered that the auriscope light didn't work. The instrument was also surprisingly easy to lift, and a quick peep into the bottom explained both observations – there were no batteries in the bloody thing. "Won't keep you a minute," I said.

In the file room, Mrs Clode was on the phone and didn't like being interrupted. "Yes, what is it, dear?"

"Have you got any batteries for this thing?"

She looked at the instrument as though trying to confirm that it was not a personal vibrator. "What you want batteries for?" she asked

"It doesn't work. There's no batteries in it."

"Just a second, love," This to her telephonic friend. "Come here," she said and, taking me by the sleeve, she drew me down until my ear was on a level where she could either whisper or spit into it as the mood took her. She smelled of old woman a bit. "Look, I know there's no batteries in it. That's the way he likes it. You put batteries in, and sooner or later, they leak, don't they? Make an awful mess. So, as long as you don't tell the patients there's no batteries in it, they don't know the difference."

"What? You mean he – ?"

"Yes. He just pokes that thing in their ears, makes a few reassuring noises and then puts them on penicillin. They're not to know the difference, are they? After all, they can't see out of their ears."

"I wouldn't put it past some of them."

"Yes, well, there you are. We haven't got any batteries, so that's it, isn't it? Anyway, what you want batteries for? What do any of you lot want batteries for? Even if you could see in her ear, you wouldn't know what you were looking at. You haven't had the training, have you?"

"Thank you so much. So sorry to have interrupted your little chat."

The most annoying part about what she had said was that it was true. The two weeks allotted to Ear, Nose and Throat diseases at medical school had been shortened to six days because Duggie had managed to convince me that you didn't need to know any ENT to pass finals. We had used the time instead to go on a long camping weekend with a couple of female physics students who had turned out to be the University of London Formation Prick Teasing Team. When I finally did show up in the ENT department, the surgeon who was supposed to teach me had an aversion to students, and the only thing I could clearly remember was the time when he described a particularly bloody operation on somebody's hooter as "a nose-pick to end all nose-picking".

The Clode woman was back yattering on the phone. All bloody right then. If that was the way they played it around here. Gripping the instrument like a battleaxe, I pulled open the door and strode back into the consulting room.

Chapter 15

"Hello! Breckleigh 2 - 8 - um - "

Beep beep beep beep. "Ah - low? Oozat ?" Click.

"Hello! Hello! God! You stupid bastard!" I put the receiver back on its rest and sat up in bed, arms folded, waiting for the thing to ring again. Extending my left leg in the darkness, I explored the bed until it reached the far edge, unimpeded. So, I'd been dreaming, hadn't I? No Bloody Avalon. To be fair, she had only said she might drop by if she was able to "sort things out", but things at the gallery were "awfully hectic" this week. A special exhibition by some talentless bum of a local sculptor, and the queer proprietor of the place had insisted - so she said - on going through the books with her.

Resting my head against the wallpaper, I counted the days it had been since I had had a chance to go through the book with Avalon. There had been the flat-warming do, of course, but since then, what? A hurried and somewhat joyless lunchtime poke after an alcoholic lunch, a quick grope and a promise in a pub car-park somewhere. It was just unfortunate, Avalon had told me, all these things coming together. Still, she had joked saucily, it would do me good to go without for a bit. She seriously suspected that I was oversexed, and a little bit of abstinence would give her time to recover, and make me appreciate it all the more once this difficult period was over. Period? Yes, that had been one excuse, but there had been others - too tired, too upset, too harassed, too busy, even a headache one day. But it was the way she said it - a cheeky little grin, a teasing little joke, a charming and devastating smile. I had to believe her.

"Yes, hello. Breckleigh 28281."

"Through now. Go ahead, caller."

"Ar - low? Oozat?"

"Breckleigh 28281."

"Ar -low?"

"Hello!"

"That Dr Chaucer?"

"No, it's Dr Fullen here."

"Is Dr Chaucer there?"

Oh sure, buggerlugs, of course, sleeping right here beside me. I'll just put him on, shall I? "No. Now listen to me, I'm – Doctor – Fullen," I explained, stressing each word and allowing enough time between each of them so that even this thick sod could understand what I was saying. "I'm – on – call – for – Doctor – Chaucer."

"Oh, I see." Muffled conversation. " He says he's on call for Dr Chaucer." "Is that right?"

"Ar-low? Can you come and see Mrs McGready, please ?"

"Why? What's the matter with her?"

"She been took bad."

"In what way ?"

"I don't know. I'm her neighbour. They asked me to ring up the doctor, see?"

"Yes, well it is now – it is now twenty minutes past two. Before I get out of bed, I'd like to know what I'm getting up for."

More muffled conversation. "Hello, doctor. We don't know what's a matter with her. She just been took bad."

"Alright. What address is it ?"

"Just a minute, doctor." Mumble mumble mumble. "Ello! Doctor? We think it's number eleven Armada Buildings, Walker Street."

"Right. Thank you so very much."

"Ar -low ? Is that the doctor?"

No, Madam, just your friendly neighbourhood rapist. The sweep of my flashlight up the crapped-on stone steps took in: sequined slippers, crumpled green socks, fire-marbled shins, egg-stained dressing gown, and finally gummy, toothless features below a crown of hair-curlers.

"Yes. Where is she?"

"I'll let you in." She hobbled crab-fashion down the steps, leaning back against the handrail and extending her toes into the murk. "We got to be bit careful, see, 'cos her husband's away at sea, like. Jus a tick. Ah, there we are, you see." She held a yale key up for my inspection, perhaps as a demonstration that she had passed some sort of test in basic key technology, and was licensed to tote one of the things - an impression not enhanced by her ham-fisted efforts to get the thing into the lock and produce the necessary degree of pronation to open it. We shuffled through into a narrow corridor smelling of boiled cabbage and baby crap, which was lit only by an unshaded forty watt bulb. There were things written on the wall, and lots of bits of peeling wallpaper about.

"She in here." The woman opened a door to our left. In the dim shaft of light, I could make out a woman of unguessable age, lying on a bed which was remarkably adjacent to the floor. The room smelled like the monkey house during the rutting season, and I had to step over the bed to get in because the door was wedged half-shut by the wardrobe behind it. It was great nit-catching territory.

"Can you put the light on?"

"Ah no, doctor, We can't have a light in here. Switch is broken, see?" She was wiggling the flail switch up and down to back up this statement.

"Thank you. That's very useful. You're Mrs McGready, are you?"

"Yes,she's Mrs McGready," the other woman said.

"What's you trouble been, exactly?"

"She's had pain in her tummy, haven't you, Shirley? Tell the doctor, love. Yes,she's had pain in her tummy, doctor."

"Has she been sick?"

"Not far as I know."

"Have you been sick?" I repeated.

The girl in the bed said, "Nyah."

"Is there something the matter with her?"

"What you mean, doctor?"

"Is she alright - in the head?"

"Yeah - she's alright. Not a great talker, are you, Shirley?"

"Nyah," the girl in the bed said.

I knelt on the floor and lifted the rancid-smelling sheets. A dog, which had been asleep on the covers at the foot of the bed, woke up and growled, then went back to sleep. I groped about for a bit, trying to hold the flashlight in one hand. Hopeless.

"Jesus Christ!" I muttered. So this was what general practice was all about, eh? Being forced by circumstances to accept - and in the end, to be grateful for - lower and lower standards of everything. Working for Jimmie had been bad enough, but at least you could see the patients, and the nursing staff could sometimes be relied on to clean off the worst of the shit before you looked at them.

"What you going to do?" the older woman asked.

"I'm just thinking."

"Oh." She took a step back and let out a few "ahs" and "I sees", as if to show that she was no stranger to watching a bit of thinking going on. "Well, what you think we ought to do?"

"Not really sure. What I think I'll do is leave her for now and come back and see her in the morning."

"She's here by herself, you know. If anything happened to her, there'd be nobody here to look after her."

"Suppose we could try to get her into hospital."

"I think that's best, don't you, doctor? Doctor'll get you into hospital, Shirley my love."

"Right. Can you wait here until the ambulance comes? I'll pop down the end of Walker Street and give them a ring."

"Alright, doctor. You leave that to me."

"Hello! Which firm is on surgical take tonight?"

"Surgical take is ah - Mr Materson."

"Who's his houseman now?"

"Mr Materson is - Dr Henry."

"Can I speak to Dr Henry then, please?"

"Hold on."

After a few seconds, a distant voice said, "Henry".

"Ah, good evening, Dr Henry. My name's Fullen. I - I'm a GP - out at Crosshills." That seemed enough of the potted biography. If in fact Henry realised that I was the same Fullen who had just finished Materson's housejob, he gave no indication of it. I had never met Henry, because our terms of office had been separated by a one week basic-English-only Arab locum, but three o'clock in the morning didn't seem like a good time to strike up a discussion about Great Shits I Have Worked For.

"I've just been to see a woman called Mrs Shirley McGready. She's got a history of - um - abdominal pain for a few hours. Hasn't been sick - I wondered if you'd take her in for observation?"

"Observation?"

"Yes. Well she lives alone, you see, and - "

"Yes, but how d'you mean - observation ? What's she got?"

"Well, it might be all sorts of things."

"Such as?"

"Well, you know, appendicitis - um - ovarian cyst - "

"Ovarian cyst?"

"Well, maybe not ovarian cyst, but, anyway - "

"She got a temperature?"

"Er - no. Her temperature's normal."

"She got any signs of any sort?"

"No, not really."

"And you expect me to take her in just because she's got bellyache?"

"Yes, well you see, she lives alone. Her husband's at sea, and - "

"Look, mate this is a hospital we're running here, not a lonely hearts' club. I'm not having her, so that's that." There was a click and an electric hum, through which the noise of an all-night radio station was just about audible. "If yew evur leave me" some man with a pretend American accent was singing "Ah weel sewerlee dah-ee".

"Did you get through to Dr Henry?" I know that voice, I thought. The old boiler - Duggie's cast-off. She who lays down and screams for it.

"Hello. Look, it's Bob Fullen here."

"Oh yes?"

"Who's the surgical registrar on take?"

"Just a minute - Yes, it's Mr Barrington."

"Can I speak to him, please?"

"Yes, hello? Barrington." By no stretch of the imagination the voice of a man suddenly awoken from a deep sleep. Was it possible that Barrington never slept - passing his nights, vampire-like, reading what Simpson and Wellbeloved had had to say about it in the British Journal of Boring Old Rubbish?

"Oh, hello. It's - ah - Bob Fullen here."

"Yes, hello, Bob. What can I do for you?"

Rolling over in bed, I registered that the little hand on the clock was pointing somewhere near the four. "You sods - why can't you leave me alone? Yes? Hello! What is it?"

"Ah, good evening. Do I have the pleasure of addressing Dr Fullen?"

"Who is this?"

"Good evening to you, Dr Fullen. It's Dr Henry here, from the Infirmary."

"Oh yes?"

"I hope I haven't woken you from your slumbers or anything like that."

"Look, what d'you want?"

"I wonder if you could cast your mind back about an hour or so, Dr Fullen. Do you remember by any chance speaking to me about a lady called Mrs McGready? You do? Good, because I thought we might have a little chat about her, especially since you went to all that trouble to send her into one of my beds over my head."

"Oh yes, well I can explain - "

"I think you will remember that I asked you whether this lady had got a temperature, and you said she hadn't. Well, a very funny thing happened. As soon as she got onto the ward, her temperature suddenly shot up to thirty nine point one."

"Oh, really?"

"Yes, really, Dr Fullen." In the background I could hear the sound of female sniggering. Henry was performing for an audience - either the nurses on the ward or some slag of his own. "And I thought you'd like to know that she gives a history of three days vomiting and abdominal pain. She's got foetor, abdominal rigidity, absent bowel sounds, and marked rectal tenderness. Hello! Are you still there?"

"Yes."

"I was very interested to read your letter, because it - "

"Ah yes, well, I didn't actually send a letter, because - "

"I was really interested to read it, because it was so full of all those interesting physical signs you said she didn't have any of. Did you notice, for example, when you were carrying out your thorough medical examination, that she was deeply jaundiced?"

"Look, matey, if you're trying - "

"And when you were taking your detailed medical history, you seem to have missed the very minor detail that she's been under the care of the Grosvenor firm for the past six months for cholelithiasis." This time a snort and a loud guffaw - a male one - could be heard coming from Henry's audience. Not Barrington, surely? Yes. Barrington, surely. "Apart from that, you seem to have got everything - oh, except for the tiny detail that she happens to be twenty weeks pregnant - otherwise I don't think you did at all badly. Let's see: you got her sex right, didn't you? And you scored about eighty percent on her name - "

"Listen , Dr Henry - "

"No. You listen to me, Doctor Fullen. You never bothered to get out of your pit to see this woman, did you?"

"Of course I did. I wouldn't send somebody into hospital without - "

"It sounds like it, doesn't it? You ring me up and tell me you've seen a woman with no physical signs. When she arrives, she's a walking bloody pathological museum. You've never set your nasty little eyes on her, have you, Dr Fullen?"

"Of course I have. I wouldn't send her into hospital without seeing her."

"Oh? And why is there no letter, then?"

"Have you ever tried writing a letter in a pitch-dark rat-hole in the middle of the night?"

"Yeah, I know. You GP's have always got some excuse. Why don't you admit it? You were too bloody idle to – "

"You jumped-up little bastard! " I screamed. "Who the hell d'you think you are? A piddling little houseman! You think you know everything. Let me tell you what it was like in that – "

"Yeah yeah, we've heard it all before."

"You little bugger! Hospital bloody doctors! You think you're God's gift to – You think you know everything. I'll report you to your consultant, you cheeky little sod!"

"Right. You do that, my old mate."

"Don't think I'm joking!" I shouted. "I'm a personal friend of Mr Materson's. He'll hear all about this in the morning."

Chapter 16

"Yar, it's something he does particularly well, I think," Avalon was saying. "We were most orfli pleased to have the commission."

Her customers, or clients or whatever, peered at the lump of rock more closely. "And how much did you say?" the man asked. He was a short-arsed geezer with goggle-like spectacles and big turn-ups on his trousers.

Avalon threw a long hank of hair over her shoulders, put her hand on her hip and arched her back slightly. She was a good foot taller than him, and as she stood there, feet confidently apart, you had to admit it - great legs. "Just a moment. I'll check," she said. Please, please, whatever you do, don't bend over I was thinking, otherwise I'll have an orgasm just watching you.

Avalon bent over. The neat navy blue skirt rode up over the long thighs, to a point at which the pattern on the royal blue stockings started to give way to the denser weave of the stocking tops. I caught my breath and looked away, only to find that I was now looking at a washed-out pastel drawing of a naked girl. She had a saucer-like belly, small, high, jutting breasts and a great main of long dark hair which partially covered her face. No, I told myself, it couldn't possibly be - Could it?

"Can I help you at all?" a voice behind me asked. The speaker had a red and white spotted cravat and matching face. It was, I think, of the male persuasion, but only just.

"Ah, no. I was just looking," I said.

The androgyne gave me a look which said that he knew about people who just looked at pictures like that one. He didn't go away, though, and after a bit I said "Actually, I was waiting to speak to Avalon."

"Avalon? Oh, I see." Say no more - Avalon. "There's a gentleman here wanting to see you, Miss Death. When you get a minute."

Avalon didn't really need to be told that. She had spent the last five minutes adjusting her orientation so as to keep her back more or less turned towards me. Now she simply nodded at him in a business-like way and said, "I think you'll find it a terrubly good investment."

Old short-arse wasn't so sure, and I must say I didn't blame him. Eight hundred and fifty quid for a fossilised dog-turd doesn't strike me as a particularly good investment.

"Could we talk it over for a few minutes ?" his wife asked.

"Shirley," Avalon said. "Take as much time as you like."

You are wasting your time with that pair, Avvers me old darling, I thought, so why don't you stop pissing about and come over here and talk to me? I cleared my throat and looked pointedly at my watch. "Will you excuse me?" Avalon finally had to say, "while I attend to this gentleman?"

She crossed her arms loosely across her chest and strode over to the little alcove of screens where I was lurking. "Really!" she said like some ruffled Sunday school teacher, "I have asked you before not to disturb me while I'm at work."

This, I hoped, had been put on for the benefit of the queer owner - if that was what he was. Apparently satisfied that Avalon was about to give me a bollocking on the firm's time rather than, say, a blow-job, he withdrew up a curtesy spiral staircase, and I felt free to turn on the charm. "This you, is it?" I asked, cheekily raising my eyebrows and nodding in the direction of the pastel nude.

"No, it most certainly is not," she said primly. Oh, come on, Avvers, me old darling, where's that legendary wit and bounce? Where's the girl who used to see the funny side of things?

Avalon inclined her self backward to glance round the edge of the screen at the useless wasters in the gallery. "What is it you want?" she asked.

"Can I see you tonight?"

"It's very - difficult," she said. "Things are very - confused at the moment. Please - don't harass me. I need time to think."

"Time to think? What about?"

"Just - time to think."

"You've got somebody else. Is that what you're trying to say?"

"Please, Bob. It's very - difficult - "

At this, the waster stuck his head round the screen. "We'd like to have a little longer to think it over," he said. "Might we pop back again tomorrow ?"

"Shirley," Avalon said again. "We're open from 9.30 to 12.30 and from two to half past four."

"Thank you very much, Miss."

"You have one of our cards, have you?"

"Ah, yes, thank you," the man said, waving a buff-coloured document. "See you tomorrow, then."

They went out, the old-fashioned bell over the door clanging behind them. "That's the last you'll see of them," I told her. Avalon permitted herself a wry smile at that, and I took the opportunity to ask "Oh, come on, love. What's wrong?"

"Nothing!" she said angrily, making an exasperated gesture with her hands. "I'm perfectly alright. I just need time to think, that's all."

"What about? Is there somebody else?"

"No, it's - it's not as simple as that," she said. "Just give me a little time to sort myself out, OK?" She looked up at me, and I could see that there were tears in the corner of those big green eyes.

"You know I love you, don't you?"

"Please, Bob - Don't. I can't handle it. It's all too - too difficult.

"When am I going to see you, then ?"

"I don't know.I don't know."

"Hello, Avalon!" The queer person was crouching on the staircase, peering down at us from over the screen. "There's a Mrs Horton on the phone about some Cotman prints."

"Won't be a second. Look, I'll have to go" Avalon said.

"Ring me," I said.

"I'll try, Bob."

"Please."

"Honestly, I'll try."

Chapter 17

"That's alright, m'dear. Just a bit of rheumatism in the gallbladder. That'll clear up in no time." Chaucer clamped a modified arm-lock on his patient and coerced her towards the door of his consulting room.

The woman hunched her shoulders with a look of dog-like gratitude on her face. Her first name was Bessie, and she looked just as lumpy and sweat-sodden as somebody of that name deserved to look. "Thank you ever so much, doctor. How's Mrs Chaucer?"

"Getting along nicely, my dear, thank you. Goodbye now," Chaucer said, all in one breath, and he shut the door briskly behind her, forestalling any attempt on her part to press on further with that line of conversation. "Rather nice old dear, isn't she?" he asked me.

In fact, the woman looked like a picture from a textbook illustrating severe thyroid deficiency – the sort of diagnosis you ought to be able to make at a distance of two hundred yards. "Well, as a matter of fact," I said, "I was thinking she looked a bit myxoedematous."

Chaucer paused to take this in, and then said, "Yes, I was just going to say that. She has got a slightly myxoedematous look about her, hasn't she?"

"Have you done a T4?"

"I'd thought of sending it off several times, of course," Chaucer tried to tell me, "but somehow I never got round to it." This was the kind of statement that gave me a powerful urge to reposition Chaucer's dentures somewhere in the back of his throat, especially now, when he followed it up by scribbling "T4 next time" on her card, as though this action followed on perfectly logically from the inconsequential, yokelly little chat he had just had with the woman. He brought his left hand over to shield the words from my eyes, at the same time giving a nervous little cough and gazing out of the window, possibly thinking that this clever bit of distraction would prevent me from seeing what he was up to.

"Yes, I've thought for a long time that she's been looking a bit – myxoedematous. What do you think?"

What I thought was that the shagged-out old lush on my right talked like - and obviously thought he was - some sort of Brain Cell Gymnast, some mute, inglorious Professor of Obscure Diseases, slumming it as an ordinary GP in British West Crosshills. This morning's surgery, for example, had been billed - not as a surgery - but as a "Teaching Session", the idea being, presumably that he would teach me, rather than the other way round. Certainly you could never tell him anything, because he would insist on pretending (after you'd told him) that he'd known about it all along.

This process ended, as in this case, with the final trick of asking my opinion about what I'd already told him, so that in a few short phrases, he had apparently completed the transformation from informee to informer.

In a way, this was worse than being back with bloody Barrington. At least Barrington had picked up a bit of useful stuff along the way, and if you hung around him long enough, sooner or later something of real interest would fall in your direction. The bloke now occupying the swivel chair and looking like Solomon after a crafty bit of wisdom-dispensing had failed his medical finals at the crummiest medical school in England - eventually getting his licence to kill in the form of a set of letters given away free with a pint of Guiness in the Irish Capital City. I had been unable to find out anything about his hospital career, but it seemed fairly certain that someone had seen to it that it had been kept as brief as possible before sending him off to rot here. "Yehhs, you can always tell a GP - but not much!" as Jimmie had told me on quite a lot more than one occasion.

"Hmm, yes. I think you're probably right," I said, deciding not to make an issue out of the thyroid thing. It was an even bet that Chaucer had forgotten what myxoedema was and that, even when he found out, he would then have to look up T4 to find out what that stood for. "I was wondering, though, about the - "

"About the - ah - gallbladder , eh? Haha! Well," he gave my hand a patronising little pat. "There you have it, you see. That's where the art of medicine comes in. You young chaps - they fill your heads with ideas about medicine being a science, don't they?"

"Oh, and?"

"Well, it's not a science, it's an art, dear boy, an art" Chaucer said. Now I have to say that Chaucer was not the first person to try to sell me this I-may-not-know-much-about-science-but-I-know-what-I-like argument. At medical school, I had served three months as a clerk on the firm of an old geezer, affectionately known as "Hawkeye", who used to fill in the gaps between outpatients with an amazing line in false-modesty chat, ("Won't be here next week - apparently the Royal Society wants to give me a gold medal or something - Her Majesty is insisting on giving a silly old buffer like me a Life Peerage - goodness knows what for" sort of style), but there the similarity ended. Hawkeye had a lot to be falsely modest about; Chaucer didn't. Let's face it, to describe Chaucer as pig-ignorant would be an insult to a very noble farm animal. How would it be if mathematicians, say, gave up science and started making artistic guesses at the right answer?

"Now take, er, Bessie here. What would you say her trouble was?"

"Well, it's a bit hard to - "

"There you are, you see. Can't put a name to it," Chaucer crowed. "Can't put a name to it because her sort of trouble doesn't appear in the textbooks. Trouble is that you chaps think the patients are going to read the books as well and stick to the rules."

"All the same, I don't see why you have to tell her something like that. I mean to say, rheumatism of the gall bladder - "

"Well, what else are you going to call it?"

"I don't see that you have to call it anything."

"But of course you've got to call it something," Chaucer insisted, using his folded spectacles to tap on the top of the desk. "That's what the patient comes to see you for. What sort of fool d'you think they imagine you are when you can't even tell them what's wrong with them?"

"Yeah, but 'rheumatism of the gall bladder' sounds like - "

"Well, at least it sounds better than 'tummy ache', doesn't it, old boy? I wonder if you'd be good enough to ring for the next patient? Now she'll be able to tell her friends that she's got rheumatism of the gall bladder."

And they'll all go on about what a bloody marvellous doctor old Doctor Chaucer is, which is why the old fool goes on believing it himself. At least in hospital you had characters like McLeod and Barrington around to use as a yardstick of your own ignorance. In the Land of the Anencephalics, the man with one brain cell is king. "So why not go the whole hog and tell her she's got cholecystitis, or something like that?"

Chaucer gave a knowing shake of his doddery old head. It was a shame to take the money. "Oh dear me, no," he said. "Much too dangerous. Much too dangerous. Next thing you know, she'll go and look it up in Reader's

Digest or wherever, find that her symptoms don't fit, and then she'll be back on you like a ton of bricks. At least she won't find rheumatism of the gallbladder in a medical dictionary, will she?"

"No, I suppose not."

"You see, they've got just enough knowledge of their own anatomy to believe what you tell them. They've got a rough idea that your gall bladder's here, your kidneys are in your back, your bladder's down the bottom, your heart's up here. So, you've got an organ for just about every symptom plus a few left over - like your spleen and your pancreas - that they're not sure about. Oh, hello, do come in, Mrs Padgett. I hope you don't mind if I teach a young colleague of mine? This is Dr Fullen. Mrs Padgett is the lady I was telling you about, Dr Fullen, you remember? The lady with arthritis of the colon. How's it been, my dear?"

Chapter 18

I'm beginning to understand what it is that motivates people like Barrington and McLeod to go on bashing the books the way they do. We've become institutionalised: nineteen years at school, five at medical school, a year living in hospital - things like that are bound to affect you. When you're suddenly thrust out into the big, bad world of British West Crosshills, you begin to miss the predictability, the routine.

Last week, for the first time in my life, I opened a medical journal, not because I had to but because I wanted to. It was a chatty little comic called The Lancet.It was a jolly good read. There was even this story about some teenage girl in France who was allergic to seminal fluid. Just imagine that. There's always somebody worse off than yourself.

The truth is that I still miss Avalon like hell. The ache colours my dreams, wakes me in the early hours, hangs over my mornings, torments my afternoons and makes my evenings unbearable. Apart from that, I hardly notice she's gone.

She didn't ring me - I never really thought she would- and in my spare time - I even get some of that nowadays - I have taken to hanging around outside the Gallery in Welbeck Street. I'm not sure why this is. It's not that I'm spying on her. I'm not hoping to bump into her accidentally; it's just that if I'm not there in person, I'd be thinking about her anyway.

For fuck's sake, you pathetic, cunt-struck weed, go out and find yourself some other tart to stuff! Sure I could. But I would feel that I had been disloyal to Avalon in some way. After all, it's not as if it's over or anything like that. I am simply giving Avalon a chance to sort herself out. Once she's had time to think things over, she'll be back.

Chapter 19

A notice on the wall of Cadogan Street Flats enjoined its residents not to indulge in football, cricket or any sort of balls games (the "s" in balls being written backwards in felt tip pen). This seemed sensible advice, considering the hazards to which players of such games would be exposing themselves, such as being smothered by half-clean laundry, being garrotted by low-slung clothes lines, slipping on piles of dog shit, or being eaten alive by the giant untrained mongrels that had deposited them there.

The sides of the rectangular communal area were formed by grey concrete buildings five storeys high. No-one who lived in these flats seemed to have a job: consequently they had nothing better to do with their time than be ill, and during one of my frequently-enforced visits, I had christened the place "Colditz". Chaucer had not been amused. One thing you learned on your first day was that the lifts never worked, so I entered the first doorway and began my climb to the third floor, trying to avoid the attention of a a bit of borstal fodder that was doing its best to spit on my head at each turn in the staircase. As I passed flat 11C, there was the sound of crockery being smashed and a male person telling a female person to do something which sounded anatomically dangerous. The door to flat 11F was opened by an unshaven yob with chewing gum intermittently visible in his gob.

"Yeah?" he wanted to know.

"Mr Peters, is that right?"

"Yeah." He looked me up and down. "Yeah, whaddaya want?"

"Did you ask for the doctor to call?"

"You the doctor?"

He was addressing this question to someone holding a stethoscope in one hand and a large black bag in the other. Of the various replies that suggested themselves"Yes that's right, " was the answer I came out with.

"Yeah, well, it wasn't you we wanted. We sent for Chaucer."

"Well he can't come, so I'm here."

"Yeah, well, ah - we don't want you, see?" He jerked his head dismissively. "Alright? You follow?" and he shut the door in my face.

I knocked again.

"Yeah?"

"Look, I don't know if you heard me. I'm calling instead of Dr Chaucer."

"Yeah, I know. I heard you, squire. It's not you we want to see. Go and get Chaucer to come round."

"I'm not some sort of errand boy, you know."

"You deaf or some ink? We don't want you, squire, so piss off."

"Yes, it's for this one," said Mrs Smart, a walking heap of lard, pointing at an unnamed child on the broken-springed sofa. "He's had a norful cough and he keeps saying he's got pains in his chest."

"Alright. Oh shit!" I said as I knelt on an upturned roller skate. "How old is he now?"

"You what?"

"How old?" I repeated, trying to make myself heard over a man on the television who was telling Mr Smart about some horses that were going to go for a bit of a run at a place called Chepstow. "How - old - he?"

"Oh - um - four and a half."

"Let's have a listen to him." The child's vest was pulled up by the mother, pulled down by the child and finally wrenched up by me as I clamped the coldest part of the stethoscope onto the only visible bit of skin. All I could hear was the chat about the horses, but at least I'd made the gesture they expected of me. "Got a bit of an infection in his chest."

"Got what?"

"Infection - chest. Give you medicine."

"Oh, I see. Doctor says he's got an infection, Jack." Mr Smart, or whoever he was, nodded a few times without taking his eyes from the screen. "And while you're here, can you take a look at Gran's fingers?"

Looking pointedly at my watch, I was led into a bedroom where a leather-skinned old woman in a beaten-up armchair sat gazing out of the window at a gas-holder and an advertisement for laxatives. "Hey - what's this?" she asked as I grabbed hold of her hand and recited the words, "I'll give you something for that as well."

"And something for Tracey's hair," Mrs Smart said, waddling back into the sitting room and cutting off the girl's attempt to make for the door. "Come and let doctor have a look at your hair, my love."

"No. Don't want to."

Neither do I, dear, neither do I. "Christ! This looks like scabies to me. Scabies, you know, little bugs in the skin. You've probably all got it, haven't you? Thank you. Don't cough in my face, dear."

"What?"

"Bugs - hair. Write - something." I started to write a prescription for a skin preparation. Pretty useless: she'd probably give it to her to drink, anyway.

"Right: well if that's - "

"Oh yes, and can I have something for my back?"

"Whereabouts on your back?"

"What?"

"Pain - back - where?" She pointed to some part of her fat self, and I began writing as an automatic reflex.

"State, in no more than sixty words, why you want to become a doctor." I once had to do that on my application for medical school. Wouldn't it be wonderful if the people who wrote questions like that were to let us read some of the answers? How many pimply sixth-formers wanted to relieve suffering and do something to help humanity? Duggie claims that he put down "I want to examine lots of naked women", but I don't believe him. One thing I can tell you, though: playing pass-the-pills with a load of smelly layabouts like this lot never came into my reckoning. "There you are. We'll open a supermarket, if you think that might help. Then you can come down and help yourself to whatever you want."

"And then there's Jack. He's been off work since Wednesday. He'll be needing a certificate."

"What's his trouble been?"

"Eh?"

"What - trouble - his? Why - off - work?"

"His nerves. All the noise and that at work was upsetting him."

I weighed up the man in front of the television. A refusal, although justifiable in principle, wasn't worth the physical risk involved. He was quite likely to belt me one, and anyway he'd only go up the surgery and get one off Chaucer, so I wrote out a certificate saying that J. Smart was unfit for work by reason of nervous debility, and snapped my bag shut on a note of over-optimistic finality. "Right: well if you think you can persuade him to stagger down to the surgery in about a week's time, we – "

"And there is one other thing. We was going to ring you, but we knew you was coming anyway. Me Dad's been sent home poorly from work. Can you just pop over and have a look at him before you go?"

"Where's he?"

"He's over in Wellington Flats. Hang on a bit, and I'll come with you." She slipped a stained navy blue raincoat on over her apron and followed me down the stairs.

"Look, I've got rather a lot of calls to make. I'm in a bit of a hurry."

"It won't take you long. It's just over the road here." She stopped, out of breath, resting her fat red legs and clutching at a stitch in her side. "Mr Percival, he's called. 48J, Wellington Flats. You go on ahead and I'll catch you up."

Wellington Flats. Stalag Luft 48. I toyed briefly with the idea of making a dash for the car and then, if challenged later, making up some balls about losing my way, but with her flat-footed waddle, the big bag was managing to keep me in sight, and I knew I'd never get away with it.

The door of 48J Wellington Flats stood ajar, so you could see straight into the living room. This was occupied by the sort of furniture you normally saw people being paid to cart away, and on the far wall there was a picture of some blokes in superseded clothing, sitting about with clay pipes in their mouths and looking pretty pleased with themselves. There was no sign of current human occupation.

"Hello . . . Mr, er . . . ?"

There was a noise from the bedroom like somebody washing up very clumsily, but no other reaction, so I gave the bottom of the door a couple of full-blooded whacks with the toe of my chelsea boot. " 'earearear. What's this?" A little man staggered out of the bedroom. He was wearing a pyjama jacket beneath the broad leather braces on his corduroy trousers, and swinging a wine bottle in one hand. "Wha's the idea?" he demanded.

"You wanted to see the doctor?"

"Wha's the idea?" he asked again. "Tryin' to smash the house down."

"You wanted to see the doctor?"

"Yeah, but tha's no - tha's no reason f'you to go smashin' the whole bleeding house down." He was swinging the door about and peering at the hinges. "Council property, this."

Mrs Smart had now hauled herself onto the landing. "What you doing still up? You oughta be in bed, dad."

"This Herbert's been trying to smash the door down."

"Yes, well look, if you don't mind - "

"Doctor's in a hurry, Dad."

"I should bleedin' well think he is in a hurry. Tryin' to - um - tryin' to smash the whole - er - "

If, by the time I count to ten, he hasn't shut his face, I walk off and leave the old fool to it.

"Tell him what happened, dad."

"No. It don't bleedin' matter now."

"Don't be silly, of course it does."

"No: it don't matter. I'll leave it out for now." He swayed forwards as he said this, and the sickly sweet smell of fermented grapes hit me in the face.

"Well, that suits me fine," I said, "because I didn't really want to - " Just then, Percival did a trick I had never seen before. He turned his skin a greeny white colour, covered his face with his hands and staggered back against the wall, breathing noisily. "There you are, doctor, you see what I mean? He's been like that ever since he come home from work."

"Better get him to bed." I put an arm round his shoulder and started to guide him towards the bedroom.

"Gercha bleedin' hands orfa me!" Percival shouted, using his elbows on my ribs. "Don't need no help from you." He did his funny little stagger back into the bedroom and collapsed onto the sagging bed.

"He's been sick something awful" Mrs Smart said.

"How many times?"

"How many times you been sick, dad?"

"Bugger off, both of you."

"How much have you had to drink, Mr Percival?" Rolling about underneath the bed were at least four empty bottles of the type he was still managing to keep a grip on. "How much of this stuff have you had?"

"Look, bugger off. I asked her to get Chaucer. You can bugger off."

"How much alcohol have you had?"

"That bottle was full this morning," Mrs Smart said.

"Well, I think it's more than likely that that's what his trouble is, then."

"You think that's what it is, doctor?"

"Well, obviously I can't say for certain, because he won't let me examine him," I muttered, "but I think it's more than likely."

Mrs Smart looked doubtfully from me to Percival and then back again. "Yes, but he had the pains and sickness when he come home from work, and he hadn't been drinking then" she said.

"Well, I think he probably had a bit of a tummy upset to start with, and he's gone and made it worse by drinking so much." I felt fairly proud of this, the sort of gambit Chaucer might have come out with. "Are you going to let me examine you, Mr Percival?"

"Bugger off."

"Right well I'll give you something to settle his stomach, and I'll ask Dr Chaucer to come round and see him tomorrow morning." I wrote up some of the white stuff and headed for the door. Somehow, healing the sick and comforting the aged had lost a lot of its appeal. Here was someone who apparently fell into both those categories, but so far as I was concerned, he could drop dead just so long as he let me get home for lunch.

"Hello! Breckleigh, mumble mumble mumble."

"Hello, dear. Mrs Clode here."

"Yes? Well? Whaddaya want?"

"Oh, there's friendly for you! What's the matter, dear: have I disturbed your tea or something?"

"Oh, shit!" a brown sauce-laden slice of luncheon meat had chosen that precise second to glide out between two thickly buttered slices of bread and slide gracefully down the front of my shirt. In the mirror I could see that my shirt had a long narrow brown stain on it, reminiscent of underpants. "My breakfast, actually. I'm having my breakfast at 4 o'clock in the afternoon, thanks to Dr Chaucer and his bleeding house calls."

"Yes, well look, dear, I've got a Mrs Smart on the phone. She says can you come down and see Mr Percival again? He's got a lot worse since you saw him."

"Christ! Not that old bastard. I've already been out to see him once today."

"Yes, well, she says he's not very well."

"She said that earlier and the silly old sod wouldn't let me examine him."

"Well, she did sound a bit worried, dear. If you could just pop down and set her mind at rest."

"Look, what the hell d'you think I am? I've only just got back from doing house visits. I've got two hours to have my breakfast-lunch-dinner, and then I've got to help Chaucer with the evening surgery. Tell her to get knotted. No, I'll tell you what. The old fool asked to see Chaucer. Tell Chaucer to go down and see him if he likes, and I'll start evening surgery for him."

There was a silence from the other end of the phone, and then Mrs Clode said "Yes, well, I was just coming to that, you see. I'm afraid he's gone out, and he says would you mind doing the surgery by yourself this evening?"

"Would I mind? Of course I bloody mind! Tell the bastard – "

"It's too late now, dear, he's already gone. He'll be half way to Bournemouth by now."

"Bournemouth?"

"Yes, dear: he's gone to a concert there with Mrs Chaucer. What am I going to say to Mrs Smart, though?"

"Tell her to get knotted."

"He does sound a bit bad, though, dear."

"Tell her to give the old bugger some more of his medicine, and then if he's no better, ring me back in the morning. No, make that ring Chaucer back in the morning."

"Well, alright, dear, if you're sure."

"Of course I'm bloody sure."

"Well alright, dear. See you at six, then?"

"Christ all bloody mighty!"

Halfway through evening surgery, I was chatting to one of Chaucer's interesting cases of strained kidneys. Sounded more like a recipe than a disease, but what the hell. "Oh yes, m'dear – hhmmm, hhmm – Oh dear" even the inflexion of the voice was contagious. The telephone extension rang. "Excuse me a moment, m'dear. Yes, hello. Fullen."

"Ah, good evening, Dr Fullen. I wonder if you remember me? My name's Henry. I work at the Infirmary."

"Yes, I remember you. What d'you want?"

"I believe you went out to see a patient of yours today – a Mr Harold Percival – am I right?"

"What the hell has that got to do with you?"

"Well, I just happened to be in Casualty when they brought him in, Dr Fullen. His daughter called an ambulance, you see. I've just certified him dead. I thought you'd like to know."

Chapter 20

Breckleigh Royal Infirmary was built on the site of an eighteenth century workhouse, and its main buildings betrayed its origins - two storeys of small multi-paned windows set in crumbling walls of some greyish-coloured stone. As the twentieth century had progressed, the need for additional accommodation had been met piecemeal and in a bewildering variety of materials and styles. The clap clinic, for example, was housed in a couple of portable, flat roofed cabins, hidden behind the Pharmacy, presumably so that the afflicted could come and go disguised as drug reps.

I skirted the outside of those buildings and walked on beside the green painted wooden hut - more cricket pavilion than anything else - where Jimmie inflicted his out-patients and sounds clinics. A short walk across a small crowded car park brought me to a quaint Gothic building of no great size, which was surmounted with a bell tower, for reasons which nobody could now remember. Perhaps it had had some religious significance in the past, but now it looked more like a scale model of Dracula's Castle. This was the mortuary, the House of Truth, where everyone's biggest mistakes could be dissected, both figuratively and literally.

The heavy oak door slammed shut behind me and I tiptoed warily down the terrazo floored corridor in the direction of the post-mortem room. As I rounded the open doorway, the man wielding the saw looked up and asked briskly, "Looking for something, are you?"

"Yes, I'm - Dr Fullen - I've come to watch Mr Percival's post-mortem."

This did not seem entirely to satisfy him. Still, these mortuary workers must spend half their lives worrying about potential necrophiliacs. "Coroner's case," he said. He was an evil-looking bastard: a great fat bearded bugger with tinted specs, tattooed forearms and gold crosses dangling from his ear lobes. His greasy black hair was tied back in a pony tail.

"So I believe."

"Yeah." He prised the top off the skull and got going on pulling the brain out of its box, with lots of fiddling and slashing away with a big knife. "You involved with this, were you?"

"Yes, I was his – um – family doctor."

"Oh yeah?" The squelchy pink football was now sitting in the pan of the weighing scales, the man peering myopically at the dial, his knife poised like an unpopular butcher about to announce a bit over, that piece, madam. "Going to be a bit of trouble about this one, isn't there?"

"Trouble?" The cold of the room suddenly made me shiver.

"Yeah. Relatives kicking up a fuss or something."

If ever you needed a motive for staying alive, I thought, it was the dreadful thought that somebody like this might get his hands on you when you were dead. "I hadn't heard."

"No? Well I expect you will. You were his GP, were you?"

"Mmm."

"Yeah, well, I expect you will then. If I was you, I'd – Watch out, he's here – Afternoon, Dr Rudman." This greeting was directed at a little hunchback with a nose big enough for two people. He was wearing the sort of sweaty raincoat normally worn at dirty film shows and peering at us through a pair of jam jar bottoms mounted on spectacle frames. He looked at me as though I had no right to be there, and then disappeared into an office off the fridge room. "You met him before?" the technician asked. "No? well you want to watch out for him. He can be a right bastard when he wants to be."

I brought the back of my hand up to my nose and sniffed it in an attempt to rid my nostrils of the smell of rotting cabbage and something much worse which permanently hung about this room. According to Duggie, this was why pathologists chose to do pathology. In the post-mortem room, they could fart as much as they liked, and nobody noticed.

Rudman shuffled through from the fridge room, tying the cord of a rubber apron which reached down to the toes of his big black wellies. The sleeves of his frayed grey shirt were rolled up to reveal his skeletal arms, and a hand-rolled cigarette hung limply from one corner of his mouth.

"Afternoon, Dr Rudman."

"Yes, Mr – er – And who have we the –?" This mangled phrase was an invitation to introduce myself.

"My name's Fullen, Dr Rudman. I was Mr Percival's GP."

"Have you come to watch the -?"

"Yes, if you don't mind."

Rudman was pulling on a pair of rubber gloves."You seem to have become very diligent all of a sudden, Doctor. Seem much more prepared to come out and see your patient now he's dead than you were - when he was - when he was still - "

I coughed and shuffled my feet nervously. "Yes, well, I - "

He removed the cigarette butt from his mouth, took it in a pincer grip and set it down on the edge of the enamel table. Exhaling slowly, as though the process required a great deal of concentration, he said, "Yes, Doctor, from what I hear, the relatives asked you to - er - to come out, and - D'you see? And you didn't take the - take the trouble to - "

"That's not true. I did go out to see him."

"Knife please, Mr - Um," Rudman said, and with an impatient slashing action, he scooped the tongue out from below the jaw and then tore the insides out of the chest. With a splash, he dumped them in a washing-up bowl at the bottom of the table. "Yes, well, it all sounds most unsatisfactory to me. Of course, it's not for me to make any ethical or - ah - moral, as it were - D'you see?"

There was a draught from behind me and two white-coated figures entered the room. The big one was Duggie who had threatened in the pub the previous evening to come down and lend his moral support. The little one looked like an off-duty SS officer of the particularly enthusiastic type. He was minus the jackboots but plus the swagger, the gold-rimmed spectacles and the look of contemptuous fanaticism.

"Yes, well, that all looks - " Rudman said, wiping the surface of the heart with a big sponge. "Ah, good afternoon. Can we - ?"

"Yes, hello, Dr Rudman. My name's Henry. I'm Mr Materson's houseman," the little geezer said. I recognised the accent from our telephone calls. He was from Yorkshire, at a guess, but he was trying not sound like it. "I certified this man dead."

"Yes, and you, Doctor -?"

"I just like watching bodies being pulled to pieces," Duggie said.

Rudman pretended not to hear that. "Yes, well I've just been explaining to this doctor here that the relatives might well have grounds for - pot, please, Mr - Um - " He had been slicing sections through the heart and was now balancing one or two choice tit-bits on the end of his knife. "Yes, there are certain irregularities, you see, certain - discrepancies." He picked up the smouldering cigarette butt and put it between his lips. "Now then, you went out to see him, you say?"

"Yep."

"Did you notice anything - untoward? Anything - ?"

"Not really. I thought he was drunk. He wouldn't let me examine him, actually."

Rudman screwed his eyes up against the curl of smoke from his cigarette and began splitting open the windpipe with a pair of stout kitchen scissors. "Most unsatisfactory - cough cough. Most unsatisfactory, Doctor. At the Inquest, that's not going to sound very - Well, that looks all quite - um - " I noticed that Creepy Henry was actually nodding in agreement that it looked all quite 'um'. "No sign of any - ah - " Henry shook his head at the total absence of any 'ah'. Rudman picked up the opened lungs and began to squeeze them in both hands. "Bit of fluid here, Mr - er - better take a sample."

"You're Fullen, are you?" Henry hissed. I pretended not to hear the little twerp, but he went on, "Let yourself in for it this time, haven't you?"

"Meaning?"

"Well if you don't know, I'm not going to tell you, mate."

"Right. Well you saw him in Casualty I believe, Doctor?"

Henry stepped forwards and I could swear the little turd actually clicked his heels. "Yes, that's right."

"Was there anything about him that struck you as odd?"

"Yes, there was one thing," Henry said. "He seemed as though he'd been frothing at the mouth."

Rudman seemed to be quite impressed with the idea that he might have been frothing at the - er, because he repeated the phrase to himself several time. What the hell was that supposed to signify? Rabies? Myxomatosis? Shaving foam overdose? "Yes, well, that's very helpful, doctor. And you, doctor, you didn't notice anything when you claim that you went out to - ?"

"I did go to visit him, Dr Rudman, but there wasn't anything to see then. And, as I say, he wouldn't let me examine him."

"That's all very well. That's all very well," Rudman said, "but don't you see there might be a question of professional negligence here? There's a possibility of – "

"Oh, it's professional negligence now, is it?" Duggie interrupted. "Suppose you tell us then – straight out – what he died of?" He had stepped up to the side of the enamel table and was leaning on the edge, peering over Rudman's shoulder.

"I beg your pardon!" Rudman spluttered, and he swung round to find his eyeline roughly on a level with Duggie's waist. As he craned his neck to look up into Duggie's belligerent features he added, "What was that you said?"

"Come on, what killed him? You know as much as Bob did when he went out to see him. Well, come on then, if you know so much, let's have your diagnosis."

"I don't see what this has to do with you, Doctor – Um -"

"It has a hell of a lot to do with me. You start accusing my friend here of professional incompetence, as if you've got brains coming out of your backside. What's this great diagnosis he's supposed to have missed?"

Rudman darted his eyes around the room, as though he expected two men with white coats and a net to appear and drag Duggie away. "Look here," he sputtered "what did you say your name was?"

"I didn't say what my name was. Come on, cut the crap. What was the cause of this bloke's death?"

"I don't really see that this is any of your business, Doctor. And I don't have to tolerate your presence here, behaving like some – "

"You don't know, do you?" Duggie jeered. "You're blustering! You've got no idea, admit it."

"Look, for Christ's sake, Duggie," I muttered. "Get out and leave us alone."

"He doesn't have any bloody idea, Bob. Clever bastard pathologists! They think they know everything. He's bullshitting because he's got no idea himself!"

"Right. That's enough," Rudman said suddenly, waving his long-bladed knife in my direction. "Out you get, the pair of you. Go on, both of you. Outside! This is a post-mortem room, not a – not an – um – This is my department and I don't need to tolerate behaviour of that sort. Go on, both of you. Out!"

"Look, I'm sorry, Dr Rudman. I only – "

"Yes, well as for you, Doctor," Rudman said, rather more calmly, "I presume you are a member of a medical defence body? Well I'd get in touch with them straight away. I really would, if I were you."

Outside the mortuary, skipping round a line of parked undertakers' wagons, Duggie was behaving like a punchy middleweight. "There you are, you see. He hadn't got a clue. You've got to stand up to them. You don't want to let the bastards talk to you like that."

"Thanks, Duggie, a whole lot," I said. "You've no idea what you've just done for me."

"You want to stand up for yourself, mate." While he was saying this last bit, Duggie's brand new, all-singing, all-dancing bleep went off, and through a hail of static, a distorted female voice said, "Dr Rossiter, prolapsed cord on Delivery Floor One. Can you get there in a hurry, please?"

"Shit! I'll have to go," Duggie said. "Look, I'll give you a ring later."

I watched him jog off in the direction of the maternity block. Well, at least all that was behind me now. Ya loses some, ya wins some. I walked slowly and thoughtfully to my car and got behind the wheel. Rudman had been acting like the biggest bastard left unhung, but he wouldn't dare behave like that at the Inquest, surely? After all, where's your professional solidarity, Rudders old mate? He bloody well might, though. Now that Duggie had gone, perhaps I'd better go back in and put up a toenail-chewing demonstration of remorse; tell Rudman how brilliant, witty, good-looking and all the rest of it he was.

Just as I was thinking this, I happened to look in my driving mirror. An obsolete white sports car with a black roof and very shiny chrome bumpers had just come through the hospital gates, and was making its way at walking pace along the front of the Nurses' Home before making a right turn at the far end. In a flash, I was out of my car and sprinting round the near side of the Nurses' Home. A short cut between two of the biochemistry pre-fabs brought me out behind the kitchens. Another twenty yards and I was standing, out of breath, at the front entrance to Bleak House.

"Hello, Avalon" I said. Avalon halted in the middle of a leggy stride and lost her composure for a few seconds. "He's not up there," I told her.

Give the girl her due: she didn't give me any of the "Who's not up there?" sort of crap.

"Where is he?" she asked.

"There was an emergency Caesarean Section. He'll be gone for at least an hour."

Avalon just said "Oh, I see."

"You've got a key to his room, I take it?" After all, why not? She used to have a key to mine. Avalon lowered her eyes and nodded. Instead of saying – as I should have done – "Good, let's go up there and have a quickie before he gets back," I said, "Can we talk about this, please?"

"Where? Not in Duggie's room, shirley?"

Seemed like an unimprovable idea to me, but I heard myself say. "Let's go for a drive, shall we?"

We walked in silence to my car. I was over-polite, anxious not to brush up against her, allowing her to go first through all the narrow bits and I even held the car door open for her to get in. She smelled of nice clean hair, the old familiar perfume and, well, just a nice Avalony sort of smell, really. Was it something about the way she held herself, or just the idea that she had come here for the specific purpose of letting the Dirty Doctor do dirty things to her in his dirty little room? Whatever it was, it had the effect of distancing her from me, of allowing me to view her more critically, more dispassionately. Her front teeth, I noted for the first time, were not so much white and even as white and jutting forward just a fraction. Her skin was not as clear as I remembered it and she had a spot on her chin. Not a very big one, but it was a spot. All the same, there were only three words to describe an Avalon way below par, an Avalon with obvious imperfections on view: absolutely fucking stunning.

"Well this is cosy, isn't it? " I said after a few minutes of aimless driving. "Talk about keeping it all in the family."

"Please, Bob, don't take it like that."

"Oh, I haven't to take it like that, have I? OK, that's that disposed of. No more worries on that score." I was becalmed behind a silly old bugger who had chosen to stop at a yellow traffic light, and could not now get his ancient, cherished automobile to start functioning again. I gave him a quick blast with the horn and asked, "Look, is it serious? You and Duggie, I mean?"

Avalon thought about that one and then said, "I think so - It is for me, anyway."

"And for him?"

"You know him better than I do" she said. "Is anything ever serious as far as he's concerned?".

"I shouldn't think so for a minute. He just fucks people on the might-as-well principle. Another bearded clam speared, another notch on the old pork sword. And then it'll be time to move on." We had arrived in a narrow one-way street. The only way out was to drive all the way back to the hospital, or to turn into the car park on the left. I chose this option.

"What's this place?" Avalon asked.

"The Little Sisters Of The False Assumption," I adapted from the blue and white sign. "It's either a brothel or a nunnery, I shouldn't wonder."

"The funny thing is," Avalon told me, "I don't even like him orfli much."

"Well, who could, come to that? Not very much about him to like, is there?"

"I thought he was supposed to be your best friend?"

"That would please you, would it, to think that? To think that my "best friend" - my best buddy pal - had stepped in and stolen you off me? Is that what "best friends" are for, do you imagine? No, he's not my "best friend". He's never been my "best friend". He's just someone I've known for a long time, that's all. I suppose the trouble is that I could never work up enough enthusiasm to hate him as much as he deserved."

There was a little black trickle of mascara visible on the part of her face that was turned towards me. OK, so it's self-pity time, is it? Try this for size, then. "It's all irrelevant now," I began haltingly, "but I'll tell you anyway - just for the record - you were my best friend. There was nothing I wouldn't have done for you."

"Please, Bob - No - "

"There was a time when I would have died for you if you'd asked me to, you know that?"

I say, steady on. That's going it a bit strong. Seemed to work, though.

Now there were real, wet tears welling up. She turned her face towards me, and the edges of her eyes were red, but the words she spoke next came from a pair of full, red lips that were half-smiling.

"Now I'll tell you something, shall I?" she said "When you get down to it, he doesn't particularly like me, either."

"Then why the – ?"

"Why do I do it? It's not the sort of thing you have any control over, is it? I know what he's like. I know he's a bastard. I know it will all end up wrong, but I can't help myself. I always fall for that type."

Bloody hell, woman! What d'you want me to say? You want me to sympathise? "Just tell me, out of interest, how did it all start? Did you ring him or what?"

A couple of real-live nuns came wandering past at that moment. They were as ugly as only a pair of nuns could be. They seemed to want to know what we were doing in their car park, and the nearer one went to the trouble of peering down under the steering wheel, just to check that Avalon wasn't giving me a quick one off the wrist.

"That Sunday," Avalon said when they'd gone, "you remember, when we were sitting outside. You must have said something about the Gallery. I suppose Duggie took it all in."

"Oh, well that explains it then. It was all my fault. Mentioned where you worked. Well, I deserved all I got then, eh? And next day, he was up there like a ferret up a drainpipe, I suppose?"

"No, he rang me up and talked to me. He was really very amusing, very witty. He can really be so charming when he wants to be, you know."

"When he wants a bit, you mean. So what happened then? "

"He asked me out. I knew how you'd feel about that, and I tried to tell him no, but he kept on and on at me."

"Wow! That's really flattering. You managed to hold out for a whole two minutes, I bet."

"Bob, look, things were nice with you. I really liked you. I still do like you. You were kind, you were gentle and you were fun – especially in bed."

"Oh yes?

I was hoping she'd go on a bit more about what a big cock I'd got, and how much better than Duggie I was at muff diving and so on. Instead, she added, simply, "But let's face it, it wasn't exactly the romance of the century, now was it?"

"Oh, wasn't it?" That hurt more than anything else she could have said. "I got the impression that I was taking it pretty seriously."

"I know. And that's maybe what was wrong. You were always getting so – I don't know – so dewy-eyed, so hopelessly soppy about me. I couldn't handle it."

"There we go. That's sorted all that out then, hasn't it? Just don't be so soppy and dewy-eyed and fucking serious next time, Fullen. Why can't you just fuck like normal, sensible people do? Stop getting yourself involved, you pathetic bastard. Stick it in, pull it out, wipe it dry and then move on to the next one." I paused, debated for a second and then went on, "You know what gave you away don't you? You know when I first realised what was going on?"

Avalon's face had already crumpled during that last bit. She looked like a frightened and bewildered lost child, and if she'd so much as touched my hand at that point, I would have forgiven her. Yes, I would. I would have hated myself for what I was about to say. Instead, I would have put my arms round her and told her it was alright, because I understood how it had been for her. I would have cried and shared her upset with her. But she didn't. She didn't even look at me, so I said "The stuff, you know, the KY jelly. That afternoon on the stairs. I wondered where it had all gone to. Couldn't even tell him to buy his own, could you? You had to use mine. That just makes me feel so – so cheap and foolish and ashamed for letting myself believe that you ever – "

"I knew you wouldn't understand," Avalon said, quietly shaking her head. "That's why I couldn't tell you about it. I knew you'd react this way."

"Ah dear, silly old me. The Dirty Doctor screwing the brains out of the only woman I've ever really felt anything for, and I can't see the funny side? Well that is really – "

"Please, Bob, don't. I can't go on if you – "

"OK, I won't. Incidentally, while we're on the subject of not getting involved, I wonder if you could explain something to me. You don't like him, he doesn't like you, so what the hell are you doing, going up to his room?" And don't for Christ's sake tell me it's because you love him, you cow, otherwise I will really begin to hate you.

"I can't help myself," Avalon said. "You see, I think I love him."

Chapter 21

"Take the book in your right hand and read the words on the card."

"Um – I'd like to affirm if that's possible."

"Witness wants to affirm, sir."

The coroner peered at me over his bifocals. "For what reason?"

"No religious belief."

"No religious belief?" he echoed, as if I'd just admitted to being a raving pederast. "Yes, alright." This whole Inquest business was beginning to piss me off. For a start, Chaucer had never stopped going on about it in one vein or another. When he wasn't being patronisingly understanding or offering unsolicited advice, he was being openly malicious. The Smart family had asked him if they could change doctors – something that had never happened before in all his eight hundred and ninety years experience. A man called Palfreyman, who was employed in some capacity by the local rag, had taken a keen interest in this business and kept ringing him up on his evenings off – did I think the Medical Defence Society could be persuaded to do something about it, old boy? After all, he was entitled to his evenings off just like everyone else, old boy, old boy.

The Medical Defence Society had other fish to fry, or more accurately, a very slippery fish to catch. A letter and several phone calls from them complained that the pathologist who had carried out the post-mortem was being unco-operative. When he wasn't spending his time being un-contactable, he was being cagey about the cause of death. Did I know why this might be? I had a bloody good idea, but I didn't tell them about it. Having a psychopath for a friend and, knowing him to be a psychopath, allowing him to attend a dodgy post-mortem with a shit of a pathologist was as good as an admission of insanity, and something to be admitted only at the risk of having one's membership of the Society forcibly terminated.

Not that the Society's track record was all that brilliant. My first contact with their lawyer – a perpetual worrier called Cawthron – had been two minutes before the Inquest, when he suggested we might have a a quick ten minute chat. Frankly he couldn't understand it all, doctor. It was most unusual for the pathologist not to be more helpful, most unusual. We'd better just hope that the cause of death had been something untreatable, hadn't we? Meanwhile, I was in enough trouble as it was, so the main thing was to sit tight and leave the talking to him. Did I think I could manage that? Good. We'd better sit down now because the Coroner had just come in. Oh, Crikey! Just look at that. The relatives had got bloody Ingrace representing them. Why did nobody tell him these things? This wasn't his normal line of work, and, frankly, Ingrace had got a bit of a reputation in the aggrieved relatives sort of stuff. Oh my God, he hoped they wouldn't drag this thing out. He had a dental appointment at eleven thirty.

"Your name is Robert Anthony Jeremy Fullen?" Cawthron now asked me.

"Yes."

"You are a Bachelor of Medicine, a Bachelor of Surgery, a Licentiate of the Royal College of Physicians and a Member of the Royal College of Surgeons?"

"Yes, that's right."

"Then we may take it that you are a fully-registered medical practitioner?"

"Um - yes."

"Not necessarily," interrupted Mr Smarty Aleck Coroner. "It doesn't necessarily follow. Are you fully registered?"

"Yes, I am." This was the second time I had come across the Breckleigh Coroner in the flabby, broken veined flesh. He had some name like Itchcock-Scratchit, and he was a member of Jimmie's sailing club. Surprisingly - since coroners must obviously get to know about surgical cock-ups - he still felt enough confidence in Jimmie's professional abilities to be a private patient of his. He looked pretty arrogant sitting up there now, but I had seen that same man, stark bollock naked with his legs in the air and his willy on show to the world. Haemorrhoids, it was. Pity he was unconscious at the time and so wouldn't remember it.

"Now then, Dr Fullen, we have heard evidence from Mr Percival's workmates about his condition when he was sent home from work. I believe that you went out to see him at about three o'clock?"

"That's correct, yes."

"Would you like to tell us about his condition when you saw him?"

"Right, well - " I coughed and cast a quick glance in the direction of Percival's family. Mrs Smart stared back resentfully at me. Stay cool, man. "He - ah - appeared reasonably OK. He was a bit unsteady on his feet and he smelled of alcohol."

"Was there anything else about his demeanour that suggested to you that he had been drinking?" Cawthron asked.

"Yes, his - er - speech was slurred. He was a bit abusive, and - um - there were empty wine bottles under the bed. "

"So now, doctor, would you like to tell us what your general impression of your patient was when you visited him on that occasion?"

"Well, I thought he was, you know, a bit - "

"Drunk?" suggested the Coroner. Pissed as a newt would have been nearer the mark, your honour, but I simply said, "Mmm."

"Thank you doctor. You formed the impression that Mr Percival's illness had been brought on by drink, and so what treatment did you prescribe?"

"I thought it might have brought on a slight stomach upset, so I prescribed a mild intestinal sedative. I advised the relatives to keep him in bed and to stop him drinking any more alcohol."

Cawthron was looking down at the pathetically thin sheaf of papers in front of him. By contrast, Ingrace had a dirty great box-file full of bumf that he could leaf through. "And did they follow your advice?" Cawthron asked.

"I'm not - um - sure actually."

"But as far as you were concerned, there was no reason to think that Mr Percival had anything more serious than a stomach upset brought on by drinking alcohol?"

"Yes, that's right."

"Thank you, doctor." Cawthron gave a worried sort of smile and flopped back onto the bench beside the Smart Family.

Mrs Smart was almost unrecognisable in a pill box black hat with a veil and a dribbled-on black suit that smelled death to flying insects within half a mile of the place. Her husband looked as if he'd been poured into a crumpled blue spiv's suit with ludicrously wide lapels. His shirt collar, several sizes too big for him, was badly fastened with a loud, shiny yellow tie. What do they call a resident of Cadogan Street Flats who wears a suit? The defendant. Smart was gaping vacantly at the coat of arms over the Coroner's chair, as though he was not quite certain what its function was. Next to him sat the tall, rangy figure of Ingrace, who now got to his feet.

"Dr Foowan," he lisped, sweeping an effeminate lock of blonde hair from his overlarge forehead, "I'd like to go into this business of your visit to Mr Percival in more detail. Now you say that you formed the opinion that Mr Percival was -ah - inebwiated. Can you tell me in what way you, as a doctor, awived at that diagnosis?"

"Sorry? I don't quite - "

"Perhaps I can help you," Ingrace said, and he gave me an oily smile. Turning over a couple of sheets of paper, he went on, "If a layman wants to know if someone is inebwiated, he might look for certain signs - a smell of alcohol on the breath, perhaps, a slurring of the speech and so on. It doesn't take a medical education to form a cwude opinion like that. On the other hand you, doctor, had been asked to see Mr Percival in a pwofessional capacity, and so naturally you would want to exclude other - more serious - causes for his condition. Do you not agwee?" I nodded weakly. "You do agwee? Thenk you: then would you like to tell us what sort of physical examination you made which enabled you to say with certainty that Mr Percival's condition was due to inebwiation?"

There was a silence which, I suddenly realised, I was supposed to fill. "Yes," I began. " Well - I didn't actually - "

"Could you speak a little louder?" the Coroner asked.

" I didn't actually examine him in any great detail."

An expression of barely suppressed glee came over Ingrace's face. "Not in any gwate detail," he repeated. "Could you be more specific and tell us in what detail you did examine him?"

"Well, I felt his pulse - "

"He never!" A stage whisper from Mrs Smart.

"And I - er - "

"Yes, doctor?"

"Well, actually it was very difficult, you see, because Mr Percival refused to let me examine him." The Coroner cleared his throat and scribbled something on his pad.

"I see, so you did not, in fact, examine Mr Percival as well as you might have done?" Ingrace persisted.

"I don't think that's strictly – "

"In fact, would it not be twue to say, doctor, that you did not examine him at all?"

"I don't think that's strictly – "

"In other words, Dr Foowan, you awived at the conclusion that Mr Percival's illness was due to inebwiation without actually performing any kind of physical examination?"

"Um – "

"Well, doctor?"

I looked over towards Cawthron for help, but he was looking at his watch and worrying about his impending upper dental nerve block. That wasn't right, and I felt like saying so. He was getting paid a hell of a lot by the MDS – a firm that took my money every year for just that purpose. The Smarts, on the other hand, had got Bloody Ingrace on Legal Aid, buckshee, on the rates, and he was obviously so much better at this sort of thing than Cawthron. Private enterprise wasn't all it was cracked up to be.

"Well, no, I formed the opinion on – "

"I want to turn now to something in Mrs Smart's statement," Ingrace went on, making a big thing out of rustling his papers. "She says that when you told her that you thought her father's condition was due to alcohol, she replied 'This trouble cannot be due to drink, because he was ill even before he started drinking'. "

"Something like that."

"Yet that did not stwike you as stwange? That did not cause you to question your diagnosis?"

"Yes, of course it did." There was a girl on the press bench – a sort of blonde version of Avalon, with long legs, wide thigh separation and all the rest of it. Earlier on, she had been swapping lingering glances with me, but now she was fixing me with a frosty stare and pressing very hard with her pencil in her little notebook.

"And yet is it not twue to say, doctor, that in spite of what Mrs Smart said, you still did not feel inclined to perform a physical examination?"

"That's not true. I asked Mr Percival if he would let me examine him and – "

"Well I'd like to consider what happened after this. About an hour later, Mrs Smart telephoned the surgewy and asked you to come and see Mr Percival, did she not?"

"Er – "

"And what was your weaction to her wequest?"

"Well I – er . . . "

"Look, you really must speak up a bit, you know," the Coroner said.

"I said that – um – I didn't think his condition warranted another visit."

"I see. You spoke to Mrs Smart personally?"

"Well, no, not actually. I – um – passed a message on to her by way of my receptionist."

"How, then, could you judge Mr Percival's condition to decide whether or not he warranted a visit?"

"Well – the message was passed on to me."

"I see. So let me get this quite clear," Ingrace said, stroking his chin and turning his gaze to the window. "You decided, on the strength of a second-hand telephone message, that it was not worth your while to visit a man whom you were *told* had deteriorated since your first visit, all this in spite of the fact that you had not seen fit to examine him on your first visit?"

Put like that, I could see his point. "Well, no, it wasn't like that at all. You see I – er – "

"Thank you, doctor."

The Coroner looked round the court. "No more questions? Right, well you can stand down now, but I may need to recall you later."

When I got back to the bench, Cawthron was tutting and shaking his head. "What should I have done?"

"You should have kept your mouth shut like I told you to. You've really dropped yourself in it."

"You were a great help, I must say." Rudman was now in the box, wearing a black skull cap and inviting some Jewish deity to strike him dead if he breathed so much as a word of a lie.

"Yes," Cawthron said. "Well, if you'd just made the token effort of going out to see him, neither of us would need to be here in the first place."

"Thanks very much. How much are they paying you for this little effort, incidentally?"

" – all substantially normal, apart from slight engorgement of the lungs and viscera." Rudman was reciting all of this out of a little black notebook. Suddenly, he paused and cleared this throat. "However, on the basis of history provided by the doctor who certified death, tests for certain chemical toxins were performed." This time he raised his eyebrows, and turned to face the scribblers on the press bench. "As a result 'f this, one hundred an' five milligrams strychnine hydrochloride recovered from the stomach contents, twenty five milligrams from the liver, one point two milligrams from the contents 'f the bowel and blah blah blah – "

A murmur of the kind that runs through courtrooms ran through the courtroom. Ingrace was nodding smugly to himself, as if he knew all along that this was coming. Cawthron, needless to say, wasn't. Instead, he gave a low whistle and scribbled a note which read "symtoms strikinine poisning?". His writing was also atrocious. I shrugged my shoulders and looked blank, so he gave a despairing moan and wrote "Possible to confuse striknine and alcohol?" I overcame an urge to correct his spelling mistakes and write something pretty rude in reply.

"And so what, in your opinion, was the cause of death in this case?" the Coroner asked.

"'my opinion, death's due to acute strychnine poisoning."

"Have you any idea as to the total dose involved?"

"'would estimate something in the region 'f two or three grammes."

"And that would normally be enough to kill a man?"

"Ooh, yes. Lethal dose anything from fifteen to thirty milligrams."

"Thank you, doctor. Any other questions?"

Ingrace got to his feet. "Doctor Wudman, in your opinion, should the signs and symptoms of acute stwychnine poisoning be wecognisable to the avewage medical practitioner?"

"Oh yes, mose defnutly. Diagnosis of strychnine poisoning should be within capabilities 'f any – er – should be recognisable to any – "

"And yet we have heard that Mr Percival's own doctor failed to make that diagnosis. He ascwibed the signs and symptoms to alcoholic intoxication. Would you tell us if the two conditions could be weasonably confused?"

"Well, not really," Rudman said, inhaling deeply and hooking his thumb in the top of his waistcoat. "Would be very difficult to confuse the – ah – "

"And yet, as we have seen, Dr Foowan did manage to confuse the two conditions. What would be your opinion as to the pwofessional competence of a doctor who managed to perpetwate such an error?" This is where Cawthron ought to have been on his feet doing his stuff, surely, but he just sat there, blinking through his glasses.

"Wehhl – 'snot for me to sit in judgment on a colleague," the old hypocrite mumbled. "Would just repeat that the diagnosis of strychnine poisoning should be within the capabilities of any doctor."

"Thank you, doctor."

"Challenge him on that!" I hissed. "That stuff about recognising strychnine poisoning. It's a load of rubbish."

Cawthron got to his feet. "No questions," he said.

"Right, Dr – um – Fullen," the coroner said. "In view of the evidence we've just heard, I think it might be an idea if you came back into the witness box."

I agreed that it was an idea, but a pretty rotten one. "Now, we've heard Dr Rudman's evidence as to the cause of death. With the benefit of this knowledge, can you now say whether you noticed anything on your first visit to bear out the diagnosis of strychnine poisoning?"

"Well, not really. He had none of the usual signs."

"What d'you mean – usual signs?"

"Well, none of the usual signs of strychnine poisoning."

"I see."

This was just what Ingrace had been waiting for. "Er, Dr Foowan, I wonder if you could just enlighten us by telling us what *are* the pwinciple signs of stwychnine poisoning?"

"Well, vomiting."

"Yes?"

"Um – "

"Yes, doctor?"

"Vomiting, um - " Being abusive to your GP? Being smelly and offensive?

"Doctor, could you answer one simple question?" Ingrace asked. "Do you know anything at all about stwychnine poisoning?"

"Well, yes, a bit."

"I'm afwaid you're not giving me that impwession, Doctor Foowan. You are giving me the impwession that you do not know the first thing about the subject."

Cawthron stood up. At first, I thought he was going to ask to be excused because of an urgent dental appointment. "I really must protest at this attack on Dr Fullen, sir. The function of this court is to establish the cause of death, not to apportion blame."

"I do feel, sir, that it is important to establish the weliability of Dr Foowan as an expert witness, since he was the only medically-qualified person to see Mr Percival before his death."

"Yes, I think that's quite reasonable," the Coroner said.

"Well, you've heard Dr Wudman's evidence. He tells us that the diagnosis of stwychnine poisoning ought to be within the capabilities of any doctor. Can you suggest, therefore, why you failed to make the diagnosis?"

"Yes, alright, that's a reasonable question, and I'll give you a reasonable answer," I said. I leaned forwards and rested my elbows on the front of the witness box. Taking a deep breath, I began quite slowly and quietly, "Dr Rudman is a pathologist. He obviously never has to deal with real live patients, otherwise he wouldn't make such stupid statements."

Rudman, who had been messing about with his briefcase, suddenly sat up and began to take notice. The pencils on the Press bench began to scribble furiously. "When I go out to see a man who's reeling round all over the shop, brandishing a wine bottle and stinking the place out with alcohol, I tend to jump to the conclusion that that man is drunk, because nine hundred and ninety nine times out of a thousand, that man will be drunk. I have to ignore that one chance in a thousand because, with all the malingerers and hypochondriacs and scrimshankers and the general trivia of general practice, it's necessary to cut a few corners to get through a day's work."

Cawthron had opened his mouth to speak, but I beat him to it. "And what's more, if that stupid, drunk, offensive little man is abusive and generally rude to me, and refuses to let me examine him, that doesn't worry me too much. Frankly, I prefer not to get too close to people who don't wash themselves." Out of the corner of my eye, I could see the expression on Mrs Smart's face. She looked not so much hurt as thunder-struck. Good. I was beginning to enjoy myself. Raising my speed and my volume, I went on, "And if that same rude, offensive little man sends me away without seeing him, and then decides an hour later that he might as well get me back to see him again, I am more than a little inclined to tell that little man what he can do with himself. Look, what is it you want from me? I'm only human. So I don't know the effects of strychnine poisoning. Did any of you lot – before today? I'd like to bet there are plenty of doctors who qualify for a gold watch without ever knowing anything about the subject – and why should they? It's not as if people make a habit of dying from strychnine poisoning. It's alright for some clever character to come along after it's all over and say the cause of death was so-and-so, and what you ought to have done was such-and-such. What I want to know is – where was he when I needed him? If he was as clever as all that, he'd be in a job where they'd actually trust him with live patients."

This last bit was an insipid reflection of what I had really wanted to say. In my mind, I had planned a heavy crescendo, strong on sarcasm and innuendo, and referring to Rudman as "Superjew". Even so, the bowdlerised version caused Cawthron to wince visibly, He got up and started to blurt out some old balls about wanting to apologise for my outburst. I could hear him saying that I had been under a lot of strain lately and that my behaviour was something or other.

"OK," I went on, "so I made a mistake. Big deal. Don't you think I'm entitled to make a mistake from time to time? I mean, what do you do for a living? Have you never made a mistake? You live in a different world from me. You go to bed at night knowing that nobody's going to wake you up. You don't have to grab your meals on the run, you can sit down without having to worry that the phone will ring, or your bleep will go off, or that you'll have to drop everything and run off to a cardiac arrest. Christ! I'm not even allowed to go to the bog in peace. If you get busy, you delegate. I don't even have time to defaecate."

"Doctor, just one moment," the Coroner interjected. "This is neither the time nor the place for you to – " but I was getting into my stride and old Piles Bottom wasn't going to stop me now.

"You'd think that a society that imposed that sort of lifestyle on its doctors would make some sort of allowances, but oh no! When you deal with people in shops and offices and so on, you get used to a basic level of incompetence. You expect to have to write several letters on the same subject because office workers are habitually careless, incompetent and slap-happy. You regard it as perfectly normal if shop assistants are rude, inefficient or inattentive. It's par for the course if your bank messes up your bank statement. 'They're only human', we say. But if you're a doctor, nobody makes allowances like that. Doctors are not allowed to be human. Being much better than average isn't good enough. You've got to be perfect all the time."

"Something seems to have escaped your attention, doctor," the coroner had the nerve to interrupt again: "a man who was supposed to be under your care has died – "

"Which just goes to show, doesn't it, what a difficult job I've got?" Dare I have a go at the working hours of the legal profession? No, better not risk it. "Society ought to be supporting and making allowances for people with difficult and dangerous jobs, not waiting to jump on them, not waiting to make a public spectacle of them the moment they make a slight miscalculation."

"Yes, well, you see, doctor," the Coroner said: "the reason you're having a public spectacle made of you, as you put it, is because a man has died."

"And I suppose that's my fault?"

"Let me finish, doctor, if you don't mind," said old Raspberry Buttocks. "The reason we are here today is because a man has died. Our purpose is to determine the cause of death, not to apportion blame."

"You could have fooled me."

"Yes, doctor, well, since you seem either unable or unwilling to help us any further, I suggest you sit down."

Chapter 22

What the hell am I doing in a bloody pub, allowing bloody Rossiter to buy me a bloody drink? I wondered as I sat in a bloody pub, allowing bloody Rossiter to buy me a bloody drink. Not just any old pub, either, but the Puking Pig; the Puking Pig in whose snug bar I had once brought Avalon to a crafty, silent, lip-biting orgasm with my left middle finger.

The Puking Pig was not the name by which the brewery would have recognised this hostelry. A circular from the Medical Staff Committee, dated some months earlier, had mentioned the place by its official name, in the context of officially putting the pub out of bounds to junior medical staff while on duty. Sure, the bleeps would just about reach that far, but it was the opinion of their lordships that a partially – or totally – pissed junior doctor would not be able to stagger the four hundred yards back to the Infirmary fast enough in an emergency.

Duggie, who, as it happened, was the duty gynaecology SHO that evening, had expressed the contrary view, to wit, that the Medical Staff Committee knew where it could stuff its circular. So, shortly after eight o'clock, we entered that same snug bar. How did I end up there?

Duggie has promised to have full and frank discussions about the Avalon situation, and I'm so cunt-struck that I will travel miles even to talk about the woman.

"Here y'are," Duggie said. "Where shall I put it down?"

I indicated the table in front of me as being a likely sort of place. Duggie plonked himself beside me, slurped his lager, wiped his mouth on the back of his hand and began to mouth the words of the popular song coming from the juke box in the public bar. The words said something to the effect that when a man loves a woman, she can do no rang. I put up with this for a couple of verses and then I said, "Go on then."

"Go on what?"

"What was it you had to tell me?"

"What? About Avalon, you mean?"

"What d'you think?"

Duggie lit up a cigarette. "Look, Bob, I didn't want it to be like that."

"Oh, for Christ's sake! I've already had this conversation with Avalon."

"Alright then. I'm sorry," Duggie stressed, as though that was his final offer. "Does that make you feel any better?" and he sighed in exasperation, crossing his legs, closing his eyes and leaning back against the red plush of the bench seat.

I looked at him critically. Those hands, I thought. Those hands with their dubious fingernails have been mauling bits of Avalon. That tongue, those hard, cynical lips have been exploring her slippery pink bits.

"That's wonderful," I said. "You say 'Sorry I fucked your girlfriend' and that's supposed to make it alright, is it?"

"Well I am sorry. I mean I didn't do it on my own, you know. She was there at the time. She must have wanted to do it as well, mustn't she?" He was right, of course. By my reckoning, Avalon had the most to answer for, really. But she wasn't so easy to get angry with. She'd got much the nicer legs for one thing.

"Not for the same reasons as you, though, eh? Another score, another one for the old memoirs?"

"Look, I warned you about her, didn't I? I told you what she was like." As he stretched his legs, the bulge at his crotch came into prominence and I could almost picture Avalon with her long, slender fingers and her bright pink nails, reaching for his zip. The idea of what must have come next was too horrible to contemplate.

"Yes. Let me think now. What was it you described her as - a medical groupie, wasn't it?"

"And so she is. I mean, why do you think she's so happy to flit about from one to the other of us? I don't think she can tell the difference, frankly. If it's got a stethoscope and a white coat, she'll fuck it. She's just a scrubber, not worth arguing about."

"My God; you really respect the women you go to bed with, don't you?"

"What the hell's respect got to do with it?" Duggie genuinely wanted to know.

There was nobody else within earshot, so I might as well make a complete idiot of myself. "Shall I tell you?" I asked, "You see, I didn't just like fucking Avalon. I really liked her. Can you understand that?"

"*Liked* her?"

"Yeah. Mind-boggling, I know, but I really enjoyed talking to her, having a laugh with her – "

"Oh, having a laugh with her," Duggie said with relief, as though he could understand that. "Yeah, she was alright, I suppose. No different from a lot of others, but alright."

"You say was?"

"What?"

"You said she *was* alright. You know – past tense?"

Duggie looked at me as though I was barmy. "Didn't she tell you?" he asked. "I thought that's why you'd agreed to come this evening."

"Tell me what?"

"I cooled her."

"When was this?"

"Ooh, I dunno. Couple of nights ago."

I felt something lurch inside me. It was bound to happen, of course, but you never anticipate the totally anticipatable. "What happened ?" I asked.

"Nothing much. She was getting a bit heavy: wanted me to go up to Wolverton for the weekend to meet her bloody family, would you believe? Her old man's a bishop or something, did you know?"

Bog off and ring her up now. "A vicar," I said.

"Whassa difference? Same load of useless cunts."

"This one isn't. He's alright, is old man Death."

"You mean you met him?"

"Yes, I went up there for the weekend once."

Duggie simply couldn't believe this. He shook his head and asked, incredulously, "You mean you let her take you for a family inspection?" I nodded. "What are you? Soft in the head or something? You don't let them pull that kind of stunt on you."

"I know you find this hard to understand," I said gallantly, "but I was really fond of Avalon. I really cared about her. She really mattered to me."

"None of them matter," the Dirty Doctor said. "They're just tarts. You have one, you use it, you get tired of it, you get another one."

"Like sheets of bog paper, you mean?"

"Something like that. Anyway, if you're still interested, you can have her back, mate." There was a look of sheer arrogance on his face as he added. "I give her to you. For old time's sake." I was silently rummaging in my pocket to find a coin for the phone box when the door to the Snug Bar opened, and in walked Jimmie Materson, followed closely at heel by Creepy Henry, who was in the process of telling Jimmie what his father always used to say about some knighted member of the Council of the Royal College of Surgeons.

Jimmie darted his gaze about the room, as if seeking for an escape route. Realising that we were the room's only occupants, and that it was too late to withdraw, he said, "Oh, hullo you two. What're you having?"

Duggie uncharacteristically took him for only a pint, but it gave me time to work out what would cost Jimmie most. After all, he owed me. He never used to buy me a drink when I was doing his housejob, but then I didn't have a father who knew members of the Council of the Royal College of Surgeons, did I? I named a proprietary mixture of alcoholic and non-alcoholic fluids. Jimmie, with a little disapproving grunt, rolled up to the bar and tried to catch the attention of the surly barman with a combination of throat-clearings and hand-signals. Having repeated our orders a sufficient number of times for the man to understand what he was talking about, he leaned back against the bar with his elbow gratifyingly centred on a pool of spilt liquid and said, " By way, Fowler: doan know if you've met Cedric Henry, have you?"

Cedric? This could not be, surely? "Yes, we have met."

"I'll say we have."

"Goo' lord," Jimmie said, not with surprise at this last exchange, but at the unpleasant sensation of being informed by the barman how much my drink was going to set him back. I watched him return his loose change to his pocket and, with some reluctance, extract some of the folding stuff from the depths of his wallet. "Yehhs. Well now, how's general practice treating you?"

"Not too bad, I suppose."

"How'd you get on at the Inquest today, then?" Henry asked.

"What Inquest this, Cedric?"

"Oh, sorry, sir. Talking shop," Henry said, giving me a triumphant leer. "Don't know whether I should have – "

"Whassit all about, ah, Rodney?" Jimmie asked. It took me a few seconds to realise that the old buffoon was trying to resolve the christian name/surname anomaly by having a crack at remembering my first name, something he hadn't attempted since a similarly unsuccessful attempt at the beginning of the Five Ports Race.

"Nothing really. Just an Inquest on one of my patients that died."

"Yehhs, slurp, could hardly have an Inquest on him if he hadn't died!" Jimmie laughed. So the old man hadn't lost the knack of not being able to make jokes.

"Strychnine poisoning or something, wasn't it?" Henry asked.

"Yes, as it happens. Why? You some kind of expert?"

The eyes behind the SS glasses screwed up into something resembling a smile. "No, but I can recognise the signs of strychnine poisoning when I see them."

Having had no chance to go away and look it up, I decided against calling his bluff by getting him to give me a full and detailed account of the effects of strychnine poisoning right there and then. "It's a pity you didn't mention it at the post-mortem, then."

Doctors, you see, don't know very much. Oh sure, there are these smart arses on the television who know all the answers, these strange coves who write columns in women's magazines – "A Doctor Writes" – that sort of crap, but the reason they know all the answers is because they've been told what the questions are going to be, and they've had time to go and look it up. I know, because there was this GP in Breckleigh who used to do a regular radio Doc Spot. He was always ringing people at the hospital to "pick their brains". Then all he had to do was churn out – parrot fashion – whatever he'd been told to say.

There is this legend that medical students absorb and retain vast amounts of information. Well, the human brain just doesn't work that way. You learn one new fact, you forget one old one. That's only common sense. No, doctors only retain enough information to get them through the day in their particular specialty. A cardiologist wouldn't know his calf from his elbow, any more than an orthopaedic surgeon would know a heart murmur from a bucket of shit. They don't need to know, you see. And as for GPs: "Ask your doctor for advice". In most cases, you'd be better off getting the book out of the library and cutting out the middle man.

Jimmie looked craftily from one to the other of us. "Some sort of needle going on here?" he asked jokingly.

"No, it's not needle. It's just that I object to clever sods who're always wise after the event."

"Now come on, you two," Jimmie said. "Cedric, you know Fow - You know Rodney here was my houseman before you, doan you?"

"Yeah, so I gathered. GP out Crosshills way, or something, aren't you?" Henry asked. I confirmed that I was what he said I was, and not something even nastier. "Oh yes. D'you remember Mrs McGready, sir, three or four weeks ago?"

"Oh yehhs, slurp, I remember her."

"It was you that sent her to us, wasn't it?"

"Yes, as it happens."

"You remember the one I'm talking about, sir?"

"Oh - yehhs!" Jimmie laughed. "Now I remember! That Mrs McGready! Ahur ahur ahur. Yehhs, slurp, well we all make mistakes sometimes."

Even Creepy Henry seemed to agree that we all make mistakes sometimes, and, after Duggie had managed to persuade Jimmie to buy him a cigar, the old bugger announced that he would tell us all about a mistake he made once. This account had all the usual features of a Jimmie story - over-protraction, a high degree of inaudibility, extreme human suffering as the high point of its humour. Where it differed from the general run of Jimmie stories was that the perpetrator of the foul deed turned out to be not some incompetent, and probably illegitimate, alien, but Jimmie himself.

It concerned a time when Jimmie, as a surgical senior registrar, had operated on a road-accident victim. In the bloody mess of his abdomen, Jimmie had lost his way. Under the impression that the right kidney was grossly enlarged by bleeding, Jimmie chopped the organ out, only to discover that what he had actually removed was the patient's liver.

"Course, the chap died," Jimmie said. "Thought there was goin' t'be an awful stink about it, but fortunately, slurp, happened to know pathologist who did post mortem."

I turned my beer mat over and read the joke on the other side. "What did they call the chinaman who went into the ladies' lavatory? – Wong Loo."

"Wehhl, this chap knew the Coroner wassen awfully bright, so he stands up in court and says, slurp, 'Examined the contents of the abdomen. Stomach and duodenum normal. Pancreas healthy. Spleen absent. Liver absent. Small and large bowel normal, appendix absent – ' Slipped it in in the middle, see?" Jimmie explained for the benefit of any subnormals listening.

"Gosh! You're kidding!" said Creepy Henry.

"Yehhs . . . slipped it in in the middle, slurp, so the chap din notice. Result was," said Jimmie, knocking back his G & T in one gulp, "liver wassen mentioned again, an goddorf without any embarrassing questions."

"Jolly good!" said Creepy Henry.

And what would have happened, I wondered, if Rudman and Ingrace had been on that case – crushing the living day lights out of Jimmie's promising surgical career with their amazing double act: "Recognition 'f the liver – largest organ 'n human body – should be within capabilities 'f any surgical senior registrar." 'Then tell me Dr Wudman, what would be your opinion as to the pwofessional competence of a surgeon who managed to excise the whole of that organ without knowing what it was?' "

"O' course, things were very different then," Jimmie continued, precipitating an acute attack of deja vecu, the phrase being an almost verbatim quotation from a speech Chaucer had made only a few days earlier while he was bemoaning the disappearance of diphtheria as a useful child-killer. "In those days, if you did a housejob, that meant you were on for six munce. Six munce, slurp, twenty four hours a day, seven days a week. Nowadays, you ask a house surgeon t'give up an evening orf – " he paused, but very decently did not specify any particular house surgeon by name, " 'n you'd think you were askin' f' the moon."

"You didn't get paid, either," Duggie volunteered.

"Thass right. You din get paid. You did it f' the experience, knowin' you were gettin' a damned good training in the basics of medicine and surgery, slurp."

"You were happy to get the job," Duggie added.

"Yehhs. There were precious few of them about then. You chaps nowadays -"

"Mollycoddled," Duggie said.

"You chaps nowadays, you doan know when you're well orf."

"Mollycoddled."

"We'd never have dreamed 'f having evening and weekends orf the way you chaps do."

"Aye, tha gives t'workers half a crown: they doan't know they're born."

Jimmie, like an aging bear becoming aware of a terrier at its heels, turned to face his aggressor. "Look here – er – wassyername?"

"Wheer will it end, that's what I'd like to know?" Duggie asked, hooking his thumbs round his lapels in what had now become his full-blown trubble at t'mill performance. "You mark my word, it's t'thin end of t'wedge is yon – "

Jimmie sat through the next sequence with a pained grimace on his face, realising that any attempt at a serious rebuttal would only make him appear to be what he actually was: a great pompous oaf. In the gaps in Duggie's harangue, he tried to frame a laugh that didn't come off. "Suppose you're one of these chaps. Junior Doctors' Association or whaddever," he said eventually, " talkin' 'bout Industrial Action, as though you were some kind of navvy."

"Oh? And what's so bad about that?" Duggie asked, suddenly dropping back into an accent not too unlike the one he had been putting on.

"Draggin' the profession down to the level of the shop floor," Materson spluttered, the last two words broadcasting a fine rain of spit over a wide area. "How're you goin' to maintain the patient's confidence when they see you arguing and bickering like a load 'f shop stewards?"

Duggie brought his face very close to Jimmie's and said, slowly and deliberately, "Actually, Mr Materson, I couldn't give a shit about the patient's confidence. They don't give a toss about my welfare. So long as I'm there to wipe their backsides for them, they couldn't care less whether I've been to bed in the past week."

"Part of the job," Paterson said. "You knew about that when you went in for it."

"Oh, part of the job, is it?" Duggie mimicked. "Listen, there was a woman a month ago who had an anaphylactic reaction. She was as near as *that* to snuffing it, and I saved her life. Is she grateful? Is she buggery! I'll tell you what she's doing: suing me. That's what she's doing. Suing me because she was allergic to the tube that saved her life. They actually like it better if we're exhausted and run off our feet - you know that? That way they can complain or make a bit of money on the side by suing us."

"Part of the job,"Materson repeated.

"Well, if that's the job, Mr Materson," Duggie said, "you can stick it. I didn't sign up to be a martyr. I'd rather be well-paid than well respected."

"Well-paid!" Jimmie exploded, "My God, you doan know when you're well off!"

"Well off? Well off, you call it?" Duggie shouted, and he produced his dog-eared pay slip from his top pocket.

"Take a look at that, chum. I've lost nine years earnings, working to get my degree. I come out, I work a hundred-hour week in conditions that would bring any self-respecting industrial workforce out on strike inside a day, and what do I get at the end of it? I'll tell you what I get. Look! Fucking peanuts! Christ, I could earn more than that sweeping out the bogs at Ford's five mornings a week."

"You doan know when you're well orf!" Jimmie spluttered, swatting aside the proffered payslip like a troublesome mosquito. "When I was a houseman, you lived in the hospital for a year, you got your board and lodgings free, and that was all. In those days, housemen knew their place, and they were glad of the opportunity - "

"Christ! Don't we bloody know it! And just because you were all too stupid to do anything about it, you think we've got to put up with the same crap. You, I am pleased to say, Mr Materson, are a a rather silly, rather senior, senior consultant, and the sooner your type gets pensioned off and buggers off to Cheltenham in your wheel chairs, the sooner we'll be able to get down to forcing this crappy country into giving us our basic rights. Joke money like that isn't enough to persuade me to go on flogging my guts out and taking the risks and responsibilities this job involves."

"Yes, well of course, Medicine requires a certain amount of dedication" Jimmie blustered, "but of course you wouldn't know anything about that."

"Ah, come on!" Duggie shouted. "Cut the crap! You're only in this game for what you can get out of it, so don't come the dedication shit with me." He was now on his feet, towering threateningly above us. "Sorry, Bob, I'm going. I can't stand any more of this bullshit. Him and that creeping little toad of his, they turn my guts inside out." He drained the last of his free beer and strode out of the room, slamming the door behind him.

"Extraordinary chap!" creepy Henry whined.

Jimmie turned to me. "Goo' Lord, whassa matter with that chap?" he asked, " 's he a socialist or something?"

Chapter 23

Chaucer walked into the consulting room after morning surgery next day, brandishing a well-thumbed copy of the Breckleigh Morning News. "Oh hello, old boy," he said "Did you manage to read this, I wonder?"

Oh sure, I've got time to laze around all morning reading bloody newspapers when I've got to do all your work for you as well, you old cunt. "No, I didn't. Is it the – er ?" The paper fell open of its own accord at page five, and Chaucer spread it out on the desk, indicating the article in the top right hand corner.

BRECKLEIGH MAN DIED OF STRYCHNINE

An open verdict was returned at the Inquest yesterday on 65- year old Mr Harold Percival of 48J, Wellington Flats, Churchwall, Breckleigh, after it was stated that death had been due to strychnine poisoning. Pathologist Dr Harry Rudman said Mr Percival died following a dose of two to three grams of strychnine which had been put in a cup of tea at his place of work – Thomas Stringer Chemicals Ltd – where Mr Percival was employed as a time-keeper.

Dr Robert Fullen of The White House, Crosshills, said that he had seen Mr Percival on the afternoon of his death, but had formed the opinion that Mr Percival was inebriated. Asked by the Coroner, Mr John Hiscock-Barrett, why he had not answered a subsequent call to see Mr Percival, Dr Fullen replied that he considered Mr Percival's condition did not warrant a further visit.

"MUCH TO BE DESIRED"

Mr Hiscock-Barrett said that Dr Fullen's conduct left much to be desired. The diagnosis of strychnine poisoning should have been within the capabilities of any doctor. Dr Fullen had not only failed to make the diagnosis: he had made no effort to substantiate or refute his own perfunctory diagnosis of alcoholic intoxication.

My eyes raced ahead over the blocks of words, but I could see no reference to "Family Doctor's Outburst In Court". I wasn't sure whether that made me feel annoyed or relieved. Why had they written nothing about it? Why were they scribbling it all down so fast if they didn't intend to publish it? Who had written all this bollocks anyway - Chaucer's Mr Palfreyman or Miss Wide-Thighs-Separation? Thinking about her naturally made me think about Avalon. I didn't get up the courage to ring her after all. Anyway, what could I possibly say to her? She had been so maudlin and fucking wet when Duggie was still poking her - what on earth would she be like now?

"Doesn't read too well, does it?" Chaucer asked, sounding distinctly as though he was about to launch off into another of his "you young chaps" monologues.

"No, I suppose not." The part that read particularly badly as far as I was concerned was the bit where the coroner said he personally took a serious view of my actions, and he had little doubt that they would have serious repercussions in other quarters. What other quarters was he getting at?

"Patients don't like reading that sort of thing," Chaucer told me.

"Yeah, well half of them can't read, can they? So I shouldn't worry too much on that score."

Leaning over me with his hand on the desk, Chaucer read through the article again, slowly shaking his nasty old head. I had never really seen him this close before. The skin of his hands, like the skin of his head, was dotted with little red spots, freckles and patches of cruddy, discoloured skin. He had that indefinable smell of old person about him, and there was an audible wheeze when he breathed in. He must be bloody ancient.

"Hmm," he said after a bit, "it's most unfortunate that you had to use this address, you see."

I felt an uncontrollable blind rage welling up inside me. "Oh, why's that, then?" There were one or two things I had been meaning to ask this old sot about this case, anyway. It had been obvious from the evidence, if not from the verdict, that Percival was a complete and utter nut case. He'd attempted suicide at least twice before, once by trying to hang himself with a piece of mouldy rope that wouldn't support his weight, and once by sawing at his wrists with a blunt penknife. Chaucer's record system naturally failed to make any mention of this.

"Well, it tends to bring disrepute on the practice as a whole, doesn't it?"

"Tars you with the same brush, you mean? Drags you down to my level?"

"I wouldn't go so far as – "

"Christ! You make it sound like I've got some sort of disease," I said. "I mean, after all, what have I done that you wouldn't have done – except do a bit of work, perhaps? I've just had a bit of bad luck, that's all."

Chaucer put his hands in his trouser pockets and wandered over towards the french window. "Bad luck," he said. "Bad judgment, perhaps – "

"Bad judgment? Are you trying to tell me that you'd have done any better?" I asked, and I got up from the desk, and moved round to confront him. "Are you trying to tell me that your knowledge of medicine is so much better than mine that you'd have – "

Chaucer clearly felt physically threatened, which was the effect I was aiming for. "No, no, no, dear boy. Not that," he said, and he began to retreat towards the desk. "Lack of experience, perhaps. You're a newcomer to this game. When you've been at it as long as I have – "

I grabbed him by the shoulder and turned him round to face me. "Experience? Is that what it is?" I demanded. "And precisely how many cases of strychnine poisoning have you *experienced* in your career? You think you'd have been any better at spotting it? You think you'd have been any keener to go out and see him the second time? No, because you'd buggered off to Bournemouth for the night. That's how much use you were. And don't think I haven't heard about you and your night calls. You dirty old lush! Don't you think it's a miracle you haven't ended up in the law courts before now?"

Chaucer's eyes hunted the room for an escape route."Now look, Fullen – "

"Then you have the bare-faced nerve to talk to me as though I've got some disgusting disease that you don't want to catch."

"Yes, well look: I don't think now is the best time to discuss this," Chaucer said, grabbing his newspaper from the desk and backing towards the door. "You're obviously still upset about – "

"I am not upset! " I bellowed. "I am not upset! I am just sick and tired of the hypocrisy. The number of armchair bloody diagnosticians who've been telling me my job. I'd just like to see how any of them would have reacted if they'd been in my place."

"Yes. Look, calm down, old chap – "

"Don't you 'old chap' me, you pathetic old sod. I'm not your 'old chap'. I'm not anybody's 'old chap' yet, thank God!" I grabbed my bag and swept past him. "Get out of my way, you silly old bugger!" I stormed out of the house and didn't stop fuming until I got to Broadgate.

Chapter 24

The door of Beau Vista was opened by a little scrubber of - how old? - thirteen maybe. "Doctor, is it?" she asked. "Just a minute." She shouted back into the house "Mam! Mam! Doctor's here!" I noticed now that she had breast buds under her tee shirt , and that she was wearing shoes that looked like surgical boots made for someone with both legs shorter than the other.

I checked my watch. This was only the second visit on my list, and it was already past noon. In Broadgate, I had been detained by a well-meaning but filthy old pensioner who insisted on giving me a scalding hot cup of tea. Halfway through pouring this, the teapot had blocked, so he put his foul bronchitic mouth to the spout and blew it clear. I could still taste the mucus.

"Mam! Mam! Hang on a minute," the girl said, and she disappeared inside the house, closing the door behind her.

Then there'd been the problem of finding this place. Thirty seven minutes. It was partly Chaucer's fault, of course, for accepting absolutely anybody onto this list. East Park Estate, apart from being too new to appear on my Breckleigh Street Map, except as a grey splodge marked "new development", was nowhere near British West Crosshills.

Goddo had taken a hand in things, of course: scattering a complicated network of red traffic lights, illegally parked cars, major road works and idiot learner drivers in my path. All the same, I put most of the blame on the residents of East Park Estate, who preferred cutesy names to house numbers.

Beau Vista was OK as a name, I suppose, so long as you didn't object to the mixture of languages and genders, but there was no logical reason why it should come between Dunraven (a clapped-out schizophrenic, perhaps?) and Izzaners. It's official name was 88, Leinster Gardens, but, I reflected, as I stood and looked at its already-battered front door, some more descriptive name, such as The Hovel or The Dump would have made it more easily recognisable from a distance.

The door opened again, and the child said, "She's not in. I forgot.

She's gone out shopping."

"What d'you mean, she's gone out shopping? She asked for the doctor to call. Why isn't she here?" On the carpetless staircase, three or four smaller children were playing a game that looked promisingly dangerous.

"There was some things she wanted from the shop."

"Yes, well, you can tell her I called, and if she wants anything, she'll have to come down to the surgery for it."

"She's here now."

Coming across the open-plan weed-patch and skirting round the wheel-less Dagenham dustbin was a broken-down old bag carrying a string shopping bag filled with crisps and other foodstuffs of low nutritional value. Her belly was stuffed with something else, and it protuded through a coat that was pretending to be part of a dead animal. Mrs Ward was in the club again.

"Mrs Ward?" I asked, advancing towards her. "I'm calling on behalf of Dr Chaucer."

"Oh yes?" She pushed past me into the house. The floor was littered with toys and bits of discarded food, through which a mangy cat was picking its way. The place stank of stale beef dripping. Children, generating a lot of noise, were much in evidence.

"In here," Mrs Ward said, gesturing for me to go into the front room. There was a cot in one corner, containing a baby, mercifully asleep and in any case far too young to appreciate what a rotten deal had been meted out to it by the circumstances of its birth. Letting down the cot side, I asked, "What's his trouble been?"

Mrs Ward looked at me as though I was potty. "Over here," she said. She rolled her sleeve and indicated part of her forearm. "This rash here ."

"You mean it's for you?"

"Itches like mad sometimes. I need something to put on it."

"You mean you've got me all the way down here just to look at that?"

"I've got it on the other arm as well."

I counted up to ten and then asked, "You've just been out shopping, haven't you, Mrs Ward?" No answer, so I repeated, "I said you've just been out shopping? Why couldn't you come up to the surgery with it?"

"Look, I've got eleven kids to look after."

"I'm most frightfully sorry to have to point this out to you, Madam, but the idea of visiting is to help people who aren't mobile enough to get to the surgery. If you can go out shopping, you're perfectly capable of – "

Mrs Ward wasn't all that interested. "Look," she said, "are you going to give me something for this, or aren't you?"

"You've got to be joking."

"Right!" she said simply. "Out you get !"

She threw open the door as the baby let out a high-pitched wail. "Go on, out you get !"

"Oh no, you don't get rid of me that easily. You don't drag me down here, waste a couple of hours of my time and then chuck me out because I won't slobber around giving you whatever you want."

"Are you leaving, or do I have to get my neighbour?"

"I think it would be rather fun if you got your neighbour."

She stormed out into the back garden, scattering children and animals on all sides and shouting, "May ! May !"

From the adjacent house, a brawny charwoman with a net in her hair appeared, arms folded ready for action. Mrs Ward filled her in on the background to her complaint, and started to point at me like an exhibit in a side-show. "He won't go," she complained. "He won't see me and now he won't go." The charwoman gaped at me, unable to believe this. "Said I ought to go up the surgery. I can't go, can I? I've got eleven children to look after."

"She's got eleven children to look after," the charwoman said.

"The fact that you've got eleven children is hardly my fault. If you want to live off the State, that's your business, but don't try and put me to any extra inconvenience on your account."

"We do not live off the State!" she shouted. "We do not live off the State. My husband gets a good wage."

She had now been joined in the garden by four of her brats, who were staring up at me with their dirty little faces agape. It was all far too much like a cartoon: the low-browed look of slack-jawed lumpishness was common to the whole family.

"Oh, I see. I hadn't realised. I do beg your pardon. What does he do, exactly, your husband? Chairman of ICI, perhaps? So you won't be drawing family allowance, then? No free milk, housing subsidies, rent rebates, income supplement - And I presume that you pay for all your own maternity care?"

"We didn't ask for the family allowance."

"You don't refuse it when it's offered though?"

"Would you?"

"No, but then I wouldn't allow myself to get into a situation where I had to rely on charity."

"I'll have as many children as I like!" she screamed.

"Ah, I see. You did want them all, then? It's not just that you're too stupid to do anything about stopping them ?"

"I'll have as many children as I like!"

"Of course you will!" I said. "I mean, it's not as if the world is over-populated or anything like that, is it? We really need good-looking, intelligent people like you to breed like flies."

"She'll have as many children as she likes!" the charwoman said.

"Sluts like you bring children into the world that you don't even want. You feed them on chips and bread and margarine, and then you shove the poor little buggers off into some filthy factory before they can't even read their name on their wage packet."

"She'll have as many children as she likes!" the charwoman repeated.

"Well! What an attitude!" said Mrs Ward.

"What an attitude for a doctor!" said the charwoman.

"Dr Chaucer never treats me like that."

"No, I bet he doesn't, because he's too feeble and ineffectual to say what he thinks. Now, I'm telling you, you're a stupid, ignorant, selfish old bag, and if you want to go on behaving like that, I suggest you change your doctor."

"Don't you worry. I will. I wouldn't come to you again, even if I was dying."

"Oh, God! What a horrible threat! I don't think I can stand it. What will I do without you buggering me about with your grouses and your bellyaches?"

"I wouldn't come to you again, even if I was dying."

"Nothing would suit me better. The fewer patients like you I have, the happier I'll be." I turned to walk back through the house.

"No, you don't!" shouted Mrs Ward. "You don't go back through there! You go round the back."

I walked on. Inside the front door there was a framed picture in unrealistically bright colours, showing a geezer with long hair, a beard, and light of a golden colour apparently shining out of his lugholes. Underneath, there was a thinly-disguised invitation to scroungers, the first part of which said that if you asked, you would receive.

"Not this time, though, my old son," I muttered, slamming the front door behind me with insufficient force to shatter the glass.

Chapter 25

"Hello?"

"Please – "

"Hello, Breckleigh 28281."

"Can I just – ?"

"Who's that?"

"Is that Bob?"

"Yes, who's that?"

"It's me."

Well, I thought, if we're going to play it that way, let's make a meal of it. "Who's me?" I asked.

"It's Avalon."

Avalon Who? would have been good, but maybe overdoing it a bit, so I settled for, "Oh yes?"

"Bob, please can we talk?"

"Talk? What about?"

"Just – talk."

"Fine, off you go, then." Why am I bloody doing this? I've been shitting myself for ten days, not daring to ring her, and now here she is, ringing me up and wanting to talk, for Christ's sake. Why don't I just say it's fucking good to hear your voice again, Avalon, my darling, the love of my life, come on round straight away and I'll give you one?

"Please, Bob, don't – I'm so – " There was a catch in her voice, and I caught the sound of a sob or two.

"So what?"

"So – very – unhappy."

Well that just fucking well serves you right, you stupid cow, I should have said, but I'm a sucker for a crying woman. "Oh, come on, it's not as bad as that, surely?"

"Yes, it's every bit as bad as that. Has Duggie told you?"

"Yes, of course he has."

"And I suppose you thought how funny it was, that you'd got your own back or something."

"No, actually, I didn't. When I heard, I nearly rang you up to say how sorry I was."

"Oh, Bob, why didn't you?"

"Why didn't I? Well, I don't know why I didn't. I suppose it's something called pride. But you haven't really left me a lot of that, have you?"

"Oh, Bob, I've been so stupid."

Too bloody right! "Well, I can't really say that it was totally unexpected. You knew what he was like."

There was a pause. One of us had to make the first move. "Look, I – " I began.

"Bob, over this past week, I've begun to realise what it was that I've thrown away with you. I know I've been an absolute bitch – "

"No, no, you haven't – "

"Yes, I have. I don't deserve you ever to speak to me again. If you want me to go and never – and never – I'll understand."

What? And pass up the chance of another of your blow-jobs, Avalon? "No, I'm just being silly," I said. "Of course I want to see you again."

"Really and truly?"

"Yes, really and truly, but look, I'm just on my way out. I've got to do evening surgery, and I'm on this evening. What about coming round to the flat, tomorrow at sevenish ? We could go out and eat somewhere. Talk it all out."

For a few seconds, I thought she was actually going to turn me down, but after a bit of a silence, she said "Yes, Bob, I'd like that very much."

"Tomorrow at seven, then?"

"Yes – And Bob?"

"What?"

"Thank you for being so nice to me."

"Avalon?"

"What?"

"I love you, you know."

"Thank you." Not and I love you too, my darling, my dearest, I cannot live without you, but at least it was a start.

Chapter 26

"And I mean, it upsets her a lot more than it would some people, doesn't it mother? You see, doctor, she's always been such a clean person all her life."

Smelly old women and their waterworks, not the most fascinating of subjects at the best of times, but I couldn't keep my mind on anything during surgery that evening. Avalon's phone call had made me feel jittery, but that wasn't all. I couldn't get the Mrs Ward incident out of my mind. Not that I was feeling any guilt for what I'd said to her. No fear. My only regret was that I hadn't taken the opportunity to say more to her while I had the chance. By now, I'd stockpiled so many unused insults that I was half- tempted to drive back down there, fling open the door and start "And another thing, Mrs Bloody Ward – "

"And to tell you the truth, doctor, what mother finds most troublesome is, well – the odour. The odour is what upsets you, isn't it, mother?"

Odour was indeed what upset mother, so I frowned and tried to look interested. They were a relatively posh pair as Chaucer's patients went: the daughter in middle-class uniform of Paisley prints and sensible shoes, the mother in elderly but expensive church bazaar tweeds. Just as the daughter started off on some other tack, this time about her mother's increasing forgetfulness, the telephone on the desk rang.

"Bob? Duggie. Look, are you on tonight?"

"Supposed to be. Why?"

"Well they can stuff that. I've got to see you. Something's come up."

"What? What is it? What's happened?" Duggie has decided to take Avalon back. Avalon is in the club and Duggie is going to make an honest woman of her. Avalon has shot Duggie. No, wait, Duggie has shot Avalon. Avalon has been killed in a car-crash. Avalon has died after an illegal operation carried out by Duggie.

"Look, I can't talk now. See you in the Puking Pig at nine, right?"

"Yeah, but I'm supposed to be – "

"Nine o'clock, got it?" He rang off.

The monologue from the other side of the desk had been brought to a halt by the telephone call, and I took advantage of the silence to say, "Alright, I'll see what I can do." I got up from my chair, signalling the end of the interview. "I'll write and ask Mr Fountain if he can bring her appointment forwards."

"Thank you, doctor." We got the old dear onto her feet and started to manhandle her towards the door. "She doesn't do too badly for her age though, does she, doctor? Have a guess. Just tell me how old you think she looks."

This was a bloody futile game. I could work out - to the nearest day - how old she was, since her birth date was written on her card. I had an infallible formula for bringing any "guess how old I am" nonsense to a premature end. Take patient's actual age and add ten years, "Oh, about eighty five, I should say ."

"Eighty five?"

"Yes, good evening to you, ladies."

One up to me. Settling back into the swivel chair, I rang the bell for the next patient, but there was no response. Thank God for that. Time to bog off, but first I got out a packet of not-particularly special cigarettes, set fire to one of them and smoked it thoughtfully and rather well right down to the finger-grip. Smoking was something I hadn't done a lot of since I was at school, but I was beginning to find that I couldn't get through evening surgery unless I promised myself this kind of break. It was more of a hobby, really, something to do with my hands that didn't involve touching unwashed human flesh. Perhaps Chaucer had taken up gin-swilling from similar motives.

Should I ring Avalon? Nah, be cool. Plenty of time to say - and do - all that tomorrow. Not too much wanking this evening, then. Besides, I'm much better at all that when I'm not on-call. The real bugger about being on-call is not the actual work, it is knowing that you can be interrupted - dragged from your pit, the meal table or even the bog - at any moment. Sometimes, actually being made to work comes as a relief. Being at everybody's beck and call is a Sword of Damocles that hangs over your day, sapping your energy and putting a damper on most things, especially your libido. Fountain, in one of his rare philosophical moments, had once told Duggie that an obstetric house-job was the best contraceptive he knew.

I stubbed out the cigarette, gathered together my on-call gear and left the consulting room, clunking up the old brass light switch as I left.

As I groped my way along the murky passageway to the front door, I had the unpleasant sensation of suddenly coming upon Chaucer who had been lurking in a crevice between the dark oak hall stand and a tub of moribund vegetation, like a stone fish waiting for its poisonous spine to be trodden on.

"One minute, if you could, old boy," he said, making an ambiguous gesture with the stem of his pipe. "If I could just have a moment or two of your most valuable time." He was speaking in a way that - even for him - was curiously formalised, like somebody reading it from a script. "If you'd like to step into the, ah, study, for a few minutes. There's something rather important I'd like to discuss with you."

This was all pretty polite, considering that my last words to him that morning had been to warn the old fool to keep out of my way. Had he already forgotten this? He pushed open a chocolate brown door and led me into a room containing lots of the sort of things I would have expected Chaucer to have lots of - faded pictures in dusty frames, a Vienna regulator giving only a very rough approximation of what the time was, a rug made out of a dead animal, warped shelves groaning with decaying books on various decaying subjects, including one doing its best to be satirical by calling itself Recent Advances in something or other. The rest of the furniture was old, rather than antique. There was a rack of implements for messing about with, and eventually setting fire to, tobacco and, in the fireplace, a pair of black spelter horses were rearing up on their hind legs and doing their best to trample on the inadequately-clothed men holding on to the reins.

The only things I had expected but didn't see were the gin bottles - full bottles, empty bottles and bottles in the process of being converted from one sort into the other. Only the smell of the stuff was detectable as I sat down on the hard leather chesterfield. It was an indication of something or other that, although Chaucer lived over the shop, this was the first time I had been invited into any part of the White House not directly concerned with the processing of patients. I felt none of the apprehension that this sort of situation ought to have caused, though. After all, it was only Chaucer I was dealing with, wasn't it? And the most enormous advantage about Chaucer being content to be just Chaucer, as against him managing to be, for example, Jimmie Materson, was his relatively puny sphere of influence. Unlike Jimmie, he could not whistle up an army of fellow shits and have me blacklisted over a substantial part of the British Isles.

Chaucer sat himself down opposite me and had the gall to start talking about the bloody weather. A desire to hit him over the head with one of his horses welled up inside me. "You had something important you wanted to tell me, " I interrupted.

"Oh, I wouldn't put it quite like that. Not really vitally important, old boy. I just thought we could have a chat generally."

"Well, if it's not important, I'll leave if you don't mind. I've got other things on this evening."

"Ah, Dr Fullen, Dr Fullen," he laughed, shaking his doddery old head at what a wag I was. I stared coldly back at him and he was suddenly serious. "There are one or two things I have to say to you about the practice," he announced.

"Such as?"

"Well, I'm sure it won't come as a surprise to you that I've had one or two patients coming to me with - er - reports about things you've been saying or doing in the course of your work here."

"Complaints," I translated.

"Yes, 'fraid so, old boy. Now look, there's no need for all this bad feeling you've been creating round here." He leaned forwards, and in his confiding voice he said, "I got a letter this afternoon from Miss Heather Bradley."

I knew perfectly well who Miss Heather Bradley was, but I asked "Come again?"

Chaucer put on a don't-piss-about-with-me look and said, "Miss Bradley. You refused to give her a sickness certificate on Monday, so I understand."

"Oh yeah, the Virgin Queen. I remember her." My first mistake had been in addressing her as "Mrs Bradley" and the second had been in asking why she couldn't get one of her grown-up children to lend her a hand during her declining years. The chronological age of this decrepit walking scarecrow had turned out to be thirty five.

"Miss Bradley tells me that you called her a neurotic, frustrated old spinster."

"I most certainly did not," I said. After all, there were no witnesses, were there?

"Oh?" Chaucer asked, and he produced from his inside pocket a sheet of lined azure blue writing paper, which he opened out on his knee. Holding this in one hand, and tilting his spectacles forwards with the other, he went on, "so I presume you didn't call her a 'stupid, shiftless old bag', either?"

"Absolutely not!" I said. "I was simply trying to encourage her to go back to work."

"I'd like you to know that Miss Bradley is a rather special and a rather delicate case," Chaucer said. This evening, beneath the ever-present thornproof sports jacket with its leather elbow patches, he was wearing a purple bow tie and a bright scarlet waistcoat. There was a psychiatrist at medical school who would have had something to say on that subject: people who dress like that are trying to compensate for their lack of personality - did you know that? "Without going into the home background and so on, I wouldn't expect you to understand. She's a very lonely woman who needs to be handled with very great care and tact - "

"She's a malingerer, Dr Chaucer," I said simply. "There's nothing wrong with her back. She been using that as an excuse not to work for five years now."

Chaucer was silent for a few seconds while he re-read the letter in front of him. "Did you use the words 'work shy'?" he asked experimentally.

"Nope."I said, "I ask you-does that sound like me?"

"Bone idle slut? Lazy slag?"

"She's making it all up," I told him. Chaucer seemed to have lost himself in the depths of Miss Bradley's letter, so on a let's-get-it-all-over-with basis, I suddenly said, "Actually, while we're on the subject, I think I ought to tell you that I had words with another of your patients this afternoon, a Mrs Bernadette Ward."

"Ah yes, I've just been speaking to Mrs Ward on the telephone," he said.

"Small world."

"Yes - Mrs Ward," Chaucer repeated. "I was going to have a word with you about Mrs Ward." He'd just better not be planning to rake up the Harold Percival episode again, that's all, otherwise Mr Bloody Palfreyman could start work straight away on an article headed "Breckleigh GP Dies From Fist In Throat". "Now Mrs Ward is a lady with a large family - "

"You can say that again."

"Yes, well, that's as may be," Chaucer said, taking out a stained leather tobacco pouch from his jacket pocket, "but the fact remains that it is not our place to pass judgment on the social rights or wrongs of large families, is it?"

"Who's place is it then ?"

Chaucer paused in the process of stuffing his pipe into the pouch. "I beg your pardon?" he asked.

"Who's place is it?" I repeated. "You don't think she actually wanted all those kids, do you? She's just too stupid to realise what's causing them."

"Look, old boy, you're approaching this from quite the wrong end. Mrs Ward has a perfect right to decide these things for herself. It's not our place – "

"Don't tell me. 'Not our place' to interfere. 'Not our place' to tell her she's a stupid cow. No, our place is to dish out the pills and come running every time she snaps her fingers." While I was saying this, I realised that something was annoying me. On the shelves to the left of the fireplace, there was a set of cruddy old books. They were uniformly bound in blue cloth with gilt lettering, and they were called The Golden Principle – A Library of Health and Hygeine. The disturbing thing was that they were not neatly aligned, as shelf furniture of that unreadable nature ought to be. Rather they lay at odd angles, in the manner one would have expected from a frequently-consulted and well-loved work of reference. Now why was that? Surely not even someone as clapped-out and fossilised as Chaucer could have a use for such books as those.

"There's such a thing as good will, you know," Chaucer tried to tell me. That was it. A couple of the volumes stood proud from their fellows, and in the murk behind them, I could just make out the gleam of green glass. So that was where he kept it. "Mrs Ward and her family have been good patients of mine for over twenty years."

"You what?" I had being trying to appear at ease on the chesterfield, but the slippery surface and the generally fucked-up nature of its springs was tending to tip me forwards onto the floor. I sat forwards with my elbows on my knees. "Good patients? What's so flaming good about that lot? "

"Not always considerate, perhaps, but they've stayed with me faithfully for those twenty years."

"You're talking like they're doing you some big favour, Dr Chaucer. Can't you understand? They don't respect you. To them, you're just the mug who gives them what they ask for. Don't you realise, people are laughing at you behind your back? They think you're a soft touch. They think you're so old and out of touch that you don't realise you're being taken for a ride."

At this, Chaucer's face sagged, as if he had just heard that the Chancellor had slapped an extra pound on a bottle of gin. "Well, at least we know now where we stand, don't we?" he said. "It seems we have very different ideas about the function of the family doctor. I have always felt that our role goes beyond that of diagnosis and treatment, that we are here to help in a – moral and spiritual capacity as well – "

The old dodderer had actually gone off into a glassy-eyed reverie this last bit, and he now followed it up with an even-more nauseating load of cant, the purpose of which was to demonstrate what a fucking nice chap old Dr Chaucer thought old Dr Chaucer was. An old lush, perhaps, but at least a kind and lovable old lush, whereas I was nasty and uncaring and cynical, the sort of person about whom little old ladies would say I'm glad he's not *my* doctor. *My* doctor doesn't behave like that, they would say; *my* doctor doesn't think like that.

But the little old ladies would be wrong, you see: he *does*. He may not tell them that he does, but he does, alright.He gets tired and bored and angry, just like me. He gets no more pleasure than I do from fingering a sore arse-hole, sniffing an incontinence pad or paddling through somebody else's vomit. Betcha he doesn't *really* like it when someone phlegs or farts in his face, leaves him with a handful of smegma or squirts pus down his tie. I'm not all that much of a monster. I don't dislike people all that much. Heck no: I don't always dislike *patients*, come to that.

If I could have been bothered, I might have told Chaucer, for example, about that time those bereaved relatives wrote a letter to old Medmay describing me as "saintly". Oh yes;some relatives really like me.There are even *patients* that like me, for Christ's sake.Even Duggie – poor old, confused, psychopathic Duggie – has had his moments of playing a real live doctor; of showing genuine compassion and a real interest in the problems of his patients. The only real difference between us and Luke Devlin is that Luke can keep the act up all the time, and we can't. There are times when we get as tired and ratty and short-tempered as the next man.

"Oh, now I get it" I said, smiling broadly at Chaucer: "You picture yourself as a sort of Healer of the Sick, Comforter of the Aged – except when there happens to be a concert in Bournemouth, of course – evening and weekends only by appointment: no calls after ten pm, please."

"I'm not sure what you – "

"Oh, come on now. I'm not one of your half-witted patients, you know. Let's not pretend. Neither of us really believes that ."

"Believes what ?"

"Neither of us believes that you've got some sort of divine mission to the neurotics and layabouts of the great unwashed British public. It's just a matter of convenience."

He had set down his pipe and was clawing at the arm of the chair. "Convenience? " he squeaked. "How d'you mean – a matter of convenience?"

"The patients tell you what they want, you give it to them. Everybody's happy. No complaints. No nasty scenes. Very nice and convenient."

"You stupid young idiot!" he said suddenly. "Here you are, still wet behind the ears, and you come in here and try to tell me how to run a practice. I've been in this game for forty years, boy! I was running this practice before you were born. You haven't been here more than a month, and you're already throwing your weight around, upsetting the patients. I know things about dealing with patients that you never dreamed of."

"Too true!" I said, "Too true! You can't teach me anything about medicine, that's for sure. The only thing you've learned in forty years is how to skive out of work, how to keep your patients quiet with a load of old balls about 'low blood pressure' and 'rheumatism of the kidneys' – "

"Why! You cheeky – "

"You could be done for misleading advertising, you know that? Pretending this is your practice. Pretending you're the boss. This isn't your practice, old fruit. We're just the skivvies around here. The patients crack the whip and we jump. Oh, except, of course, when we put on our funny Irish voice and pretend not to be who we really are, because we don't want the patients thinking we're skiving out of work, now do we?"

"Well, I don't know. I really don't." He was shaking his head, and I realised that this was the first time I'd heard him admit to not knowing anything. "I just cannot understand a mentality like yours. It's take, take, take with you and to hell with your patients. In my day, it was understood that a doctor had a sense of vocation. We worked eighty and ninety hours a week and were paid nothing for it – "

"More fools you for putting up with it."

"Money, money, money, that's all it is with you."

I stood up, knocking a heavy glass ashtray to the floor. "Don't come the self-righteous bit with me," I said. "There's no question of high principles behind anything you do. The only reason you go on dishing out the pills to your load of skrimshankers is because you're scared that if you don't, they'll up and take their custom elsewhere."

"You wait," he said. "You wait till you've had my experience. Then we'll see. Then we'll find out how your little theories work out."

There was a silence. I half expected him to begin another tirade about how tough it was when he started, and how medicine used to be an art before all these new-fangled drugs took the sport out of it, but Chaucer just took off his spectacles and started to wipe them with a big red silk handkerchief.

"I suppose you'd like me to leave at the end of the six months?" I said, replacing the fallen ashtray on the sofa table. Talbot Hotel, Dorking, I noticed. Could there ever have been a time when this pathetic old wreck would have had enough balls even to steal an ashtray from a hotel lounge?

"It won't be necessary for you to work the full six months."

"Right, alright then," I said, waving my hands about for extra effect. "I'll be leaving at the end of the week, then." I uttered the sentence with a touch of histrionics, leaving time for Chaucer to start licking my boots and begging me to consider.

He tapped his pipe out on the ashtray. "Yes, that would be ideal," he said quietly. The word "ideal" made it sound like too much of a good thing. All I wanted was for him to say it was acceptable.

"Right, that's it. End of the week, then."

Chaucer yawned and scratched his ear. Finding myself without a punchline, I turned and flounced from the room, dislodging the ashtray again as I passed, and catching my toe in the draught-excluder as I went through the door.

Chapter 27

"How d'you mean – he's given you the push?" I asked.

Duggie cleared a space for his empty whisky glass in among the assorted glassware on the table in front of him. "What d'you think I mean? Just that – Fountain's given me the push."

"Not seriously."

"He has," Duggie confirmed, oozing self-pity. "He took me into the Sister's Office in the middle of the list this afternoon, gave me some crap about my work not being satisfactory and gave me a month's notice."

"Ah, come on," I said. "He can't bloody well do that." Over the rim of my glass, I looked around the lounge bar of the Puking Pig. Thursday evenings were never popular here. Friday was your traditional jazz night, when bowler-hatted garage mechanics strummed darky melodies for the benefit of adolescents from the adjacent technical college. Monday was Folk Evening, and to be avoided at the risk of being forced to rub shoulders with bearded men who wore green socks under open-toed sandals. Saturdays, an old woman with a colostomy played Ivor Novello's greatest hits on an out-of tune piano while middle aged couples laughed loudly, spilled beer, discussed the menopause and vainly tried to remember the words. But Thursdays – There was a quite a row coming from the public bar where there was a darts match in progress, but at ten minutes past nine, Duggie and I constituted fifty per cent of the clientele of a sedately silent lounge bar.

"He can, though. I've been into it with the administration," Duggie said. "You see, I never got round to signing a contract. He can do what he bloody well likes."

"What? Just like that? It's primitive, like something out of the nineteenth century." I tried to sound genuinely sympathetic, but other people's problems are never quite as pressing as your own. I suppressed a yawn. Dare I look at my watch? Even though Chaucer and I had agreed to go our separate ways–to pursue our individual careers as solo performers. The group has had artistic differences – I was still on-call, and so had some sort of legal obligation to my patients. Politeness dictated that I should lend

Duggie a sympathetic ear for twenty minutes or so, and then I intended to go home and get my beauty sleep. Tomorrow I've got places to go, people to do.

"Yeah, but that's not all" Duggie winged. "He said that there'd been complaints about me. It was his considered opinion that there was no place for me in gynaecology, and he was afraid he would be - what was it? - 'unable to help me in obtaining another job elsewhere'."

"Bastard," I said obediently. That was all Duggie was after, presumably, a bit of brotherly solidarity.

"Yeah, and you know why he did it, don't you?" Duggie.asked, putting one of his great paws heavily on my shoulder and breathing all over me. God, I hate people when they're drunk.

"Jimmie?"

"Yeah. I'll bet that old bastard fixed it for me because of the other night."

"Aw, no," I said, almost jovially. "Jimmie wouldn't do a thing like that.Honest, he was alright about it after you left, even tried to make jokes about it. He wouldn't hold a grudge like that."

"Like hell he wouldn't. He fixed Winters for your Casualty job, didn't he?"

"Yeah, well, that was different. That really was about my work - I think." Or did I think? I didn't really think. No, I really believed that it had been a straight reprisal over the boat business, and if Jimmie wasn't behind Duggie's dismissal, where had Fountain picked up that expression about there being "no place" for him in gynaecology?

"He's a bloody vindictive old bastard. If Fountain really felt like that about my work, he wouldn't have given me the flaming SHO job in the first place." Duggie shook his head angrily and, surely, those are not tears we see in his eyes? Psychopaths may not give a shit about other people's feelings, but they can still get very upset when their own selfish needs are frustrated. So it says in Bluff Your Way In Psychiatry, anyway.

"Yeah, but supposing he really has had complaints?"

"Well of course he's had bloody complaints, and we know who from, don't we?"

"You serious? You really think Jimmie did it for you?"

"Don't you?"

"Well if he did, if he's chucking you out because of a personal grudge," I said mechanically, "it's unethical apart from anything else." Look Duggie, I'm terribly sympathetic and all that but I've got my own problems, not that you'd be interested. "Why don't you get in touch with the MDS?" I suggested.

"And do what? They could do bugger-all. You think Fountain's going to own up? Yes, sir, sorry, sir, I did give him the boot because Materson told me to? What proof have I got? Consultants always close ranks."

"There must be something you could do."

"Don't bloody bother, Bob. I'm sick to death with this crappy hospital anyway. I'm sick to death with this piddling provincial peeping-tom town. I'm sick to death with bloody medicine. And I've had it up to here with moaning, groaning, bellyaching bloody patients." He stood up and surreptitiously wiped his cheek on the back of his coat sleeve. "It's like being a vet, working in this place. You get about as much intelligent response out of your patients as you would out of a herd of Jersey cows." That last comment was curiously out of place, the words of a man who at least seemed to care what his patients thought about him, but it didn't last long. He went on, "I'm glad I'm out of a job. The country can keep me for a change. Come on, give us your glass, I'll get you another one of those."

I tried to register a genuine protest at this idea, but Duggie was not having it. He rolled up to the adjacent bar, and pushed his way in between the two people sitting there. Being British, they pretended not to notice, carrying on their conversation by craning their necks round the side of him. They were vaguely familiar to me, something to do with low grade hospital administration.

One of them was confirming his extremely-boring-person status by telling the other one, "Wonce yew soyn that chit, it's roit out of your hands. It goes roit through the machinery."

"Piss off!" Duggie told him.

Duggie persuaded the barman to come out of the public bar by shouting "Oi!" several times, gave this man our orders and turned back towards me, leaning unsteadily against the bar and dragging on a battered cigarette. "Why don't you chuck your job in as well?" he suggested in a fairly loud voice. "We could bugger off somewhere and do some grabbing for ourselves for a change."

"Don't worry, I already have," I announced almost gleefully. "I told

Chaucer to stuff his job."

"No! Honest? When?"

"This evening. He was laying down the law about some old bag who was trying to use me as a public convenience, so I told him he could get stuffed."

"Right. That settles it then," he said, clearing a space for the glasses. "We bog off tomorrow. No point hanging around any longer. We get right away from here, make a fresh start." What followed was a series of suggestions for making ourselves rich, which included, in ascending order of improbability: opening up a medical employment agency in London, getting jobs as ship's doctors and shafting up the rich old biddies, setting up an abortion clinic in Ireland, setting up an abortion clinic in Brazil, using our medical qualifications as a cover to smuggle narcotics, running (and possibly acting in) a pornographic film studio in Germany.

"Because only a mug would stay in fucking medicine," Duggie opined finally. "Hospital doctors are divided into two types: you've got your big fat, arrogant bastards and your nasty little creeps who suck up to them." The chit-signers had stopped their conversation and had joined me in listening to what now sounded - in volume, tone and delivery - like a public lecture.

"Next slide, please," I muttered, but what happened next was even better than that. As if to illustrate what Duggie had just been talking about, a prime specimen of each of these two classes of hospital doctor came in through the door. The nasty little creeps were represented by Hauptmann SS C. Henry, and the big fat bastards by Dr M. Washbrook. They had in tow two individuals who were just about recognisable as female - the fat geriatrics woman and a chinless midget who looked desperate enough not to object to being mauled by someone like Henry.

"Hey, looks who's here!" Washbrook leered. "It's the Dirty Doctor and his mate."

"The diagnostic king of the western hemisphere," Henry smirked.

"We was just talking about you, kid."

"What's this I hear about you and Fountain?" the geriatrics woman crowed, making as if to sit at our table.

"Naff off!" Duggie told her.

"Ooh! He's a bit rude, in't he?" Washbrook said. "I don't think we'd better sit near him. Let's go and sit over here."

The great barrel of blubber made an elaborate show of shifting the adjacent table towards the middle of the room, allowing enough space for the geriatrics woman to negotiate a passage between it and the bench seat. Henry, meanwhile, stepped up to the bar and rattled off their orders - orders which he clearly expected to be obeyed without question at all times. The geriatrics woman turned her back on Duggie and went on telling the midget about the fubulous time she'd had with these murvellous people who had a yut parked somewhere in the South of France. Washbrook headed off in the direction of an archaic looking juke box, which dispensed equally-archaic music. Oldies but mouldies. He did all that was required of him, and in a few seconds, a stunted scotsman was singing us a song about a military fellow-countryman of his who wandered far away, this soldier far away. All this had one good effect, which was to stop Duggie talking so loud. Selecting a match from the box on the table, he put it between his lips and tried to strike a cigarette on the side of the packet.

"Arthur Hall Peer Sinew Anchors," he appeared to say. "Jester Puncture Arsenic-ink Reaps." He threw the match onto the floor and attempted to discover which of the glasses in front of him still contained fluid.

The geriatrics woman was now going on to say that she was hoping to have a furtnight in the Buhurmas in Novumber. The music on the juke box changed and Duggie grabbed my wrist. "Listen!" he ordered, cocking his ear and holding the index finger of his other hand erect, a method of calling for silence which he often used before doing one of his artistic farts. "Listen. They're playing our tune!" After a few introductory bars, Duggie joined in with the vocal, loud, off-key and in an accent somewhere between an Irish tenor and a Home Counties cowboy:

Ah-putta yer beeg teets ah leetle clowser teeoo tha foe -ha-ha-ha-hone!

Let's-a preetahend that ah-wee're ah-teeoo gethar awl ah- lee-own!

The critical reaction to this performance varied considerably. The chit-signer altered his position so as to turn his back more squarely on the singer; the barman looked over with a professional eye, trying to gauge the chances of an escalation of the situation; Washbrook grinned and said, "Bloody hell"; Henry smiled inscrutably behind his glasses, giving for a second the impression that he might be a Japanese concentration camp commandant seconded to the SS for lessons in cruelty.

Eef luhv ees ah-bla-heend, make up yur ma-heend

Ay-eeve got to nee-ow...

"Oh Gawd, Rossiter's pissed out of his mind," the geriatrics woman said. Which indeed he was, although whatever effect being pissed might have had on his performance in other fields, it certainly had no inhibitory effect on his ability to make a noise. With a stamina born of much practice in the back of rugby coaches, he carried on through the rest of the unintentionally-altered tune, occasionally stumbling over the intentionally-altered words, and having to repeat a line or so. By the time the beeg teets bit had come round for the third time, the geriatrics woman piped up, "Oh, for crying out loud, put a sock in it, Rossiter!"

"I'll put a sock in you in a minute!" came the riposte from the king of repartee and wit.

"Yes, look, Rossiter," Henry said, "try to remember who you are. You are a doctor, you know. Or at least, you ought to be."

"Faark off!" Duggie said. A year ago, Duggie was an anti-social, loud-mouthed, hard-swearing, hard-drinking, woman-shagging medical student, and everybody loved him. If he'd charged into the bar with a college scarf round his neck and a stuffed gorilla under his arm, they've have rolled in the aisles as the flour bombs flew through the air. He sits a couple of exams, and suddenly they expect him to undergo an overnight conversion like Paul of Tarsus, Prince Hal and Simon frigging Sparrow all rolled into one. There's no place in mythology for an anti-social, loud-mouthed, hard-swearing, hard-drinking, woman-shagging doctor, which is a pity, because they do exist.

"You ought to be setting an example," Henry was imprudent enough to go on. "You're not a child any more. You ought to be a responsible member of society now."

"Oh, I awt to be, awt I? That's what I awt to be, is it, Cedric old fruit?" Duggie said, accurately mimicking Henry's clipped northern-posh vowels. "Of course, what I awt to be, if I tried hard enough, is a shit-faced little creep with roaring faecal glossitis from the number of influential backsides I've been polishing with my tongue. Cedric, old man, old man. Where the hell did you get an artsy-fartsy name like that from, Cedric? Christ! Your parents must have known you were going to turn into a four-eyed, half-brained, brown-nosed cock-sucker."

"Hey, just bloody watch it, kid," Washbrook warned.

"It's alright. Leave him," Henry said calmly. "We're not going to have to put up with him for much longer. The Dirty Doctor's been given his marching orders."

Whoops, you shouldn't have said that Cedric old son, I thought. The one thing you mustn't do is make Duggie angry. You wouldn't like him when he's angry. I covered my eyes and grimaced as Duggie leapt to his feet. "Hey! Just a minute! Just one flaming minute! Now I get it," he cried. "That's it! You were there, weren't you? You and that shitface Materson. It was you, wasn't it?" With this, he had managed to propel himself through the few feet that separated our tables, and had hauled Henry bodily from his chair, shaking him by the scruff of the neck, like a terrier with a terrified, bespectacled rat. "It was you, you stinking four-eyed little fart sniffer!"

The pressure of the carefully-knotted medical school tie around his windpipe put any sort of reply from Henry temporarily out of the question. When Duggie did slacken his grip, Henry's face was blue and his tone conciliatory, which was understandable in the situation of being half-strangled by a totally-pissed fifteen and a half stone madman.

"Look!" he spluttered. "I had nothing whatsoever to do with Jimmie and Fountain – "

"Jimmie and Fountain! So it was that old bugger! You two did it, didn't you?" Duggie demanded, shaking Henry so that his eyes bulged and his teeth rattled. Duggie's face had become red and suffused, his chest was heaving and he was snorting through his nostrils. "You fixed Fountain for me!" he snarled.

"No! No! I had nothing to do with it," Henry bleated, feebly trying to shield his lower body from impending attack. "Look, please don't hit me. I've got a – lot of crowns, and I'm not very good at – "

"Materson – rang – Fountain – didn't he?" Duggie persisted.

"Well, yes, he – he said he might give him a ring, but I don't know whether he actually – "

Duggie didn't wait to hear any more. "You – dirty – shitty – filthy – little – bastard!" he screamed, accentuating each of the last five words by bringing part of his anatomy forcefully into contact with parts of Henry's anatomy. These were in approximate order: fist to nose, elbow to mouth, foot to groin and then, as he dropped, side of hand to back of neck and knee to chin. It was an impressive display of demolition. Henry crumpled and fell to the floor among discarded teeth and the remains of his SS spectacles, where he lay whimpering and sobbing softly.

"You tell that big fat bastard to stay out of my way!" Duggie yelled, giving him a contemptuous kick, "otherwise he'll get the same treatment."

This announcement brought the barman scurrying out of the public bar where he had retired, over-optimistically mistaking Duggie for the usual sort of lounge-bar drunk. "Bloody hell!" he shouted. "Wha's going on here?"

"It's him!" the geriatrics woman shouted, indicating Duggie, just in case a giant with bleeding knuckles, standing menacingly over a battered body and swearing strange oaths might be mistaken for an innocent bystander. "It's him. He's drunk! He's drunk!"

"I am hell as like drunk!" Duggie shouted, shaking his damaged fist and giving Henry another kick in the balls. "I am hell as like bloody drunk!"

Henry, his mouth full of blood and tooth fragments, had nothing clever to say on the subject. Washbrook had indicated an unwillingness to participate in any of the rough stuff by withdrawing to the corner behind the juke box, where he was joined by the geriatrics woman, but the barman kept coming forwards, crouching and swinging his arms like an exasperated gorilla. "Now look here, you." You don't realise just how big Duggie is until you get close up to him. As Duggie came forwards to meet the challenge, the barman began to back away, still uttering fighting words. "Watch it, mate. I've done karate, you know."

"Wow! Bhhig deal!"

"Don't take liberties with me. I know how to handle myself – "

Duggie chased him twice round the room. "Come on then, chum. You want bother?"

"You'll get bother! You'll get bother! I'll get the police onto you!"

"Great! Wonderful! Go on, then!" At that point, the bead-wearing midget slipped out of her chair and insinuated one of her legs between Duggie's ankles. Duggie tottered – mainly from surprise and the effects of Scottish distillery – and slumped backwards over a table. With a grunt of triumph, the barman leapt on top of him and seized him in a stranglehold.

"Somebody call the police!" he shouted.

"Come on then!" Duggie shouted to me. "Get the bastard off me!" I hesitated, then lurched forwards, grabbing the barman by his gristly neck.

"Gehhd orf me! I'm warning you!" the barman snarled, making as if to take a bite out of my hands.

"Let go of him!"

The midget had taken off one of her sandals and was using it as a hammer on my shins. "Drunken hooligans!" she screamed. "Drunken hooligans!"

I got my foot against her flat chest and thrust her away from me, forcing an agonised "Ooaarh!" from her and scattering beads across the floor. Shrugging off my feeble hold, the barman took hold of a fistful of Duggie's hair and began to bang his head against the table. "Teach you!" Bonk! "Come in here - " Bonk! "Start smashing - Bonk! " - place up - grooaargh !" This last expression was a cry of pain as Duggie brought his knee up and caught him in the crutch. He doubled up on the floor, grasping at his beer belly, and Duggie was on his feet again.

"Let's get out of this bloody place!" he shouted, and, as a parting gesture, he grabbed the edge of the table next to him and overturned it, bringing down a cascade of empty glasses, bottles, beer and tomato juice.

We pushed past the chit-signers and made for the door. "Here, just a minute! "one of them shouted, as if a last-minute appeal to reason was going to halt Duggie's progress. In a few seconds we were outside the pub and inside my car.

I put the headlights on full beam, revving noisily and pointed the nose of the vehicle at the spotlit figures of Washbrook and the barman. Washbrook was straining his vocabulary to the full, shouting out not only things like bloody daft and bugger, but trying his hand at one or two trisyllabic jobs. Suddenly he realised I was coming at him and he made a desperate last-second dive for safety into the hedge that surrounded the car park.

Duggie was chortling away and, as we drove past, he leaned out of the window and gave a V-sign to the world in general. "Get stuffed!"

The barman, red-faced and short-winded, was after us, his arms flailing like a windmill. "Don't think you - get away with this! You wait! I know where you work! Police'll hear about this - I got your number!"

He tripped on the uneven pavement and Duggie gave a great hoot of delight. "Yah! Serves you bloody well right, you pot-bellied wanker!" he jeered. When we were out of the car-park he gave a loud guffaw and said, "Here, let's go and do the Nurses' Home."

"What you mean – 'do' the Nurses' Home?"

"Raid it – smash the place up a bit."

That, strangely enough, was a relief. Duggie's last drunken stunt involving the Nurses Home had been to climb out onto the flat roof of the three storey building and pee on the heads of people passing below. "Christ! Haven't you done enough for one evening?"

"No, come on, we could have a bit of fun. Go and scare the shit out of some of the old birds up there."

"Oh, come on, now," I said, but without thinking I had turned into the Hospital Grounds and was heading towards Bleak House.

"Hang on a bit, though," Duggie said."Do you see what I see?"

We were passing the Private Patient Wing, and Duggie nodded in the direction of the car park. There, nestling beneath a row of what were possibly elm trees, stood the steel blue Daimler with its personalised 'JMM' number plates.

"Jimmie's car!" Duggie said excitedly. "The old bastard's working late at the money factory tonight."

"Oh no!" I said. "Let's get out of here."

"Oh yes!" he said, gripping my knee hard so that it really hurt. "We'll teach the bastard."

"No, come on, this is getting serious. Anyway, look, you don't know it was him."

"I don't give a damn whether it was him or not. It's the principle of the thing. Complacent bastard. I'll wipe the smirk of his face." Before I could stop him, he was out of the car and staggering noiselessly into the car park. After a moment's hesitation, I got out of my car and followed, cowering in the shadow of the trees and watching as Duggie moved up to the side of the Daimler. He felt in his pockets and there was a glint of light as he produced a murderous-looking pen-knife from his pocket and applied it with surprising skill to the door lock. With a grunt, he forced the door open.

"For Christ's sake, Duggie. Leave the bloody thing alone and let's go."

"Naff off!" He slipped into the driver's seat and his head disappeared below the level of the windscreen. I could hear him tinkering about with the wiring under the dashboard.

"Oh, God! He only needs to walk out here – "

Duggie's head re-appeared after what seemed like an hour. "He's got some sort of anti-theft device on it. I can't get it started."

"For Christ's sake, leave it alone then."

"No fear! He's not getting away with it as easily as that." I could hear him swearing and grunting until, with a metallic wrench, he twisted the car radio from its mounting and yanked it out of the car. "Right, Mr Jimmie Materson!" said Duggie, brandishing the radio over his head. "Fix my job for me, would you?" Biting his lower lip, he pitched the radio with all his strength into the trunk of the adjacent tree, where it shattered into a heap of wires and transistors. There was a sudden scurry from behind the trees – hospital stray cats, bolting for cover – but it was enough to send shivers down my spine.

"There's somebody coming!"

"Balls!" said Duggie, after a quick look round, and then he was back inside the car, ripping through the leather upholstery with his pen-knife.

"You bloody madman!" I called. "I'm going! You're off your head! You don't know what you're bloody doing."

"Whassa matter with you? You think you owe him a favour or something?" Duggie emerged from the car, discarding handfuls of seat stuffing. "Great fat bastard!" he yelled, kicking out wildly at the headlights.

"Right. That's enough!"

"Not yet, it isn't. I'll slash his tyres for him." But then he seemed to change his mind and started scoring deep grooves in the paint work with the point of his knife.

"Come on, give us a hand!" he called.

"To do what, for God's sake?"

"Get behind the thing and give it a shove!" He had released the hand brake and was pushing on the doorframe. "Come on!"

I found myself behind the car with my shoulder to the boot, helping Duggie to push it the short distance to the car park entrance. Now we were at the top of a slope, and the job became much easier. Our pace quickened as Duggie steered the car to the right, onto the steep hill that led down towards the laundry building. There was no effort at all now. The car was running under the force of gravity, and our main problem was keeping pace with it.

"Right, let it go!" Duggie shouted, and with one final shove, the Daimler accelerated away from us down the ever-steepening slope. At the bottom, the road curved sharply to the left, and the fifteen foot drop straight ahead was protected only by a corroded wire fence. "Ge – ronimo!" The Daimler, sweeping aside the flimsy barrier, nose-dived with a resounding crash into the courtyard below. The car spun, did a somersault and ended up on its roof a few feet from the laundry door.

"Fan – bloody – tastic!" shouted Duggie.

"Now let's get the hell out of here." I could already hear voices from the direction of the laundry, and a geezer in a green beret and a white boiler-suit was hobbling over from the neighbouring incinerator building as fast as his gammy leg would carry him.

Duggie was laughing all the way back to the car. "Did you see it?" he asked. "Did you see it hit the ground? Ker- chumpff!"

"Get in the fucking car," I growled.

I was fumbling for my keys when a familiar voice became audible. "Yehhs . . . wad I always say it – prostatectomy is the operation that separates the men from the boys. The boys can do it – ahur ahur."

"Yes, very true, Jim."

Even in the dark, Jimmie's little round head was easily recognisable, contrasting sharply with Winstanley's crop of silver-grey hair. As they came round the corner, Jimmie almost walked into me. "Oh, 's you, Fowler. What're you doing here? Been to see your private patients, have you?" Jimmie's idea of a joke.

"We were just leaving."

"Oh, I see. Who's this? Oh, 's your anarchist friend. Wha's he been doing? Planting bombs in the Private Patient Wing or something?"

"No, ravishing the decadent bourgeois private nursing staff," Duggie said.

"Oh yes, hmm – Well, goodnight to you."

"Goodnight, sir."

I jumped into the car and flung open the passenger door. "Now get in and shut up!"

"No, I want to stay and watch."

"Get in the frigging car or I'll go without you."

Slowly and deliberately, he climbed in, and just before I drove off, I could hear Jimmie's voice saying, "Tha'ss funny . . . I could have sworn I left it here."

Chapter 28

The smell of the glue factory is one of the first things the casual visitor notices about Commercial Street, but we residents, we Hogdowners, get inured to that sort of thing. Hogdown is actually mentioned in the Domesday Book, when it had 5 hides of cultivated land with 32 acres of meadow, worked by 41 freemen and bondsmen. There were 8 ploughs and 2 mills in the village, and the true value of the whole parish had increased since the Conquest from 60 shillings to 100 shillings. Nowadays, it's probably not worth as much as that. It's an extremely undesirable suburb of Breckleigh, a place where joke patients live, and that's why I live there. You get a lot more for your money in Hogdown.

I drove slowly and with the exaggerated caution of a man who has had a few along the bit of Commercial Street that leads off the Breckleigh Road near the abattoir. The coming of the railways had brought a brief period of prosperity to the area, and Commercial Street consisted of four-storied terraced properties, complete with servant accommodation. The ground floors of many of these properties now housed shops of the less fashionable kind - dealers in second hand goods, purveyors of jerk-off material, West Indian grocers, Asian clothing shops, that sort of stuff, while prostitutes scurried like rabbits at all hours of the day and night into their burrows in the basements.

I found a parking space and led a not entirely incurious Duggie past a hunting pack of Brummie tarts to the door of number 87. Three laboured flights of stairs later, Duggie let himself down unsteadily into a basket-weave chair and looked critically around the room. "How much does he charge you for this place, then?" he wanted to know.

"Not a lot", I said, but still more than the place was worth.

"If you want my opinion, it's a dump."

"You might be right," I said, not knowing whether to feel pleased or angry at this assessment, "but I'd make the most of it if I were you. You could soon be a guest of Her Majesty, helping her law enforcement agents with their enquiries." Duggie made one or two alternative suggestions of ways in which Her Majesty's law enforcement agents might spend their time.

"Look, when are you going to get it into your thick nut?" I said. "This isn't the wolf cubs we're talking about. These boys don't mess about, you know. Even Constable Plod is going to be able to work out who stuffed Henry and fucked Jimmie's car up for him. We'll be lucky to get away without being locked up."

"Just let either of those shite hawks go anywhere near the sodding rozzers, and I'll fix them."

"Oh, for Christ's sake, grow up, Duggie. Or sober up, or do something. Here, d'you want a coffee?"

"Just as you like."

"Don't let me force you."

I went out into the kitchen, reorganised the pile of dirty washing-up in the sink, booted a couple of cardboard boxes in the general direction of the pedal bin and set about doing battle with the dreaded back-firing gas stove. Above the noise this necessarily created, I heard the telephone ring. I panicked briefly, thinking it was the police, but did they really operate in that way? My second reaction was to remember that I was supposed to be on-call for Chaucer's practice. When I got to the phone in the bedroom, Duggie was already speaking on the extension in the sitting room.

"Wehhll, now. Howdee doodee dair, baas!" Duggie was saying in a booming Nigger Minstrel voice.

"Hello? Who's there?" Chaucer's voice.

"He – llo dair! Who dat dair sayin who dis here?"

"Look, is that Breckleigh 28281?

"Suuure is, baas, Hmm mm!"

"Then may I speak to Dr Fullen, please?"

"Can ah take dee baas a message, sah?"

Chaucer paused and then pressed on as though having a perfectly normal conversation with someone. I could sympathise. After all, when somebody buggers about on the phone, it takes a lot of nerve to accuse them of buggering about – there's always a chance that you might be wrong.

"Well, yes, I suppose so. Can you remind him he's supposed to be on call this evening? He's not been answering his phone. I've had to answer three calls since nine o'clock."

"Ooh! Tough luck, sah!" Duggie cried. "Ah bet yuz ain't bin out to see none ob dem?"

"As a matter of fact, I've been out to see two of them, but I'm damned if I'm going out any more on my evening off."

"Oooh, bass, dat sure am tough! Real tough titty! Watcha want me ta do about it?"

There was another silence. "Look, I want to speak to Dr Fullen," Chaucer said finally.

"No, sah, de beeg whaart doctor cannot come to de phone jus' now."

"Why not?"

"Dee big whaart doctor am indisposed, baas."

"Look, is that you, Fullen? Putting on that silly voice?"

"Ooh, no baas, diss am li'l black Rossitah. Ah am dee beeg whaart doctah's faithful serbant boy, sah."

"Good Lord Almighty!" Chaucer said. "What are doctors coming to? No sense of responsibility – "

"Hey, looka heah, baas, aah gotta message for you from de beeg whaart doctah."

"Oh?"

"Him say – you stick you job up you ass hole – he ain't doin' no more night calls for you!" and with this, Duggie slammed the phone down and started hooting with laughter. "Silly old bastard! 'What on earth are doctor's coming to?'" he mimicked. "Silly sod!" He started to do a Zulu dance around the room, chanting "Zoombah! Zoombah! Zoombah! Zoombah!"

"You're a twit, Duggie," I called from the bedroom. "He can report me for not answering the telephone when I'm on call."

Duggie stuck his head round the bedroom door. "I thought you told me that old biddy of his used to do some of his night calls for him?"

"Yeah, I know, but – "

"Well, if he tries anything, you just threaten to report him for that. That'll shut him up."

"Well, I don't know. I don't like it." I pushed brusquely past him and went back into the kitchen. From there, I could hear Duggie unashamedly nosing around the bedroom, opening drawers, sliding open doors, all the while singing quietly to himself - some catchy little ditty about not wanting to join the army, not wanting to go to war. When he'd quite finished, he made his way back into the lounge. "Put a record on?" he called.

"If you like. Not too loud. The landlord lives downstairs." Using the handle of a fork, I whisked a carton of sour milk into the plughole in the sink. A week-old chunk of black pudding - the most un-Kosher substance known to man - floated to the surface and then disintegrated, and the glutinous purple liquid slurped noisily away. There is no doubt that the place lacks a woman's touch. As I set about pouring hot water into mugs, the turgid sentimentality of a thirties dance band began to filter through from the sitting room. The saxophones faded and a girl crooner started to sing in a Mid-Atlantic accent about the time the moon got in her eyes. Not my sort of music at all, but it was a record Avalon had bought me for my birthday. She had even remarked on the "lovely" lyrics of this particular track as an illustration of her theme for that evening which was, if I remember right, this house believes that they don't write them like this any more.

"Here y'are," I said. "You're honoured, you've got the one with the handle."

Duggie took the mug of cheap coffee and set it down on the carpet next to his chair. On his knee, he had the record sleeve, and on the back of that sleeve, in flowing fibre-tip, was a very personal message in the hand-writing of Miss Avalon Death. Talk about invasion of privacy. This didn't seem to bother Duggie too much. "Snap" he said, holding it up for me to see.

I looked at the thing silently for a few seconds. "What? Exactly the same?"

Duggie nodded. "Word for word," he said. For some reason, this made me feel angrier with Duggie than with Avalon. Duggie seemed to sense this. "Look, I told you, didn't I? She's not worth it."

"Not to you, maybe."

"Do you really have to find out the hard way?" he asked. "Do you want me to give you the rest of the stuff that went with it? The stuff about how every time she hears this song - " He paused, open mouthed, and raised his hands like a conductor, waiting for me to join in the chorus.

" – it reminds her of the day we met?" I asked experimentally.

Duggie grinned and nodded. "It reminds me of the day we met," he mimicked in a good falsetto. "And they're such lovely words, aren't they, don't you agree? They make me feel – "

" – all gooey and fluttery inside, like I was – "

" – a little, innocent schoolgirl on her first date," Duggie said, and he gave a triumphant, "Ha! You see! What did I tell you?"

"Bloody hell!" I said. "The cow – "

Duggie leaned forwards and patted me on the knee. "Good lad," he said. "You're learning." He raised the mug to his lips and drank noisily. "Did she give you one of those photographs as well?"

"What, the full-colour studio job, the one with the scarlet dress?"

"Bet she's got a cupboard full of the things at home."

I thought for a second and asked, "Lock of hair?"

"Yep,lock of hair, wrapped in tissue paper," Duggie nodded. "Done that one. Tick."

"You know what?" I said. "I think she missed her vocation in life. She ought to have been a man."

And that started it. That was the signal, the agreement between us that it was OK to talk Avalon. I've never been a great one for Boys Nights Out, but I got a real vicarious sexual thrill as we swapped Avalon-screwing stories: my second-hand bookshop for Duggie's church porch, my Nurses Home bathroom for Duggie's knee-trembler in a public swimming bath, my blow- job in a hospital lift for Duggie's operating theatre –

"Bloody hell!" I whistled admiringly at that last one. "What – you mean – lithotomy poles and all the rest of it?"

Duggie narrowed his eyes and nodded. "Lithotomy poles – vaginal speculum, you name it."

"Blud-dee-hell!"

"Yeah, well it was two in the morning and the night staff were all having a crafty kip," Duggie went on."There was always a chance they might have walked in on us, of course." He raised the mug of what was now stone-cold coffee to his lips. "Otherwise it wouldn't have appealed to her, would it?"

I was just about to ask him for his views on something I had long suspected about Avalon: that she would not have been in the least averse to a) going to bed with another woman, and b) having a kinky threesome with two men, but before I could phrase the appropriate question, there was a loud hammering on the door downstairs. A voice was shouting something at us from way down in the street. "Bloody hell, it's the police!" I choked.

Now we could make out the words of what was being shouted. They were, "Doctor! Doctor! Help! Come quick! There's been an accident."

"You and your bloody cops!" Duggie hissed. "Quick! Put the light out. Pretend we're not in!" He leapt to his feet, throwing up the light switch and yanking the plug of the music machine from its socket. The room slurred into a dark, eerie silence.

"Doc – tor! Doc – tor!" we could hear above the hammering.

"It won't hurt just to have a quick word – " I began.

"Stay where you are! Keep quiet, otherwise they'll bring your sodding landlord up to find us."

"Don't you think we ought to – "

"Use your common sense, man. What's in it for us? What the hell's the ambulance for?"

"But the hospital's eight miles away. And supposing nobody's called them?"

"Shut up and keep quiet!"

The hammering continued, and the voice started up again ,"Doc – tor! Doc – tor!"

The landlord had opened the outside door and was shouting up the stairs in his Bombay accent, "Hello? Hello? Dr Fullen, can you come here quickly, please?" I could hear him start to mount the stairs.

"I'm going, even if you're not." I stumbled across the darkened room and switched the lights on. My bag was by the door. I grabbed it and stepped out onto the landing.

"OK, I'm coming!"

Halfway down the stairs, the landlord breathed Prawn Vindaloo all over me. The man was like an Air-wick in reverse, you could tell which rooms he'd been in. "Man here says there's been an accident, Dr Fullen. Says he needs your help right away."

"You're a doctor, arencha?" asked a little man I had never seen before.

"Yes, what's the trouble?"

"Quick! One of the trucks has come off the rails and run into the houses on the end there. There's somebody trapped inside."

I thought for a moment. Tell little man to phone ambulance. Tell little man am intoxicated and off duty. Fall down on floor shouting "Ouch: there goes my Achilles tendon again". Tell little man to bugger off and mind own frigging business. No, there was no way out of this. "Alright. Where is it?"

"Just on the end of the road here. Good job I knew where you lived."

"Yeah, bloody marvellous." We clattered down the front steps and out into the street, then I trotted along behind him until we reached the bend in the road. From a hundred yards away, we could see it all.

My first reaction was amazement that there was so much activity going on. A Bingo Hall had just finished trading for the night, and was still discharging its customers into the street. Instead of making their usual way home, they had come upon an unexpected bonus, and they now hung about to form what was almost a crowd near the railway bridge. This grey metal structure, advertising the worst garage in town, spanned the road, towering over the houses. The orange street lighting and the revolving blue lamp of a police car lit up the scene that they had all stopped to gape at. A goods train had managed to get derailed on the bridge, and a single coal truck had slipped sideways down the grassy embankment, demolishing the end wall of the little terraced house by the bridge. What scared the shit out of me, though, was a second coal truck, which was lying on its side halfway up the muddy embankment. Any sort of disturbance looked as though it would upset the equilibrium and send the thing sliding down the twenty feet or so onto the wrecked building beneath.

The little man kept pushing people out of the way, pointing at my black bag and telling people I was a doctor. This announcement provoked a storm of public apathy. So-whatness registered on the faces of the Bingo players, but a path seemed to open up for me and I found myself getting carried ever nearer to the action. By the wall, two public employees of the collar-feeling variety were discussing the best way of getting down into the wrecked house.

The climbing of the ten-foot wall onto the embankment seemed to be the first step, but there was some debate as to how this ought to be accomplished. The larger and less athletic-looking of the men said they ought to wait for the fire brigade to get there, and at that precise moment, an ambulance pulled in to the side of the road and the two crewmen jumped out.

"Well, well, how's it going then, doc?" the ambulance driver asked me. I had never seen him before in my life. How the hell did he know who I was? "What you doing here, anyway?"

While I explained what I was doing there, his mate was being hoisted up to the top of the wall. Casting a wary eye up at the unstable coal-truck, this weedy youth crouched down and then began to slither down the bank, disappearing from our view as he entered the wrecked house. I watched the police herding the onlookers back to the safety of the far side of the road, and thought what lucky bastards onlookers were. One particularly tall onlooker was allowed through though, and it took a few seconds to recognise the flat northern vowels of a man who was saying "It's alright. Let me through. I'm a doctor." Oh bloody hell, not bloody Rossiter.

The little grey haired man by my side grabbed his sleeve. "Here ; you're Doctor Fountain, arencha? You looked after my wife in hospital once."

"No, I am not Dr Fountain, thank you so much. I have no desire to be Dr Fountain. I wouldn't be Dr Fountain even if you kissed – "

"You remember my wife – Mrs Beech? She's crippled with the arthur-itis in her knees. It's her that's trapped in there."

"Yeah,bad luck for her, that."

"She was in bed, you see, crippled with the arthur-itis. I'd only just gone up the road for a packet of fags from the machine when it happened – "

The weedy youth re-appeared at the top of the wall. "You can get down there, but it's difficult. She's trapped by her legs. They're bleeding a lot."

"That ought to cure her arthritis, then," Duggie said.

"Look," I said, " I would deem it a great favour if you would kindly bugger off somewhere. Go and give yourself up to the police or something. You're making me feel sick."

"What you want to do about it, Doc?" the ambulance driver asked.

"Is she still conscious?"

"I'll say she is. Moaning and screaming the place down."

"I suppose we'd better give her something." I fumbled in the drawers of my bag and extracted a syringe. With shaking hands, I filled it with morphine. "Have you ever given an injection before?" I called up to the weedy youth.

"No, but I'll have a go, if you like."

The ambulance driver gave a slow, meaningful shake of the head. "He's not covered for that, you know, doc. Besides, she'll need a drip as well, won't she?"

"A drip?"

"Hang on." He strode over to the back of the ambulance and came back with a drip set and needle.

"Does that mean I've got to do it?"

"Well, there is nobody else, is there? I'm not a trained paramedic, and John here's only been in the job three months."

I looked around me and saw that people were looking at me. Duggie was smoking a cigarette, slightly unsteady on his feet, and smiling benignly. The rest of them – policemen, ambulance men, bingo players, Mr Beech, an old man with a dog that regularly peed on my doorstep – they were all looking at me, waiting for me to volunteer, waiting for me to do a Luke Devlin.

"Um – You're quite sure – You don't think he could – ?"

"No chance, Doc."

"Well, then, I suppose – "

"Here y'are then. You'll need these as well," he said, slapping a couple of elasticated tourniquets into my hands.

"Hang on a minute, though. Don't you think we should – " Three or four pairs of hands suddenly seized hold of me and thrust me high into the air. Acute schizophrenia supervened. I was now outside my body, watching this luckless idiot being shoved up the side of a wall.

"Here y'are, Doc, give us those here." The weedy youth pulled the drip set and the rest of it from my hands and seized hold of my wrists, helping to lift my limp, unwilling body onto the wet, sooty grass. I lay on my belly, winded and terrified. I can remember wondering whether Luke Devlin ever went round comforting the aged in situations quite as ludicrous as this, or whether he had more sense. Trying to drag in a lungful of air, I staggered to my feet and looked down at the sea of faces. My head swam and my knees turned to jelly.

"Alright, then doc? Here's your stuff. She's down there."

The youth pointed down into the hollow. The first thing I noticed was the first coal truck, and I registered with some amazement just how big it was. This truck was lying half inside the kitchen at the back of the house where it had battered a great hole in the side wall. A dividing wall had collapsed onto the invalid bed in the sitting room. The lights in the house were out, but in the yellow sodium lights from the railway line you could make out the torn wallpaper, the crooked pictures, the smashed, cheap furniture, even the remains of a meal still lying on the bedside table. To cap it all, there was a steady drizzle of rain. It was all too sad. It took a few seconds for my eyes to pick out the grey-hair and the pain-lined features of Mrs Beech, looking up at me and bleating like a lamb. Her legs were invisible beneath a pile of rubble, and there was a lot of the red stuff about.

"You coming down with me?" I asked.

The youth craned his neck to look down into the hollow again. Mrs Beech lay directly in the path of the second coal truck. Not only that, the upper storey of the house was sagging and seemed to have no visible support. "Nah, better not," he said casually. "I'll stay up here and pass messages on."

I took a deep breath. It was now or never. From the observation post inside my head, I watched the bloke all this was happening to take a hold of the tools of his trade and start to stagger down the bank. Just then, a warning shout issued from the mouths of the Bingo players below. A fresh shower of coal dust was raining down the bank. The second coal-truck was starting to slip. Uttering a terrified yell, I threw myself onto the grass and curled up in a foetal position.

"It's alright" I heard a voice quite close to me say. "It's stopped again." I uncovered my eyes. We were still alive. "Alright, doc? Down you go, then."

"Oh, bloody hell!" I called over the pounding of blood in my ears. "I've trodden on the syringe. It's busted. I can't use it!"

"Just get the drip up, then!" the ambulance driver shouted up at me. "Get the drip up and put the tourniquets on."

I looked up again at the truck with its massive wheels and undercarriage. The sheer size of it terrified me. I swear the thing appeared to be sliding very slowly down the muddy bank. I was rooted to the spot.

Fear rushed from my pounding chest down into my jellied, useless, legs. It was like standing on a high diving board, unable to get up the courage to take those few simple steps to the edge. My brain simply wouldn't let my legs move. I was stuck.

"That truck's coming down!" I shouted urgently. "Look, it's slipping!"

"Don't be so bloody daft!" the ambulance man shouted. "Go on, get on with it!"

"Why don't we wait for the fire brigade?" I called, desperately. Anything, anything so long as it put off the moment where I had to put my head on the block.

"Go on, Doc. Get in there. This is your chance for a medal," the weedy youth said encouragingly, and he started to push me forwards by the shoulder.

"Yeah, go on, get in there, doc," the ambulanceman shouted. "You know you've got to do it, don't you?"

"Not me!" I shouted suddenly, and I shook my shoulder to dislodge the youth's hand. "It's not my job. Get some other mug; you're not getting me down there!"

"Go on!"

"No! I'm not going down there. It's too bloody dangerous!" I started to crawl back towards the edge of the wall. "Come on, get me out of here!" I shouted.

"Oh, for Christ's sake – " the ambulance driver began, but just at that moment, there was a scuffle from below. Duggie had leapt up at the side of the wall and was clambering up towards me with the same agility and shoulder-rolling determination that had almost made him a schoolboy rugby international. There was an excited murmur from the crowd. Round his neck, Duggie was wearing my stethoscope, flying like battlecolours to proclaim to the world that This Was A Doctor. Between his teeth he was gripping a loaded syringe, and as he fought his way up the rough brickwork, he looked like one of those pirates shinning up the rigging with a cutlass in his jaws. Egged on by shouts from the crowd, the policemen stepped forwards, grabbed his legs and thrust him further up towards me.

"Go on, doc!" somebody shouted. "You show 'em how to do it."

The murmur from the crowd had grown into a spontaneous outburst of encouragement and admiration. One or two people were clapping their hands excitedly.

In a few gymnastic seconds, Duggie was up on the grass bank, swaying gently on his feet and breathing noisily through his nose. "Give me those bloody things, you useless pillock!" he muttered, grabbing the drip set and the tourniquets from my quivering hands. "Now where the hell is the silly old bag?"

"Down there, Doc." The youth pointed down into the gathering murk below us.

There was a loud creaking and groaning from the truck further up the bank, a warning shout from the crowd below.

"No, Duggie!" I pleaded. "No, please don't! Look, the truck's on the move. You'll get yourself killed!"

"Piss off, you pathetic wimp!" he shouted and, shaking off my restraining hand, he crept down the bank like a commando under fire. He clambered over the pile of rubble and vaulted down into the shattered room. Down in the hollow, I saw him kneel beside the mutilated body of Mrs Beech. He lifted her shoulders gently from the bed and cradled her in his arms.

"Alright now, my old darling, I'm a doctor," I could hear him saying. Tenderly, he lifted the hank of grey hair from her face and stroked her lined cheek with the back of his free hand. "Don't you worry. You're safe now," he said. "Won't be long now, and we'll soon have you out of here."

Mrs Beech had stopped her moaning. She extended a trembling arm out towards him, as though she had seen a vision. "Doctor - oh, Doctor - Oh, God bless you, Doctor," she said.

Another rumble from above, and this time the screech of tortured metal. In a shower of coal dust, I pressed myself flat against the earth, closing my eyes tight and holding my breath. I was aware of something enormously heavy accelerating its way down the bank, and then a booming metallic clang and the huge roar of collapsing masonry. The ground beneath me seemed to come to life for a few seconds, and then there was a silence.

I looked up. The truck had disappeared, and below us a cloud of coal dust concealed a silent heap of rubble, splintered wood and twisted metal.

Chapter 29

Avalon rolled over onto her back and pulled the sheet up to her chin. "I just feel so – I don't know – so contented, so right," she said. She smiled at me – a wide, uncomplicated, matey smile. "I've been such a complete and utter fool, haven't I?"

"Oh no," I lied, "just unlucky, that's all." I kissed her on the nose. Some of the things your mouth has to do just to keep your prick happy.

"I have, though, haven't I?" she asked with a hint of real concern in her voice. "But you felt it too, just now, didn't you? You know what I mean about us?" She raised herself onto one elbow and looked down on me as I lay beside her. The sheet dropped away from her and I couldn't resist a quick peep. Nipples like dinner plates. I'd almost forgotten.

"Yes, I did," I said. If you really want the truth, sugar, that wasn't the greatest demonstration of screwing you've ever put on, but I suppose any poke with someone who looks like you is intrinsically worth having.

I did everything right – no leaping on her and ripping her knickers off as soon as she came through the door or anything like that. It had all been done very tastefully. We even talked to each other first. After all, Duggie not yet cold, it seemed the least we could do. So that's what we did, we talked about Duggie. We talked about him all the way through an awkward meeting at the flat, through a stilted car journey to the crank restaurant and most of the way through a meal of overpriced fartfood.

At first, I thought Avalon was going to ruin things by making a big thing out of playing the young widow. She was so self-pitying, so bloody reverential when she talked about Duggie, you'd have thought it was Beethoven or Winston Churchill who'd been playing hide the salami with her. I waited for a particularly maudlin bit of St Duggie the Martyr stuff, until the corners of her eyes were really beginning to glisten, and then I put my arm round her shoulder. "Death isn't so bad," I told her. "They give you an anaesthetic for it."

By the time we got to the coffee and the wafer thin mints, Avalon had started to loosen up a bit, to give me erections by crossing and uncrossing her legs, and even to smile when I made a joke, rather than give me a look that said it was sacrilege to laugh on occasions like this. Now I knew the evening was not going to be wasted. I was going to fuck Avalon again. It's what Duggie would have wanted.

On the way back in the car, things began to feel really promising. Avalon was relaxed and apparently perfectly content to be with me. She didn't actually get my cock out, but it was almost like old times. Once back in the flat, she needed very little coaxing between the sheets. She made one final gesture in remembrance of Duggie by saying we weren't going to do that, this evening of all evenings, shirley, were we? All she really needed was a little cuddle, a little reassurance. Coming right up. We started off like babes in the wood, fully-clothed and clinging to each other on top of the bedspread and ended up like wild animals, practically ripping holes in the sheets.

"Bob? What do you really think about us?"

"In what way, precisely ?"

"Well, you and me, how do you see the future for you and me?"

I looked at her critically. She was a bit blotchy from all the things I'd been doing to her, but she still looked absolutely splendid.

"Avalon, there's something I didn't tell you."

"What?" she asked, and the expression on her face lost its friendliness. "What is it? If it's something nasty, I don't want to hear it. Not tonight."

You gotta be cruel to be kind, but I couldn't bear to do it to her while those big green eyes looked down on me so trustingly. "Come here," I said, and I pulled her towards me. Cradling her in my arms, I came as near to telling someone the absolute truth as I had ever done in my life. I told her openly and honestly what a smashing-looking bird she was. I told her what she had meant to me, how much I'd missed her when she went away. That was the easy bit.

"But – ?" Avalon asked.

"But what?"

"This is all leading up to something, isn't it ?"

"Yes,it is. It's like this, Chaucer – I've had an argument with him."

"Oh, is that all?"

"No, I've resigned from the practice. I'm chucking it in."

"And doing what?"

"I don't know. I haven't decided yet. But it won't be anything in Breckleigh. Nothing anywhere around here."

"Where then?" She looked smaller and more vulnerable than I had ever seen her look before. I felt a strong flush of protectiveness and affection towards her.

"I don't know. I'm thinking of somewhere like Australia, America maybe."

"How long for?"

"I don't know that, either."

She sat up and looked searchingly into my eyes. "But you will write to me, won't you? You'll keep in touch?"

I thought for a minute, and then I said, "I don't think so. I don't think that would be a good idea, do you?"

There were no tears in her eyes as she said simply, "So this is it, is it? This is where it all ends?"

" 'fraid so. This is the end of the line. This is how it ends."

"Is this because of what happened between me and Duggie?"

"No," I lied. "Nothing to do with that."

"You - you asked me to marry you, remember ?"

"Yes I did, but that was before things - changed."

"And if the Duggie thing hadn't happened ?"

"Avalon, how do I know? How does anybody know these things?"

From the window, I watched her walking slowly and, I hope, dejectedly along to her car. Somehow she didn't look quite as pretty as I remembered her. Even so, I almost yielded to the temptation to run down the stairs, throw my arms around her and offer to share my life with her under whatever terms she wanted. I didn't, though.

Chapter 30

"I did not, myself, have the pleshah of knowing Douglas in life, but I have learned from his loved ones, gathered here with us this afternoon, that he was a very selfless and above all a very Christiyun young man, ay doctah, whose dedication to his patients came before everything else. And, indeed his final magnificent act of self-sacrifice is a lesson to us all of the powah of true Christiyun love. For greater love hath no man than this – that he lay down his life for his friend leddus pray – "

It was my idea to get old man Death to conduct the service. After all, if he had to have a Christian bury him, Duggie would have preferred to have one that didn't believe in God.

"Duggie never went inside a church in his life, you know," Mrs Rossiter said as we walked down the Cathedral steps. "Not after he was five or six, anyway. His father died of cancer of the throat when he was a little lad, and he never forgave God for it."

"No, I know he had a bit of a down on God."

"Well, that's it then." We looked up and down the crowded stretch of Cathedral Street, busy with market day shoppers. "I'm supposed to be catching the three forty back to London. The connection doesn't get in to Sedgely till a quarter past midnight."

"Yes, well I'd just like to say how sorry about it all I am, Mrs Rossiter," I said clumsily.

"Are you? I don't know, Bob. I still can't understand it myself."

"What's that?"

"Duggie doing something like that. It just doesn't make sense. It was so unlike him."

"Well he wasn't really himself that evening, I don't think." The wind began to blow colder and I felt a few drops of rain on my face. "Look, can I give you a lift to the station?"

As I helped her into the car, Jimmie, wearing a heavy black overcoat with an astrakhan collar came down the cathedral path with Fountain.

Jimmie inclined his head towards us with a polite, serious look on his face and muttered, "Fowler", then he passed by and disappeared in the crowds down towards Sheepgate.

"He was drunk, wasn't he?" Mrs Rossiter asked.

"What makes you think that?"

"They never said anything, but that's the only explanation I can see for it." She turned her lined face towards me. "He was drunk, wasn't he?"

"Well, he'd had a bit to drink."

"Yes, I thought so. You see, he wouldn't have done anything like that otherwise. It wasn't his way. It wasn't his nature to do anything for anyone."

"Oh, I don't know," I said, desperately trying to think of something Duggie had done for me. "He was alright, really."

"Yes, I know he was alright, but that's as far as it goes. I don't like to speak ill of the dead, especially when it's my own son, but the trouble with him was he was selfish. He never gave a thought for other people. Selfish, that was him."

Seated on the high wickerwork stool in the dormer window, I could see all the way down Commercial Street to the docks. Louring storm clouds had brought an early dusk to Hogdown, and temporary traffic lights gleamed brightly down near the railway bridge, where a gang with a JCB was noisily completing the destruction of a half-demolished house. The local hookers, those bastions of free enterprise, were taking advantage of the resulting traffic congestion. On the pavement below me, a haggle of fat, stunted women were ducking and peering in at the captive occupants of a queue of stationary vehicles.

What these women sold was not a thing to treasure. It was a brief, joyless experience on both sides, carried out like a surgical operation with only the essential parts bared. Of the group down there today, there was only one who wouldn't have had to pay me to do it. She was a lot taller and skinnier than the others. Through the open window of a Range Rover, she was haggling with some big fat geezer in a sheepskin coat as to the amount he ought to pay to rent her fanny for two minutes.

"Go on, Porky, git in there," I muttered. "Get it while it's hot."

The girl hitched up the shoulder of her tee shirt in a rather transparent manoeuvre aimed at demonstrating that breasts wobble about a lot unless suitably restrained.

"Yeah, go on, you can afford it," I said.

But Fatso was immune to her womanly wiles, and he drove off with a squeal of tyres when the lights changed, leaving the girl waving her arms and calling various insults after him. It was then I noticed that there was more than a hint of Avalon about her - an emaciated, pockmarked, cigarette-smoking Avalon with a critical skirt-to-belt ratio and tattoos on her forearms. Sisters under the skin.

I drained my coffee cup and looked again at the newspapers balanced on my knee. It had been a slack week for news. Duggie's death had made the headlines in the Breckleigh Morning News and the front pages of most of the national dailies. Even the Top People's paper carried an article of six column inches, including a potted biography of Duggie, but excluding the more lurid details.

The prize for trite, rubbishy journalism, though, went to The Evening Echo - "The Voice of Sedgely", which my mother had sent me. On the front page there was a head-and-shoulders portrait of the Dirty Doctor himself. I've no idea where they got it from - I'd never seen it before. It certainly didn't look like Duggie - the features were too idealised, and the facial expression was too innocent and sincere. It reminded me instead of someone else I used to know, but I couldn't quite place him.

The article underneath said that Sedgely Doctor Hero had died in train smash. After an ungrammatical and inaccurate description of the accident, a bit of local colour had been added in the form of an interview with our former headmaster, Rev. J. N. Stokoe. Stokoe went on a bit about Duggie paying the supreme sacrifice for his dedication to his patients, and then chuntered on about his exemplary school career. If in fact old Stokoe remembered Duggie, which I doubt, it confirmed what I had always suspected - that he was a bit soft in the head.

On back page, col.4, it went on:

Fellow Old Sedgeleian, Dr Ronnie Mullen, who was also present at the accident, said later : "I am naturally very shocked, but I think that anyone who knew Douglas would not be surprised to learn of his heroism. He was a very dedicated doctor, who lived for his patients."

I thought they'd like that bit. Of course, it suddenly came to me who the picture on the front reminded me of: Duggie Rossiter: Healer of the Sick, Comforter of the Aged.

On Radio Four, some woman was now telling me how to make a face-pack out of sugar and egg-whites, but the sound of the radio and all the other background noises seemed muted and distant, and a curious stillness hung over the room, like a railway station after the last train has left. On an impulse, I got to my feet and made a neat pile of the newspapers on the dining table. From the drawer of the bureau I got out the full-colour studio portrait and laid it carefully on the pile of newspapers. Lovingly and carefully, I closed the newspapers around it, with crisp folds and tidily tucked-in flaps. The whole thing made a neatly wrapped parcel which I admired for a few seconds, then tossed onto the smouldering coke fire.

In a few seconds, it burst into flames, and I began to move around the room, humming quietly to myself and throwing the last of my belongings into the open suitcase on the floor.